# PRINCE OF VICE
## BOSTON BLOODLINES

### IVY WILD

Copyright © 2023 by Ivy Wild

All rights reserved.

No part of this book may be reproduced in any form or by any electronic or mechanical means, including information storage and retrieval systems, without written permission from the author, except for the use of brief quotations in a book review.

Cover Model: Kaio

Photographer: Wander Aguiar

Promotional Assistance: Valentine PR

*To everyone trying to find their true calling.*

# Playlist

*Innocence by Flume feat. Aluna George*
*Blue Dream by ZHU*
*Heaven by Julia Michaels*
*Slow Down Love by Louis the Child*
*Show me the World by Hippie Sabotage*
*Fortune Days by The Glitch Mob*
*Sonnentanz by Klangkarussell*
*Love Letter by ODESZA*
*Gold by Chet Faker*

*Listen on Spotify:*
*https://geni.us/POV-playlist*

The heart has its reasons which reason does not understand.

— BLAISE PASCAL

## Chapter One

### *Isabella*

"Ms. Moretti, he's in cell 7," the guard grumbles as I step into the dimly lit and dank confines of the city jail. The air is heavy with despair and the metallic scent of fear.

"Thank you," I reply, my voice resolute despite the shiver that runs down my spine. I walk past the rows of cells, each one a grim testament to the human capacity for cruelty. The shadows seem to reach out for me, whispering dark secrets that I dare not comprehend.

My heels click sharply against the cold floor, each step a reminder of the weight of responsibility I carry on my shoulders. The height of the cells looms high above my shorter frame, and I tuck an imaginary strand of bright red hair back into my bun out of habit. As I approach the final corner, where my new client awaits, I can't help but feel a thrill of anticipation tinged with fear.

There, in the farthest cell, stands Primo Maldonado. His tall, muscular frame is coiled with tension, a predator trapped in a cage. Even behind bars, there is an undeniable aura of authority about him – no doubt a product of his upbringing in the world of organized crime. He looks up at my approach, his dark eyes narrowing with interest.

"Primo Maldonado?" I ask, though it's more a confirmation than a question. "I'm Isabella Moretti, your attorney."

His dark eyes fixate on me. His gaze moves up and down my body, causing an involuntary shiver to move through me. I feel judged in a way I've never felt judged before.

"Bullshit," he says, his voice a low growl that vibrates through the stale air between us. "Where's Frankie?"

"My father's dead," I say without hesitation. "Sorry you didn't hear the news. I've taken over his cases."

His outward appearance is calm in a way that doesn't seem to match the tumult behind his eyes.

His gaze lingers on me for a moment longer before he turns away, bracing his hands against the cold metal bars of his cell.

"Ms. Moretti," he says, his voice low and measured, "I'm sure you do a great job in small claims court." He leans closer, the shadows from the dim lighting casting an ominous glow over his chiseled features. "But, I don't want a rookie lawyer who's barely out of law school trying to save my neck – especially when it's on the line for murder."

I really hate guys like this. Just because I don't fit "the

mold" of what a defense attorney should look like, he already assumes I'm not cut out for the job. Even still, his words sting, and I fight to keep my composure, focusing on the rhythmic drip of water somewhere in the distance. I'm not going to let him see how much his skepticism affects me.

"You're right," I say. "You're scheduled to be arraigned in thirty minutes. I'm sure you know exactly how that process works. As soon as we get in there, I'll make a motion to recuse myself as your attorney and then I'll sit in the front row and watch you put me and my oral advocacy skills to shame. Where did you go to law school again, Mr. Maldonado?"

He crosses his massive arms over his chest, muscles straining against the fabric of his shirt, and scoffs. "How many murder trials have you won? How many high-profile cases have you defended?"

The truth of the matter is that I have experience in neither. I'd watched my father defend mobsters like Primo for years. That was his business, and he made a lot of money doing it. Until he turned up dead six months ago at sixty under suspicious circumstances. I promised myself that I wouldn't turn into my father, no matter how good the money was. Unfortunately for me though, my father died with considerable debt to his name. And not just bank debt. That would have died with him. No, he had to die owing debts to the mob. That sort of debt passes on, and of course to me.

I may be bluffing, but I need to take this case. A case

this big might be the one chance I have to clear my family's name so I can move on and live my own life.

"Who says I've agreed to represent you in your murder trial?" I respond. "I select my clients carefully. The ones who are too," I pause and give him the once-over, "difficult, I am happy to hand off to a lesser skilled attorney."

"Fine," he mutters, his gaze lingering on me for a moment longer, as if he's sizing me up. "So, what's the plan?"

I hesitate, taking a deep breath as I prepare to lay out our strategy. The truth is, I have no idea if we can succeed – but Primo doesn't need to know that. He needs to believe in me, and more importantly, I need to believe in myself.

"What do you want?" I ask him.

"To get out of this fucking jail cell," he scoffs back. "Obviously. Is this how your representation is going to go? Asking me obvious questions and charging me, what? One thousand dollars an hour?"

"Fifteen hundred, actually," I reply. "But, I'm sure you're good for it."

My heart is racing. I might be holding my own against him on the surface, but deep down I know that Primo is a very powerful and dangerous man. I probably shouldn't piss him off too much.

The smallest of smiles graces his lips. "The most I pay for oral advocacy is a grand," he chuckles. "And that's for girls who have more experience than you."

I give him a fake smile and tilt my head to the side.

"Well, it was nice working with you, Mr. Maldonado. Please enjoy representing yourself at your upcoming arraignment. It starts in thirty minutes."

I go to turn around, but his voice echoes against the concrete cells.

"Fine. You win, Ms. Moretti. But, I hope you're ready for the fight of your life. Because if you think this is just another case, you've got another thing coming."

As his words ring through the cramped jail cell, I can't help but feel a shiver crawl up my spine. But I refuse to be daunted.

"Believe me, Primo," I whisper, "I'm ready."

"Like father, like daughter," Greg Daniels says to me as we wait for the hearing to begin.

Greg is the federal prosecutor assigned to this case, and I know he thinks this is his big moment to make a name for himself. I don't blame him. He's already into his late forties, with salt and pepper hair and a bit of a gut. If he doesn't secure a high-profile conviction soon, chances are he'll be relegated to low-level matters for the remainder of his career.

He and my father had a longstanding rivalry. Probably because my father got so many mobsters out of jail cells Greg tried to put them into. His animosity has apparently extended to me, even though up until recently, I never interacted with him.

"Glad to see we're keeping it professional, Greg," I say in response, organizing the papers on my desk.

"You're representing a murderer," he says to me. "I think professionalism is mostly out the window at this point."

"Alleged murderer," I retort. "So glad to see that you've embraced the 'guilty until proven innocent' mantra."

The door opens from the side of the courtroom, and Primo is escorted in by the U.S. Marshal.

As he sits down next to me, I can feel his dark eyes on me again. He looks like he's about to say something, but he doesn't get his chance.

"All rise!" the clerk says as the judge walks into the room. Judge Dolan is an older white man with a thick mustache and a heavyset frame. Even though you never stand close enough to the judges to really know their height, you can tell that he's not very tall.

"Shit," I curse under my breath. Judge Dolan was a known hard-ass, especially when it comes to organized crime. He is one of those judges who are known for being un-bribeable, which really seems to piss off a lot of mobsters. I've always admired him for his tenacity, especially in the face of great risk to his personal safety, but the case being assigned to him is definitely going to make things more difficult on our end.

Greg makes his argument, and Judge Dolan seems to eat it all up. I have to stop myself from shaking my head several times at the bold accusations he makes with completely unsupported evidence.

When it's finally my turn to speak, I stand and try to calm my nerves. Not only are the judge's eyes on me, but Primo's are as well.

"Your Honor, the prosecution fails to meet their burden to prove that Mr. Maldonado is a flight risk or a danger to society. If you consider the crucial elements here, Mr. Maldonado has no prior criminal record, he and his family have strong ties to the community and to the area, and he is currently employed and overseeing the operations of Maldonado's Bakery, which is an iconic spot here in Boston.

"It may be a long time before this case goes to trial. There is no need to use the state's resources to house a man who has no history of violence."

As I speak, I can feel the eyes of the courtroom on me - some curious, others skeptical, and still others calculating. But I don't let their gazes faze me; I am a whirlwind of determination and focus, fueled by the knowledge that I hold the power to change Primo's current circumstances.

As I finish my argument and take a seat beside him, I can feel something shift in his expression - a subtle softening around the eyes. I wouldn't dream of thinking there was even a hint of gratitude there, but it's obvious that his view of me may have changed slightly.

I remind myself that I don't care and focus back on what's going on in the courtroom.

"Nice work, Moretti," he says to me under his breath. It's so quiet I almost miss it.

"Your Honor," Greg says, standing up and trying to rebut my argument. "Everyone knows that Mr. Maldonado is the son of Johnny Maldonado, who, may I remind the court, is currently serving a twenty-year sentence for tax evasion and fraud."

I launch to my feet. "Objection! Relevance, Your Honor? The sins of the father do not befall to their children, unless I've gravely misunderstood how our criminal justice system works."

Greg ignores my objection and continues to speak. "And, we all know that the Maldonado family has long been involved in organized crime throughout the city."

"Objection!" I turn to face the judge. "Your Honor, if the prosecution doesn't stop their paper-thin attempts to sway the court's decision with hearsay, I'm going to be forced to move for another hearing."

"Sustained," Judge Dolan grumbles. "The prosecution will do well to remember that character evidence and their own testimony are not admissible in this courtroom."

Greg nods and sits back down. I can see the anger on his face at the fact that my objection was sustained.

Judge Dolan looks over the papers in front of him, his eyes hidden beneath his bushy brows. Finally, he leans forward in his seat. My heart quakes within its cage; I can feel my argument hanging in the air.

"Ms. Moretti," Judge Dolan begins, his voice carrying a gravitas that sends chills down my spine. "I have carefully considered your arguments and reviewed the evidence presented. It is not without reservations that I grant Mr. Maldonado's release. Bond is set at $2 million, and he will be placed under house arrest."

The judge turns to Primo, and their eyes meet. "If it weren't for her," he points to me. "You'd be rotting in a jail cell until your trial. Be grateful."

"Thank you, Your Honor," I reply, my cheeks burning bright red. Relief floods through me like a sweet, intoxicating elixir. My hands tremble only slightly as I fight to maintain composure, the precarious victory still settling upon my shoulders like a tentative embrace.

"Congratulations on your freedom, Primo," I whisper, turning toward him with a genuine smile lighting up my face. He offers me a nod, but he doesn't match my enthusiasm. For a moment, I allow myself to bristle at his cold exterior, before once again reminding myself that I don't care.

I know that there is an intensely long road ahead of me, but for now, I'm riding high on the fleeting satisfaction of my victory.

The Marshal comes over and asks Primo to stand. He does, but before he's taken away for outprocessing, he turns to me. "This is far from over." His deep voice and its message resonate with me like a thunderstorm on the horizon.

I meet his gaze, our eyes locking in a moment of mutual understanding. We are connected now, our fates bound together by the threads of this case.

"Nothing worth having comes easy," I say back to him before the Marshals take him away. I gather my belongings and leave the courtroom before Greg can say anything to me.

I stand in the cold air outside of the city jail. The wind whips around me, biting at my exposed skin like a pack of hungry wolves.

The metal gate opens, and Primo comes walking out. He's not wearing his prison attire anymore. This time, he's wearing what I'm sure is an overly expensive suit, and I hate the way that it hugs his muscular frame so well.

His dark eyes bore into me, as if they can pierce through to my very soul. In the light of the day, I can see just how attractive he really is, tucked away beneath his dangerous aura. I brace myself for the onslaught of his words, a storm I've already come to expect in the brief time since I've known him.

"Isabella," he drawls, the syllables dripping with disdain. "I won't pretend that your performance today wasn't... sufficient. But let's be clear. This little victory doesn't mean I'm convinced you're the right person for the job."

My chest tightens, the familiar serpent of self-doubt

slithering through my veins. I clench my fists, refusing to let him see the tremor in my hands.

"I understand that you might have concerns," I say, my voice steady despite the tumult inside of me. "But rest assured, Primo, I will do whatever it takes to prove your innocence."

"Whatever it takes?" He raises an eyebrow, a mocking smile playing on his lips. "You're young, Moretti. And while your passion is admirable, I'm not sure it'll be enough. I need to find someone with more... experience."

His words sting like a slap across my face, but I hold onto my determination like a lifeline. I will not let him undermine me, not when there's so much at stake.

"Primo," I begin, my voice firm. "I've worked tirelessly to get to where I am, and I've earned every success I've achieved. You can choose to dismiss my abilities, but I promise you, you'll never find someone who will fight harder for you than I will."

For a moment, silence stretches between us like a chasm, and I can only hear the distant shuffle of footsteps and the concrete walls behind us. Then, Primo's laughter rings out, a sound as cold and hollow as the cell that just contained him.

"Alright, Moretti, I'll bite," he smirks, his eyes glinting with something unreadable. "We'll see if your precious little determination can hold up against the forces at play here. Come to the mansion tomorrow. We'll discuss your strategy for winning my case and I'll determine then if you're the right lawyer."

I swallow down the bitter taste of indignation, reminding myself that it is Primo's life on the line, not mine. "Understood," I reply, my gaze never wavering from his.

I know he's trying to test me already. It's far too soon to have a well-developed strategy. I hold my head up high and meet his gaze.

"See you tomorrow, then," I say.

Primo places his phone to his ear, and within seconds, a black sedan appears in front of us. He gets in and rolls the window down to address me in an overly cliché move.

As I turn to leave, I can feel Primo's eyes boring into my back, but I refuse to let his doubt define me.

## Chapter Two

*Primo*

I stand at the window, watching the sun dip low on the horizon, casting the vast and impeccably landscaped grounds of the mansion in a golden hue. The opulent estate sprawls before me, its manicured lawns and gardens, the sparkling pool shimmering like a sapphire jewel, the fountain with its carved marble cherubs spouting water into the air. It's all so beautiful, yet I feel suffocated within these gilded walls.

I think about my father sitting in prison and a small smile tugs at my lips. My relationship with my father growing up was always *difficult*, especially with him always favoring my younger brother, Constantino, to succeed him, over me. Dad seems to have gotten what he deserved. Twenty years for fraud and tax evasion. All because he decided to do business with a man, not for his business acumen, but because he was willing to sell his daughter in marriage. Henry Dimes folded like a cheap tent when the authorities came sniffing around his books, and dear old dad ended up with, for his age, essentially a life sentence.

With dad in prison and me under house arrest for my own alleged crimes, it's certainly given my brother a good opportunity to push his agenda.

The doors to my study creak open, and Carlos "Charlie" Vitale shuffles in, his silver hair combed back neatly. Charlie's eyes, sharp as a hawk's, hold decades of wisdom and loyalty. He's always been there for me, a confidant and trusted advisor.

"Primo, you're brooding again," he chides gently, straightening his suit jacket. "You should try to relax, take your mind off things."

"Easy for you to say," I grumble, my fists clenching at my sides, still staring out at the view beyond the window. "I can't just sit here while my life crumbles around me, Charlie. I need to be out there, handling the family's business."

"Primo, it's important that you stay put. Your trial is coming up, and we need you free and clear." Charlie's voice is calm but firm, a fatherly tone that reminds me of countless conversations over the years.

"About that," I say. "I'm not sure Isabella's cut out for this kind of trial. She's young, inexperienced. This is high stakes, Charlie." My heart beats faster, anxiety creeping in as thoughts of my uncertain future swirl in my head.

"So, you think you want another lawyer?"

"I do," I reply. "Can you find me someone? Someone less green?"

"I'll work on it," Charlie says. "Although, finding another lawyer might be harder than you think, Primo." Charlie's voice holds a note of caution. "With your father's arrest and the rumors about Constantino's scheming, our family's power isn't what it used to be. Not everyone will want to take on this case."

"Damn it, Charlie, I know that. But what choice do I have?" My frustration boils over, a torrent of anger and fear. I pace the room, my footsteps bouncing off the marble floor like the distant rumbles of thunder.

"Primo, calm down." Charlie's hand reaches out to steady me, his grip firm but gentle. "You have more control here than you think. Just because you're stuck in this place doesn't mean you can't still handle business."

"Handle business? How am I supposed to do that when I can't even step outside?"

"Here." He hands me a cell phone, sleek and unassuming, no doubt with an extra layer of encryption. "You can still make decisions from here. Coordinate shipments, manage the supply chain, all while awaiting trial."

I run a hand through my hair in frustration. "You really think leading from a cell phone is even possible?" My anger is boiling over, but I know it's not Charlie's fault.

"It's not ideal, but it'll keep things running," he replies calmly, used to my outbreaks.

I take a deep breath and try and calm my nerves. "Thank you, Charlie," I force myself to say. My fingers close around the phone, its presence both reassuring and burdensome. "I appreciate everything you're doing for me."

"Anything for you, kid." His eyes soften as he claps me on the shoulder.

"How did she get on my case in the first place?" I wonder out loud.

"I think it was just an oversight. Frankie's only been in the ground for a little while. Chances are the paperwork got sent to his old office and she was there to pick it up."

"What happened to Frankie?" I ask. "Other than the being dead part?"

Charlie shrugs. "He lost your father's trial."

"There was no way anyone was going to win that trial," I reply bitterly.

Charlie nods. "I agree. I believe he also owed a pretty substantial debt to the family. I can get some clarity for you on that, as well."

"I appreciate it," I say. "Hopefully you can find the right person for this job. It's hard to trust someone I barely know with my life, Charlie. Every day I spend locked away in here, I lose control of the family. And that scares me the most."

"Primo, we've weathered storms before," he says, his eyes never leaving mine. "We'll get through this together. Just have faith in yourself."

"I lost my faith in just about everything a long time ago," I mutter.

"Alright, enough with the dramatics," he chuckles.

"Now, put all this behind you and go get some work done. And remember, you're not alone in this."

"Right." With a nod, I watch as Charlie exits the room, leaving me to face my demons alone once more.

I power on the phone, messages flooding in like a deluge, each one whispering of drugs, guns, and the sprawling underworld we've built. As I sift through the information, a sense of purpose begins to rise within me. For the first time in days, I feel like I can breathe again.

But even as I work, my thoughts keep drifting back to Isabella. I try and maintain my focus, but her green eyes, that red hair, her soft voice, and her determination to save me from this nightmare is alluring. She's a beautiful woman and already proven herself to be capable. I fully expected the judge to deny bail. Yet, somehow she was able to convince a hard-ass like Dolan to let me out on house arrest.

Still, I can't shake the feeling that it might not be enough—that despite her best efforts, our enemies, both within and without, are closing in. The thought chills me to the bone, a cold wind blowing through the lavish halls of our once-invincible empire.

"Damn it," I mutter under my breath as I continue working through messages, my fingers tapping away at the screen with an almost frantic urgency. "I need to find a way out of this mess."

The responsibility bears down on me as I continue to handle the family business through the phone. My fingers fly over the screen, issuing orders and making deals, but a nagging doubt gnaws at my insides like a ravenous beast. I can feel our power slipping through my fingers like sand, and the knowledge that I am shackled here, unable to assert my authority in person, only heightens the unease.

"Everything has a price," I whisper to myself, recalling my father's most often repeated adage. And I cannot help but wonder if the cost of my freedom will be our downfall.

I send off a message to one of my men, ensuring the timely delivery of a shipment bound for Boston. "Keep an eye out for the Irish," I warn him. "They're hungry for more power, and they won't hesitate to take advantage of our current situation."

The message sent, I put down my phone and glance out the window, my gaze drawn to the distant horizon. There, a storm brews, its dark clouds a portent of the tempest that threatens to engulf us all.

"Damn these murder charges," I murmur, my frustration bubbling to the surface like water reaching its boiling point. The circumstances of my arrest still chafe at me like a pair of ill-fitting shoes. Something about it feels off, as if I've been played for a fool, and I cannot shake the suspicion that this was all part of a grand scheme to usurp my power.

"Who would dare to betray me?" I wonder aloud, my voice barely more than a whisper in the silence of the room. "Constantino? The Irish?"

But even as I voice these thoughts, I know that answers will not come easily. Betrayal is a snake in the grass, hidden from view until it strikes with deadly precision. And I cannot help but feel that the viper's fangs are poised to sink into my flesh at any moment.

Even if I were to find another lawyer, would I be able to trust them with my case? Who knows where their true loyalties would lie? For that matter, can I even be sure that I trust Isabella? Who knows whether she has ulterior motives and what they are.

I growl in frustration as I realize that I may have little to no chance of salvation in this case, no matter who is representing me.

Another hour passes by but restlessness gnaws at my insides like a ravenous beast, urging me to move. The gym, tucked away in a corner of the sprawling property, beckons to me with its promise of relief. As I stride down the hallway, my footsteps echo off the marble floors, their rhythm steady and determined.

"Sometimes, Primo, you need to burn the demons out," I tell myself, feeling the family's troubles bearing down upon me.

I step into the gym, breathing in the familiar scent of sweat, leather, and iron. My gaze lands on the figure already occupying the space—Teddy, the youngest Maldonado brother. He stands bent over a punching bag, his fists wrapped in bandages, delivering blow after powerful blow to the worn leather surface.

"Hey, Teddy," I call out. He pauses mid-punch, turning to face me with a smile. Teddy was never one to be bothered by the family's business or troubles.

"Primo," he replies, wiping the sweat from his brow with the back of his hand. "What brings you here?"

"Restless energy," I admit, running a hand through my slicked-back hair. "The walls of this mansion are starting to close in on me."

"Understandable," Teddy says, stepping away from the punching bag. Despite his role as the family cleaner, he keeps his distance from our business affairs. His loyalty is unquestioned—a welcome reprieve from the uncertainty that plagues the rest of my life.

"Constantino is making moves," I confide in him, leaning against the wall as I watch him unwrap the bandages from his hands. "He's trying to seize control while I'm stuck here under house arrest."

"Nothing new there," Teddy observes, his tone nonchalant but with an underlying current of concern. "He's always been hungry for power. Yours, specifically."

"True, but now he's got the perfect opportunity to wrest it from me," I say, clenching my fists at the thought. "I can't be everywhere at once, especially now. When Dad went to prison, I thought this was my chance to elevate the family name. Bring us back into prominence and run things that secures our future. Instead, I'm on trial for murder myself and no one seems to support my vision."

"Maybe you should have a talk with him," Teddy suggests as he tosses his bandages into a nearby bin. "Set boundaries. Remind him who's boss."

"Boundaries don't seem to mean much to Constantino," I reply bitterly, the frustration simmering within me. "He'll do what he wants, regardless of what I say."

Teddy shrugs. "I'm not going to pretend I understand the business side of things, but I still think talking to him is the way to go."

"Honestly, what good would that do? You know as well as I do that if he takes control, blood and violence will run thick through the streets. That's not what I want for our legacy or this city."

Teddy shrugs. "Better than starting a war."

"I'm not the one starting a war," I scoff. "The order of inheritance is well established. He's the one trying to push boundaries and punch above his weight class."

"Speaking of punching things," Teddy says, clapping me on the shoulder. "How about you burn off that energy? I think the punching bag could use more punishment. Maybe it'll get your mind off of things."

With a wry smile, I wrap my hands and take my place before the worn leather surface, feeling the coiled power within me begin to unspool with each strike. As I pummel the bag, I imagine it's Constantino's smug face.

I wipe the sweat from my brow, pausing for a moment to catch my breath. Teddy, noticing my distraction, leans against a nearby weight bench and furrows his brow in concern.

"Primo, there's something else you should know," he says hesitantly, rubbing the back of his neck. "Giovanni's back at the mansion."

I raise an eyebrow, surprised by this revelation. It isn't like our brother Giovanni to associate with the family business. As a legitimate entrepreneur, he has always preferred to distance himself from our darker dealings, fearing they could jeopardize his hard-earned success.

"Really?" I ask, intrigued. "What's he doing here?"

"Apparently, he got caught up in the mess down in Miami," Teddy explains. "You remember that sting operation we were both involved in? Well, when everything went south, he ended up bringing a girl back with him. She was injured during the shootout. I think she's still with the doctor, healing. But, he indicated his intention was to eventually bring her here."

My interest piques as I recall the chaotic events that unfolded in Miami. The fact that Giovanni has returned is certainly unexpected, and it sets off alarm bells in my mind. Could he be planning to use this opportunity to seize control of the family?

"Teddy, do you think Giovanni might try to take over?" I ask cautiously, weighing the potential consequences of such a power play.

"Maybe," Teddy admits with a grimace. "He's made no secret of the fact that he wants to move the family into more legitimate businesses. If he thinks he can do a better job than you or Constantino, he might make a move."

His words send a chill down my spine, and I realize

that my position is more precarious than I'd initially thought. With both Constantino and potentially Giovanni vying for power, I need to be more vigilant than ever.

"Sometimes I wonder if it would just be better for me to give it all up," I sigh. "Growing up I watched Dad make mistake after mistake that threatened our position. A position our ancestors fought for with their lives. I thought when it was my turn to lead, I could strike a balance. Grow and maintain our power, keep the other families in line, and ensure peace and good order in the city."

"Why not go Gio's route, then?" Teddy asks.

"Because his route is to give up power completely," I say, the words bitter in my mouth. "If not us, then someone with far less of a moral compass will move in. There will be a power vacuum first, though. Mob wars affect everyone. That's never something I wanted."

Teddy gives me a somewhat sad look and shrugs his shoulders. "This is why I always stay out of the business side of things. It's messier than cleaning up murders."

I chuckle at his analogy. "You might be the smartest of all of us, Teddy."

With that, I finish my workout and return to my quarters, my thoughts racing with the new information Teddy has given me. I've barely closed the door behind me when I'm hit with a wave of exhaustion, and I decide to take a shower to wash away the tension from my body.

As the hot water courses over me, my mind begins to wander to my alluring defense attorney, Isabella Moretti.

Her beauty is enough to distract any man, but it's her fierce intelligence and determination that truly captivate me. Even if she isn't going to be my lawyer, I can still appreciate a beautiful woman. I allow myself to indulge in fantasies of her, my hand moving rhythmically as images of her fill my mind.

"I hope you're as good in court as you are in my dreams," I think, my pulse quickening as my body tenses and releases in a moment of sweet surrender.

Emerging from the shower, I feel both physically and mentally refreshed, ready to face whatever challenges await me. As I dry off, I resolve to stay vigilant and protect my family's legacy at all costs – no matter who tries to stand in my way.

## Chapter Three

*Isabella*

The Maldonado mansion looms before me, an edifice of wealth and power; it's an iron fist wrapped in a velvet glove. The grandeur intimidates me as I stare up at the imposing structure, my irritation growing at the thought of how much blood money has been poured into these walls. I swallow hard, mentally steeling myself for the task ahead.

As I approach the front door, Primo is already waiting for me, his towering figure leaning against the ornate entrance. He's fierce and intimidating, with eyes that cut through me like a sharp blade. I hate that he's exactly my type.

"Ms. Moretti," Primo says, not offering a greeting but rather an acknowledgment of my presence. "We've already wasted precious time since the arraignment hearing yesterday. We should be preparing for the trial. That's strike one."

His pushiness grates on me, igniting a spark of defiance. "If this is going to work, Mr. Maldonado," I snap back, "you need to reset your expectations."

Primo smirks, unfazed by my retort. "I only ever have the highest expectations, Ms. Moretti. Most people often disappoint me, but I hoped you'd be different."

I focus on keeping my composure, refusing to let him see how much he affects me. My heart races, responding to his magnetic pull, but I can't allow myself to get lost in it. Not now, not with so much at stake. I need this case and I know to keep it I'll have to win Primo's trust.

"Then let's not waste any more time," I say, forcing a smile onto my lips. "Lead the way."

As I step into the shadow of the mansion, I brace myself for the world I'm about to enter. A world of power, secrets, and danger where I must keep my wits about me if I hope to survive – and win this case. And as much as I despise what Primo Maldonado stands for, something within me can't help but be drawn to the man himself.

Primo leads me down a dimly lit hallway, my eyes drinking in every exquisite detail of the Maldonado mansion. The walls are adorned with rich tapestries and gilded frames housing hauntingly beautiful paintings. I can't help but feel as though I've stepped into another world – one where darkness and desire intertwine, casting a spell upon all who enter.

"Allow me to introduce you to my brothers," Primo

says, his voice a low growl that sends a shiver down my spine. As we turn a corner, three men come into view, each one strikingly different from the others.

"Constantino," Primo gestures toward a man with sharp features and piercing eyes that seem to bore into my soul. His posture exudes power, making it clear he's a force to be reckoned with.

"Giovanni," he continues, indicating a more refined-looking man whose quiet demeanor belies a fierce loyalty. He stands slightly apart from the others, avoiding the spotlight and family disputes.

"Teddy," Primo finally introduces the youngest brother, with gentle eyes and a warm smile. He radiates kindness, a stark contrast to his surroundings. I immediately sense that he is the moral compass of the family.

"Isabella Moretti, our new attorney," Primo announces, "for now," he adds and I stop myself from rolling my eyes. I can't help but notice the mix of curiosity and skepticism in their gazes.

"Nice to meet you," Giovanni says warmly, extending his hand.

"Likewise," I reply, shaking his hand firmly, trying to convey confidence despite feeling like an intruder in this dangerous world.

"Let me show you around." Primo leads me away from his brothers, and I can't shake the feeling that I'm being watched.

We continue through the lavish halls of the mansion, Primo recounting tales of his family's history. He speaks of their rise to power, the legacy he's expected to uphold. I can't ignore the pride in his voice, nor the responsibility that seems to bear down on him.

"Over here," he gestures toward an ornate door, "is where our great-grandfather held court." He opens it to reveal a lavish room filled with dark wood and crimson drapes. "He built this empire, and now it falls to me, to us, to maintain it."

I observe the room, my mind racing with thoughts of the crimes committed within these walls, the lives affected by the Maldonado family's ruthless pursuit of power. And yet, there's a part of me that longs to know Primo's true nature, the man beneath the imposing exterior. In the short time I've spent with him, he's shown glimpses of it. On the outside, he's all bite, but when I look into his eyes, I can see the weariness and uncertainty there. Maybe it's wishful thinking, but it makes me believe there's a human being underneath his gruff exterior.

"Are you frightened, Isabella?" Primo asks, his voice softening slightly. The vulnerability catches me off guard, another drip in the bucket showing me that maybe there is more to Primo than what he lets the world see. I find myself trying to find the right words before responding.

"Of course not," I lie, forcing a smile on my face. Because the truth is that I am scared, *very* scared. I desperately don't want to end up like my father, and I know that representing Primo could lead me down a one way path. More than that, the very world that Primo runs, the one that I'm now a part of, is more than enough to keep me up at night.

"Indeed," he says, the hardness returning to his voice. "Let's get to work then, shall we?"

As we continue our tour of the mansion, my mind races with questions.

*You're on trial for murder, and maybe you didn't kill this victim, but how many men have died under your control?*

*What sorts of criminal enterprises are you running now?*

*Am I really capable of winning this trial for you?*

I shake off the self doubt that tries to creep in with the shadows. I tell myself that I can win this case, even if it means getting closer to Primo Maldonado than I ever intended.

The tour comes to an abrupt end as Primo opens the doors to his office, a striking contrast to the rest of the Maldonado mansion. The room is drenched in sunlight, streaming through floor-to-ceiling windows, casting long shadows on the sleek, modern furniture that fills the space.

"Welcome to your new workspace," Primo announces with an air of smug satisfaction. I take in the sight before me – my own desk, set up meticulously in front of his larger one, as if I were his personal assistant. The audacity of it all is almost laughable.

"Let me be clear, Mr. Maldonado," I say, standing as tall as my five-foot-five frame allows and locking eyes with him. "I will not be moving into this mansion, nor will I let you lord over me."

He leans casually against his desk, studying me with an amused expression. "Isabella, darling, we've already wasted precious time. If you're going to be my lawyer, you'll work on my case here, full time. It's non-negotiable."

"Actually, it is negotiable," I retort, not allowing myself to back down. "I have other clients, and I will not abandon them or my life just because you want to keep me under your thumb."

Primo raises an eyebrow but says nothing, his silence only fueling my determination. He stares at me intensely. "Strike two, Moretti. You're already proving yourself incapable of following the most basic of rules. Are you sure you really want this case? Because, you haven't convinced me."

"Fine," I relent, deciding to pick my battles. "We can discuss it later." As I settle into the chair at my temporary desk, I notice the wealth of evidence stacked neatly before me. Despite my irritation with Primo, I can't help but feel a thrill at diving into the case – unraveling the truth, piece by piece.

As I begin sifting through documents, Primo watches me intently. I can feel his gaze, but I refuse to let it distract me. Instead, I focus on the task at hand, allowing my mind to become fully immersed in the world of organized crime and courtroom battles.

"I've already sent discovery requests to the prosecution," I tell him. "A full list of interrogatories plus a lengthy request for production of documents. We should have those within three days."

Primo just continues to watch me, not commenting on anything I'm saying.

"What we *do* have is everything the prosecution presented to the Magistrate in order to get you arrested in the first place," I say, pointing to the documents in front of me. "I've gone through everything already and I have a couple of questions to ask you."

"Ask your questions," Primo says with a wave of his hand.

The evidence sprawls across the desk before me like a map of Primo's dark world. My fingers dance over photographs and documents, taking in every detail with ravenous curiosity. The sharp scent of ink mingles with the rich aroma of polished wood beneath my hands.

"Have you seen this?" I ask, holding up an incriminating photo of a rival gang member. Primo nods tersely, his jaw clenched tight. He looks like a statue, all chiseled angles and cold intensity. It's unnerving, but I refuse to let it distract me.

"Your brother Constantino's name appears here," I point out, tapping on a document that details a recent arms deal gone awry. "What's his role in all this?"

"Constantino is...ambitious," Primo says, his voice guarded. "He's always looking for ways to expand our operations."

"Even at the risk of your family?" I ask, trying to pierce the veil of secrecy that surrounds him. But before he can answer, the sound of raised voices permeate through the hallway outside the office door.

"Dammit, Giovanni!" Constantino snarls, his temper flaring like a wildfire. "You're too weak to lead this family!"

"Better to be weak than heartless, brother," Giovanni retorts, his voice laced with venom. "We need to leave this life behind, not dig ourselves deeper into the grave!"

As the argument escalates, I glance at Primo, whose face has hardened into a mask of fury. His eyes smolder with indignation, but beneath the anger, I detect a flicker of vulnerability – as if he's torn between defending his family's honor and acknowledging the truth of Giovanni's words.

*"Maybe he's not such a monster after all,"* I think to myself as I try and steal glances into his eyes, desperate to find that bit of humanity I'm slowly convincing myself exists within him.

"Excuse me for a moment, Isabella," he mutters, striding toward the door with a predatory grace. He flings it open, revealing the two brothers, their faces flushed and contorted with anger.

"Enough!" Primo roars, his voice reverberating through the cavernous room. "We have enemies at our doorstep, plotting our downfall, and you two are tearing each other apart like animals? The Irish mob is preparing to strike against us, and we're doing nothing to stop them!"

Giovanni steps forward, his chest heaving with barely contained rage. "That's exactly why we need to get out of this life, Primo," he argues, his eyes blazing. "We can't keep going down this path. It'll only lead to our destruction."

Constantino remains silent, his lips pressed into a thin line as he regards his older brother with steely defiance. His calculating gaze unnerves me, makes me feel like a pawn on a chessboard – one wrong move away from being captured.

"Focus on our real enemies, not on each other," Primo pleads, his face a storm of conflicting emotions. "This family needs unity, now more than ever."

As the brothers stand in tense silence, I watch from my chair, struck by the raw intensity of their rivalry. I've seen families torn apart by ambition before, but never one so steeped in darkness and intrigue. It's a world I never imagined entering, yet here I am, standing at its precipice.

"Very well, brother," Constantino finally concedes, his voice dripping with disdain. "But remember that our enemies aren't the only ones who can bring us to our knees."

"Is that a threat?" Primo demands, his eyes narrowing dangerously.

"Consider it... a reminder," Constantino replies cryptically before stalking away, leaving an icy chill in his wake.

"Come, Isabella," Primo says quietly, his voice heavy with a thousand unspoken words. "We have much work to do."

The door swings shut with a muted thud, sealing away the storm of contention that rages between the brothers in the corridor beyond. Primo leans against the wood as he takes deep breaths, obviously trying to regain his composure.

"Didn't know you were the type for front-row seats to family drama," he remarks, turning his gaze on me. I'm standing across the room, and his sharp eyes lock onto mine. I return his gaze, unflinching and fearless.

"Believe me, Primo, it's not my preferred form of entertainment," I reply, crossing my arms over my chest. "But I'm not going to cower in the corner either."

His low grumble fills the room. He pushes himself off the door and strides towards me. "I think I might like the idea of you cowering in the corner. On your knees, looking up at me." His voice is deep and I'm mesmerized by the way he licks his lips. My heartrate quickens and my words catch in my throat.

"Flustered, Isabella?" he asks, invading my space.

I back up slowly until I'm tripping over my desk, all but falling onto the surface. He rests his hands on either side of my thighs and I look down. I hate that I can't stop myself from thinking about what those hands would feel like on me.

"No," I stammer.

"Good," he says, standing up and returning to his desk. I take a deep breath, finally able to breathe again. "Because this is the world you've entered now, and if you aren't prepared to handle it, I suggest you find another lawyer to take over my case."

His words bring me back to my sad reality. I stand up and brush imaginary wrinkles out of my clothes. "Stop being an idiot," I retort, my voice laced with exasperation. "I didn't make the decision to represent you lightly. I have my own reasons, so don't underestimate me."

"Then tell me," he demands, his voice low and challenging. "Why did you decide to take my case at all, since you're obviously not happy about representing a mobster?"

My jaw tightens, and for a moment, I consider not answering. But then I speak, my voice resolute. "You may be a mobster, Primo, but everyone deserves a fair trial. And it's clear that there are forces outside your family trying to make sure that doesn't happen."

His eyes narrow, studying my face as my words sink in. I watch as his expression softens, determination warring with vulnerability in the depths of his gaze. I imagine that it's rare for Primo to see someone stand up to him like this. I hold my breath as I wait for his answer.

"Bullshit," he says at last, his tone curt. "There's something you're not telling me. Something to do with your father."

Anxiety gnaws at my insides. Does he know? Of course he knows. It would be foolish to think that he didn't.

"I'm sure you're aware that my father turned up dead six months ago," I begin.

"So I've been told," he replies coolly.

"Well, when he died he owed a lot of money to some dangerous people. People that are coming after me for it now."

"How much money?" Primo asks.

"Far more than I have or could make doing legitimate work in any reasonable amount of time," I admit.

Primo nods his head and a small smile lifts his lips. "Ah, so that is why you are so intent on taking this case. Do you think that if you win my case, I'll absolve you of the debts your father owes? Even to other families?" There's a hint of mockery in his voice.

"I'm not so naive, Primo," I bite back. "But, I do think that this case will give me a good chunk of the funds I need to settle the most dangerous of debts so that I know me and my sister will be safe."

"How admirable of you," Primo replies. "And you think that I'm going to let you take my case because your motivation is money?"

I grit my teeth and stare into his stupidly attractive face. "I think that you're going to let me take your case because you have no other lawyer and that money is the best motivator of all. Especially in your world where loyalties seem somewhat fluid these days."

He's on me in a flash, his thick fingers wrapping around my throat with an intensity that has me gasping.

"Oh, Isabella," he drawls. "When you overstep, you risk falling into the viper's den. It's cute that you think someone will be there to save you. Cute, but foolish."

I know I should feel fear, but I don't. Maybe it's the adrenaline coursing through me. The feeling of his fingers on my throat sends shivers through my body and I'm mesmerized as I stare into his eyes. His grip loosens on my throat and I can finally breathe again.

"So?" I say, trying to seem unfazed. "Do we have a deal?"

"Remind me of the terms you're offering?" he replies, smiling to himself as if this is all too much fun for him.

"I win your case and you give me the funds to absolve my father's debts."

"Sure thing, Moretti," he says dismissively. I hesitate for a moment, not sure if I've just managed to secure my salvation or damnation through this man.

"Alright then," I reply, my lips quirking into a half-smile as I uncross my arms and reach for a stack of documents on the table before us. Even if Primo isn't serious about this deal, I have to be.

As I dive back into the evidence, I can't help but steal glances at Primo when he's not looking. There's fierce intelligence that hides behind his even coarser exterior.

And as much as he terrifies me, I can't look away.

## Chapter Four

### Primo

A week has gone by and Charlie still hasn't found me another lawyer. Which means that I've endured a week of working next to Isabella. A week of smelling her perfume, wanting to feel her curves, and of listening to the sass come out of her pouty little mouth.

I recline in the plush leather chair at my desk, sinking into its embrace as I watch Isabella read the documents in front of her. While the lawyer's body is tempting, it pales in comparison to the dedication and intelligence she exudes. Even though she won't be the one to represent me at trial, I can't help but savor this opportunity to witness her perform under pressure. Her eyes flicker up to meet mine, and I refuse to look away.

Her attempt to negotiate the little deal of hers with me was endearing. Watching her stand up for herself and try her best to go toe-to-toe with me made my cock so fucking hard.

"Is something wrong?" I smirk, raising an eyebrow. She doesn't flinch.

"Actually, yes," she responds, her voice a mixture of annoyance and determination. "I'm trying to work, and all you're doing is staring at me."

"Are you uncomfortable under my gaze?" I ask, leaning forward ever so slightly.

"Let's just say you're the kind of person who makes people uncomfortable in general," she retorts without missing a beat.

I laugh, the rich sound filling up the room. "In my position, that's an advantage."

"Believe me, that wasn't meant as a compliment." Her eyes narrow, challenging me.

I decide then and there that I'll enjoy this verbal dance with her, pushing boundaries and breaking her down before I tire of her. By the end of the day, I'm confident Charlie will have another lawyer for me, but the thrill of bending her to my will is too delicious to pass up.

Maybe I'll even get to bend her over in other ways.

"Let's get back to work, shall we?" I suggest, gesturing toward the stack of papers on her desk. But instead of obeying, she remains fixed in place, her defiance burning like a beacon.

"Fine," she mutters, finally turning her focus back to the documents. Her fingers trace lines of ink, and her brow furrows in concentration. I can't help but admire her tenacity and wonder what other secrets lie beneath her professional exterior.

"Your dedication is admirable, Isabella," I say, my voice dripping with sincerity. "But don't forget who you're working for."

"I'm well aware of who I'm working for, Mr. Maldonado," she replies, her tone icy.

"Good," I say, leaning back in my chair once more. "Because there's a lot at stake here – for both of us."

As she continues to work, I find myself drawn into her world, captivated by the way her mind races and her fingers dance across the pages. She seems confident, and for the first time in my life, I'm not entirely sure whether I will emerge victorious or broken from this encounter.

Surrounded by the lavish decorations of my office, I'm unable to tear my gaze away from Isabella. The way her brow knits together in concentration as she pores over documents, her pen tapping impatiently against the paper, only serves to fuel my desire to see that fierce determination in other aspects of her life. Women have always been a fleeting source of entertainment for me, shining brightly for but a moment before their luster fades, revealing nothing more than a hollow shell beneath. But there's something about Isabella that makes me believe she may be different. But, I have to know for myself. Despite the seriousness of what's in front of us, I want to see just how much she's willing to take, and whether she's truly able to stand her ground, or if it was just a fleeting moment of courage.

"Are you just going to sit there and watch, or are you going to help me?" Her voice pulls me from my thoughts, and I can't suppress the grin that spreads across my lips.

"Helping sounds infinitely more enjoyable," I reply, smoothly rising from my chair and making my way over to her desk. "But, I must admit, you're nice to watch, too."

As I sit down on the edge of her desk, my legs sprawled over stacks of papers, I can see the fury smoldering in the depths of her eyes. It's perfect, and I decide to push her further. "You know, with the way you're looking at me, one might think you're the one on trial."

"Is this some kind of joke to you?" she snaps, clearly not amused by my antics.

"Quite the opposite, my dear." I lean closer to her, savoring the way her body tenses at my proximity. "I enjoy testing people, seeing just how far they can be pushed before they break. There's an art to unraveling someone, to making them submit to your will."

"Save your intimidation tactics for someone else," she retorts, her words sharp as daggers. "I'm not some mobster you need to scare into submission. Now get off those papers; I have work to do."

Her defiance is intoxicating, and I can't help but admire her tenacity. Part of me wonders if any man has ever truly appreciated the fire that burns within her, or if they've only sought to extinguish it.

"Isabella," I say, my voice low and measured as I lean forward, wanting to see just how far I can push. The shadows of the dimly lit room cast intricate patterns across her face. "You may not think I intimidate you now, but that will change." I pause, letting my words sink in. "When you close your eyes at night, you'll see my face and hear my voice. You'll be up with thoughts of me, and slowly, ever so slowly, I will creep into your mind until you bow to me."

At my words, she stands up, all five-foot-five inches of her, hands firmly planted on her hips, her eyes ablaze with defiance. "I will never bow to you, Primo," she bites out, her voice trembling with indignation. "If you think this is going to be our working relationship, then you better fire me now because that is absolutely not something I will do."

I chuckle, a deep rumble resonating from my chest. "I admire your fire, Isabella." A rosy hue blooms across her cheeks like a delicate sunrise, and I grasp onto it, eager to see where this uncharted territory might lead.

"Has anyone ever truly appreciated your spark, Isabella? Perhaps that's why you're still single – you've never found a man who can match your intensity?" Her silence speaks volumes, yet she doesn't bite back at my words. I find myself pushing further, wanting to unravel every thread of her being. "Are you just as intense in the bedroom? Would you let me see that side of you at some point?"

The quiet stillness of the room amplifies the tension between us, the air thick with anticipation. She remains silent, her gaze steady, and I push the boundaries even more. "Imagine, Isabella...the two of us, locked in passion and fury. I'd love to get you this angry, strip you bare and shove you down onto my bed. I would fuck you raw from behind until you're screaming my name, your body surrendering to mine."

The words hang in the air between us, a heady mixture of desire and defiance dancing like embers in the night. The moment stretches on, our gazes locked in an unspoken challenge, each daring the other to take the first step into the unknown. The sharp sting of her palm connects with my face, a resonating slap that reverberates through the room. My nostrils flare, my cock throbbing with desire for this fierce creature standing before me.

"Watch your tongue," she warns, fire in her eyes. "I won't hesitate to leave you without a lawyer if you keep this up."

"Is that so?" I smirk, undeterred by her defiance. "If you end up as my fuck toy rather than my lawyer, I'll simply find another lawyer. No skin off my back."

Determined not to show weakness, I invade her space, my body mere inches from hers. She doesn't shy away, but I can see the surprise flicker in her eyes. I ghost my fingers up the inside of her thigh, and though she seems taken aback, she doesn't stop me.

"Let me tell you, Isabella, all the filthy things I'd do to that sweet pussy of yours," I whisper, my breath hot against her ear. "You're already dripping for me, I can feel it. But let's not get ahead of ourselves, shall we? You have a case to work on, and I wouldn't want to be a distraction."

With that, I pull back, leaving her standing there, flustered and confused. The mixture of anger and arousal radiates off her, a delicious combination that only fuels my lust further.

I wonder just how far I can push her. Since she won't be my lawyer anyways, why not have a little bit of fun and see just how stiff of a spine she really has? One last push and then I'm fairly certain that she'll break.

Excusing myself, I retreat to the bathroom connected to the office and crack the door open just enough for her to hear my actions. Unzipping my pants, I grasp my throbbing erection and begin stroking myself, not bothering to hide the sounds of my pleasure.

"Isabella," I groan, dictating my fantasies aloud. "I want to hold you down, watch my cock disappear between your lips. I want to push myself so deep into your throat that you choke on it. I'll make you suck my balls until I come all over your eager face, turning you into a wet, fucking mess for me."

The images in my mind intensify, driving me closer to the edge. "Beg for my cock, Isabella, and only then will I rip off those panties and fuck you like the little plaything I know you are."

With a roar of her name, I reach my climax. "My sexy little lawyer," I shout as I release. Panting, I clean myself up and return to the office.

I'm shocked to see her sitting there at her desk, still working. Before I can say anything she's on her feet. I can see the fire in her eyes and it's intoxicating. Her defiance only fuels my lust for her once again. Perhaps I've underestimated her.

"If you'll excuse me," she says, "I think I need a glass of water." She leaves the office, slamming the door behind her.

I can't help but laugh, wondering who truly won this first round of our twisted game.

Whoever the winner, it's clear that playing with Isabella Moretti is quickly becoming my new vice.

## Chapter Five

### Isabella

My blood boils as I watch Primo's blatant disregard for his own trial. How dare he sit on my desk, scattering my carefully organized papers? But what infuriates me even more is when he retreats to the bathroom, leaving the door ajar so I can hear him pleasuring himself, all while describing in lurid detail the things he wants to do to me.

"Isabella," he groans, and I feel a shiver run down my spine.

As much as I hate to admit it, his words awaken something within me. It's been so long since I've been touched by another, but I refuse to let him win. He's trying to toy with me, to see if I'm truly taking his case seriously. I've worked too hard to let someone like him ruin everything.

I wait for him to finish and come back into the office because I know he's just trying to test me. I can see the shock on his face when he sees me still sitting at my desk. Before he can open his mouth to say another word, I'm up out of my seat. "Excuse me," I say, "I think I need a glass of water."

I storm out of the room, needing space to clear my head and regain control over my body's treacherous response.

I pace through the vast halls of the Maldonado mansion, feeling disoriented and lost. The opulence of the place does nothing to soothe my frayed nerves. I try to push thoughts of Primo from my mind, reminding myself that when I return to his office, I mustn't let him see how much he's getting to me.

Lost in my internal turmoil, I collide with a woman, nearly knocking her over. "Oh, I'm so sorry," I stammer, taking a step back.

"No problem," she replies, her voice cool yet sultry.

I take a moment to study her. She's stunning, with tanned skin that glows like a sun-kissed goddess and hair so dark it could rival the night sky. She stands taller than me, which isn't difficult given my height of five-foot-five. Her eyes are sharp and calculating, guarded secrets hidden behind them.

"Are you lost?" she asks, her tone implying that my presence is unwelcome.

"Ah, not exactly," I respond, trying to regain my composure. "I'm just...taking a break."

"From what?" Her inquiry is intrusive, but I can't fault her for being curious.

"Working on Primo's case," I admit, feeling defensive.

"Good luck with that," she mutters, her eyes narrowing as if she knows more than she's letting on.

As if on cue, Giovanni, Primo's brother, comes rushing over with a determined expression on his face. He stops when he sees us, and for a moment, I swear there's a flicker of fear in his eyes. The woman glares at him, pure hatred emanating from her gaze. My stomach churns with unease, sensing that something is amiss, especially given that this family is steeped in mafia lore.

"Excuse us," Giovanni says, his voice laced with tension. He takes the woman gently by the arm and leads her down another hallway, their hushed whispers following behind them.

I bite my lip, uncertainty gnawing at me. This place is a labyrinth of secrets, and I'm starting to feel like Alice tumbling down the rabbit hole. If I continue to wander these halls, I might just find myself in more trouble than I bargained for. Steeling myself, I turn and head back to Primo's office, determined to focus on the task at hand.

As I enter, Primo smirks from behind his desk, his dark eyes alluring and dangerous. Annoyance flares within me, and I wave off his game. "Who is the woman with your brother, Giovanni?" I ask, curiosity getting the better of me.

Primo raises an eyebrow. "I don't know about any woman with Giovanni." His tone is casual, but I can't shake the feeling that he's hiding something.

"Well, I just ran into one in the hallways," I retort,

crossing my arms defensively. "It looked like they were having an argument."

"Ah," Primo says, his lips curling into a wicked grin. "Giovanni isn't one for girlfriends, but that doesn't mean he doesn't need to... relieve himself. Unlike me, he doesn't have a beautiful little lawyer to admire." He winks, and I roll my eyes, fighting the heat rising in my cheeks.

"Please," I scoff, unwilling to entertain the idea. "That's not what's going on, and you know it."

Primo leans back in his chair, his expression turning serious. "You'd do well to let it go, Isabella. Some things are better left undisturbed."

"Fine," I huff, irritated by his evasiveness. "Can we please get back to work now?"

"Of course," he replies smoothly, gesturing to the papers strewn across the desk. As I sit down and begin to sift through the evidence, I can feel his gaze upon me, watching my every move like a hawk stalking its prey. Tension coils around us like a snake, and I struggle to keep my focus as we delve deeper into the dark underbelly of the Maldonado family.

## Chapter Six

### Isabella

The door to my small Boston apartment clicks shut behind me, and I immediately feel the exhaustion of the last week weighing heavily on my shoulders. Kicking off my heels, I pad into the kitchen and pour myself a generous glass of red wine. The velvety liquid swirls in the glass, casting a dark crimson shadow upon the countertop as I take a deep breath—a momentary reprieve before I face the reality of my situation.

My phone buzzes on the table, startling me from my thoughts. There's a flash of anxiety that moves through me before I look at the name. I hold my breath, hoping I'm not receiving another "anonymous" text message.

Evelina's name flashes across the screen, and I breathe a sigh of relief. My sister and I haven't always been close; our childhood rivalry inevitably led to a strained relationship.

But as we pursued our respective careers—myself as a lawyer and her as a doctor—we found common ground and reconnected. Now, she's more than my sister—she's one of my best friends.

"Hey, sis," I answer, my voice weary but imbued with warmth.

"Bella! How are you?" Her voice is chipper, despite the fact that she's likely just finished another grueling shift at the local hospital.

"Exhausted, honestly. It's been a crazy day." I collapse onto my sofa, sinking into the plush cushions.

My small living room is sparsely decorated with only a few pieces of furniture. A small sofa sits in the center, flanked by a couple of armchairs. The walls are painted a muted beige that matches the pastel rug beneath. There's a window that looks out onto the city and a bookshelf containing my favorite reads and a few family photos. The room has a cozy, inviting feel despite its minimalistic features, in stark contrast to the fancy mansion I know Primo is currently sitting in.

"Tell me about it," she says, her tone inviting and open.

"Okay, so you remember how I told you about Primo Maldonado? My new client?"

"Of course. He's the mob boss's son, right?"

"Exactly. Well, I've had my first real meetings with him this week, and let me tell you...he is something else." I take a sip of wine, gathering my thoughts. "He's this incredibly attractive man, but he's also an arrogant, controlling asshole."

"Sounds like your kind of guy." Eve teases, and I can practically hear the smirk in her voice. "Why not just use him for good sex and then move on?"

"Eve!" I exclaim, feigning shock. "There's a rule against sleeping with clients...at least, I'm pretty sure there is."

"Rules are made to be broken," she says with a laugh.

"Maybe for you, but I've got enough on my plate trying to defend him." I sigh, taking another gulp of wine. "Besides, I doubt he'd be interested in anything beyond a professional relationship."

"Are you sure about that?" Eve challenges.

"He doesn't seem like the kind of man who would let his desires get in the way of business. He's too calculating for that."

"Ah, well. You never know." She takes a pause before continuing. "Just remember, Bella, life is too short to waste time on people who don't make you happy. And even shorter when your job is defending mobsters."

"Thanks for the reminder, sis." I roll my eyes but appreciate her concern. "I'll keep that in mind. I just want this case to be over so I can finally move things in the right direction, you know? To finally distance ourselves from the crime world and focus on more legitimate cases. I honestly wouldn't have taken this case at all if it weren't for the fact that we really do need the money." I get up and start pacing around the small footprint of my living room.

"I get it," Eve replies gently, her voice softening. "Growing up, it was hard for both of us knowing that Dad always represented mobsters, even if it paid well."

"Exactly." I stop pacing, staring out of the window at the twinkling Boston skyline. "Our father's choices cast a shadow over our lives, and I just want to break free from it. I want our name to stand for justice, not crime. And, I'm tired of always looking over my shoulder, wondering if some loan shark is going to shank me."

"I'm so sorry, Bella," Eve says with a sigh. "I hate that you're dealing with the brunt of this. I wish I could help somehow."

"No!" I respond immediately. "I'm glad that they're only coming after me. I don't want you getting mixed up in any of this. It's honestly a miracle that they haven't come after you, too. Besides, you've got student loans to pay off."

"So do you," Eve points out.

"Yeah," I sigh. "But, not as many. I'll be okay."

"Dad's work made growing up so difficult for us. People at school stayed away from us because of his connections. And now it's followed us into his death."

"Yeah," I agree, my voice heavy with emotion. "We always felt like he was doing bad for society, and we bore the brunt of it. Still do."

"Frankie Moretti, the infamous mob lawyer," she muses.

It's a shame, really. Our father grew up in Italy, the son of a construction worker. He had a simple upbringing, but he was always jealous of what other people had. That's what likely led him to representing mobsters—they paid the highest amount.

And when the Italian mob asked him to come over to the USA, he dragged our entire family with him. He went to law school here, got his license, and continued to represent mobsters, despite everyone's hopes that maybe this would've been a new start for us all.

"New country, same old story," Eve laments. "But Bella, remember, you have the power to change our family's legacy. You can be the one to break the cycle."

I take a deep breath, feeling her words settle on my shoulders. "You're right. I need to focus on winning this case. If I do that I can get us out from under this debt and prove that we're more than just our father's reputation."

"Yes," Eve encourages me. "And who knows? Maybe working on this case will give you insight into how to handle your wayward client."

"Let's hope so," I say, clinking my glass against the phone in a makeshift toast. "Because I refuse to let him or our family's past define me."

"Cheers to that," she agrees.

"Eve, I'll be honest with you," I admit, as I swirl the wine in my glass, watching the deep red liquid catch the light. "I'm struggling with a lot of self-doubt. I wonder if I can handle this case by myself, but I don't really have the money to bring anyone else in. I don't even know if I would be allowed to bring anyone else into the case. I'm sure the Maldonado's don't really want their family life shared with too many people."

I take a deep sigh as I admit the feelings deep inside of me. "I'm just worried about whether I'm really smart enough to pull this off. I don't know, maybe Primo is getting to me after all. Or maybe, he's just picking up on something that's already there."

"Don't forget how hard we were pushed academically growing up. That's what's given us both our self-doubt," Eve reminds me gently. "Mom and Dad always expected perfection from us, but that doesn't mean we're not capable of handling big challenges. You're brilliant, Isabella. Don't let Primo intimidate you, no matter how attractive he is." She adds that last sentence with a lighthearted twinkle in her voice.

"Thanks, sis," I say, touched by her words. "I needed to hear that."

"Of course." She pauses for a moment before continuing. "So, tell me about your love life these days. Any other interesting prospects?"

I chuckle at her question. "Not really, and not like I would even have time even if there were. How have you been doing since the divorce?"

"Ah, yes, the great betrayal," she sighs exaggeratedly.

Eve's history with men was about as bad as mine. She married a guy just after she graduated college. I know she really loved him, but for some reason, his family did not love her. Not one person from his side even showed up to the wedding and she was devastated. Six months later and it came out that he was cheating on her with bridesmaids, a girl that she'd been friends with all through college. He refused to go to counseling and filed for divorce as soon as his affair was discovered.

I don't think she'll ever fully trust men again.

"Honestly, I've been enjoying casual dating. Just last night, I spent the evening with a guy who lives in a penthouse with mechanized curtains that open at dawn. Can you believe it?"

"Wow, fancy!" I exclaim, giggling along with her. "We've certainly come a long way from our Catholic upbringing, huh? I remember when we used to be so ashamed of even thinking about having casual sex, or any sex, really."

"God, yes," Eve laughs. "I'm glad we've broken away from that shame. Life's too short to be guilt-ridden over natural desires."

"Agreed," I say, clinking my glass against the phone again, celebrating our newfound freedom from the constraints of our past.

"By the way, has anyone else tried to approach you?" Eve asks, her voice softening with concern.

"Surprisingly, it's been quiet for a while now. But, you know, I can't shake off that feeling of unease."

My last run-in with a loan shark wasn't pleasant. I recall how he tried to physically threaten me, his hands gripping my arms tightly, leaving bruises as he reminded me that there would be consequences if debts weren't paid. I felt lucky to escape with my life that day.

I've received weird text messages and emails from anonymous numbers since then. For the most part I just ignore them, because what else am I supposed to do?

"Hey, maybe working with the mob is a good thing in

this case," Eve suggests, trying to lighten the mood. "Once they find out who you're representing, they might be smart enough to leave you alone for good."

"Ha! That would be the day," I chuckle, despite the lingering anxiety that sits in my stomach like a snake.

"Listen, Isabella," Eve says, suddenly serious. "Why don't we plan to get together for lunch soon? I'll be free after three more night shifts, and we can catch up properly, face to face."

"Sounds perfect," I agree, feeling a warm sense of comfort wash over me at the thought of reconnecting with my sister. "It's always nice to have quality time with you."

"Great! And I want to talk to you about a new real estate deal I think we should invest in together," she adds, her voice brimming with excitement. "I've been doing some research, and it looks very promising."

"Really?" I raise an eyebrow, genuinely intrigued. "Well, now you have my attention. I'm certainly open to discussing it."

"Fantastic! Let's make it a date, then." Eve's voice is filled with affection. "I'll call you after my last shift to set up a time and place."

"Looking forward to it, sis," I say, my heart swelling with gratitude for the unwavering support and love my sister provides me.

"Love you, Bella. Take care of yourself, okay?"

"Love you too, Eve. And don't worry about me—I've got this."

We exchange our goodbyes, and I feel reassured by our

bond and the plans we've made to reconnect. As I end the call, I can't help but reflect on how far we've come as sisters, breaking free from the shackles of our past, and forging our own paths.

I finish my last sips of wine and decide to just go to bed early. As I step into the shower, the hot water cascades over my body, washing away the tension of the day. The steam fills the small bathroom, enveloping me in a warm embrace. I try to reflect on the positive things I have in my life right now.

How fortunate I am to have a sister who not only supports my ambitions but shares in my struggles. Lathering my hair with shampoo, I think about how Eve has had her own battles, especially within the medical field. She's an incredible doctor, but the constant threat of lawsuits weighs heavily on her. People are so eager to point fingers and place blame; it's no wonder she's considering a change.

I rinse the suds from my hair, feeling a pang of sympathy for her. Our father never gave her the choice; he forced her into medicine because he regretted not taking that path himself. In contrast, I've always been free to choose my career. As the water courses down my body, I hope I've made the right decision in pursuing law.

The shower comes to an end, leaving me invigorated and refreshed. Wrapping myself in a soft towel, I pad into the bedroom and slip between the cool sheets of my bed. The case reclaims my thoughts as I lay there, staring at the ceiling.

There was something in the evidence folder that didn't sit right with me. A nagging thought, like a persistent itch, demands my attention. I promise myself to revisit it next time I'm at the mansion. I also need to have a real conversation with Primo, to determine his innocence and uncover what truly happened the night of his arrest.

"Is he really as innocent as he claims?" I murmur aloud, my voice barely audible over the hum of the air conditioner. "Or is this just another carefully constructed facade?"

I toss and turn, my thoughts tangled in the enigma that is Primo Maldonado. Despite my best efforts, sleep remains elusive, a mocking wraith hovering just out of reach. The sheets twist around me like silken lianas, binding me as I try to escape the torment of my own desires.

"Damn him," I whisper, beads of sweat trickling down the nape of my neck, tracing the curve of my spine.

My body throbs with an insistent ache, one that refuses to be ignored. My mind replays every interaction I've had with Primo, latching onto his dark, brooding stare and the way his muscles ripple beneath his tailored suit. I can hear his moans as he pleasured himself to the thought of me. The things he said he'd do to me...

I hate myself for succumbing to such primal urges. His arrogance is as infuriating as his charm.

"Alright, Isabella, enough is enough," I chide myself, my voice barely audible above the pounding of my heart.

I slide open the drawer of my nightstand, my fingers

brushing against the cool, silicone surface of my vibrator. It's been too long since I've allowed myself this release, and though it shames me to indulge in such fantasies, I know it's necessary if I hope to retain my sanity. Maybe by using him as material I can finally get the idea of him firmly out of my head and focus on the case.

"Primo Maldonado, you may hold power over the criminal underworld, but not over my pleasure," I think to myself, a wicked smile playing at the corners of my mouth.

With trembling hands, I guide the vibrator to my core, allowing the soft hum of the motor to coax me into oblivion. My imagination runs wild, painting vivid images of Primo's firm lips trailing a fiery path along my inner thigh, his dark eyes never leaving mine. The tantalizing combination of lust and danger sends shivers down my spine.

"Please," I gasp, my voice a desperate plea as the waves of pleasure build and crash around me.

"Only for you, Isabella," I imagine Primo's deep voice murmuring against my skin, his breath hot and teasing.

The tension within me twists tighter and tighter, each pulse of the vibrator sending me closer to the edge. My fingers grip the sheets, knuckles white as my body betrays me, drawn inexorably toward release.

"Primo!" I cry out, the name torn from my lips as the pleasure reaches its crescendo.

My breath comes in ragged gasps as I ride the emotional waves, finally allowing myself to relax in the aftermath. The shame of my desires threatens to consume me, but I push it away. For tonight, at least, I've found a way to cope with the maddening enigma that is Primo Maldonado.

"Tomorrow," I murmur, my eyes fluttering closed once more, "I'll face him again, and this time, I won't be so easily swayed."

With that final thought, I slip into a restless sleep, haunted by both the man and his secrets that still lie hidden beneath the surface.

## Chapter Seven

*Primo*

The sun spills through the stained glass windows of my office, casting a kaleidoscope of colors across the polished mahogany floor. I sit behind my imposing desk, my thoughts heavy like the leather-bound books that line the shelves. A knock on the door pulls me out of my reverie.

"Come," I say.

The door to my office creaks open and Charlie slips in, his face a canvas of worry. He shuts the door quietly behind him, as if trying not to disturb the tense atmosphere. I can tell he's bearing bad news.

"What is it?" I ask, not bothering with pleasantries.

"I haven't been able to find another lawyer to take your case." The words spill out, heavy with disappointment.

I'm on my feet in an instant, pacing the dim confines of my office like a caged animal. Panic ignites within me, a wildfire threatening to consume rational thought. "That can't be! What about Sal? Or Mickey?"

"Dead and missing," Charlie replies, his voice laced with frustration. "Every name I checked, all the same."

"Dead and missing?" I repeat, incredulous. "How is that even possible?"

Charlie's eyes flicker with uncertainty. "I don't know. Something's off."

"Is someone interfering with our case?" The question hangs in the air like an unwanted guest. "From within the family, or outside?"

"Could be," he admits, rubbing a hand over his stubbled chin. "It's suspicious that we can't find any of our usual lawyers, the ones who know how to handle cases like ours – bribing judges, threatening witnesses, that sort of thing. But at the same time, none of my sources have heard anything about threats to attorneys."

He meets my gaze, concern etched into the lines of his face. It's clear that Charlie takes this matter personally, his unwavering loyalty to the family driving him to find answers.

I take a deep breath, forcing myself to focus on the issue at hand. "So," I begin, my heart heavy with trepidation, "do you think Isabella is our best shot?"

Charlie sighs, his eyes downcast. "For now, keep working with her. I'll keep looking for another attorney, but she might be our best bet for handling all the pretrial work." He hesitates, gauging my reaction. "I'm confident I can find someone else before the trial."

I groan in frustration, the weight of uncertainty settling on my shoulders like a leaden cloak. "I don't like this, Charlie. I don't like it one bit."

"Neither do I," he agrees, his voice somber. "But we have to play the hand we're dealt, at least for now."

"Fine," I concede, clenching my fists. "What else did you find out about her?"

"Her background checks out," Charlie says, and I can tell he's choosing his words carefully. "Her father had a massive gambling debt from the race tracks. Loan sharks were after him before he died."

"Loan sharks?" I repeat. It adds depth to Isabella's story, making her situation more relatable and, dare I say, human.

"Yep," Charlie confirms. "In fact, they were the ones who killed him – not because of any mob connections, although that worked in our favor. They took care of the mess after he lost your father's trial. And now, those same loan sharks are after Isabella because she inherited her father's legal practice."

A heavy sigh escapes my lips. Isabella's story checks out, corroborating what she had told me before. It's another indication that she is, indeed, trustworthy. But can I truly trust her with my life, my future?

"Thanks for looking into it, Charlie," I say with genuine gratitude. "Keep me updated on any new developments."

"Of course." He nods solemnly before departing, leaving me to wrestle with my thoughts once more.

I force myself to sit back down at my desk and try and contain some of my anxious energy. My fingers drum impatiently against the smooth wood as I wait for Isabella to arrive.

Annoyance simmers within me at the thought of her refusal to live in the mansion during our time working together. Now that I know she's going to be handling things for the time being, she needs to fall into line. The fact that she insists on keeping her other clients only fans the flames. I want her undivided attention; I don't want to compete with anyone else for her focus. Today, I decide, I will bring this up again when she arrives.

The door swings open, and there she stands, looking stunning even in casual leggings and a top. She can sense me staring at her outfit and fidgets slightly.

"I figured we'd be working long hours," she explains, "so I dressed comfortably."

Her figure is a distraction I can hardly afford, the curve of her hips and swell of her breasts tempting me to imagine ripping off her clothing and taking her on the very desk at which I sit. She tests me, pushes me, and it ignites a primal desire to show her who's in control. But before I can indulge in those fantasies, an internal voice of reason reminds me there is much at stake. I need to focus.

"Isabella," I begin, trying to keep the edge out of my voice, "I've been thinking about our arrangement. I still believe it would be better if you lived here during the trial. And I must admit, I find it difficult to accept that you're not giving me your full attention by keeping other clients."

She arches a perfectly sculpted eyebrow, her eyes narrowing ever so slightly. "Primo, we've been over this. I value my independence and my career. I'll give you all the time and attention necessary to win this case, but I won't sacrifice everything else in my life for it. There are other people who also need my help."

"Other people on trial for murder?"

"Other people unfairly convicted of such crimes, if you must know," she says, her hands on her hips. "Among my paying cases, I also do pro bono work for the Innocence Project, trying to get those wrongfully convicted the justice they deserve."

Her defiance sends a thrill down my spine, even as it stokes the fire of my frustration. As much as I want to reach out, to pull her close and make her submit to me, I know that's not what she needs right now. We're partners in this fight, and I must respect her boundaries. At least until someone else can take over.

"Fine," I relent, gritting my teeth. "But remember, Isabella, I'm trusting you with my life. If you can't handle it, let me know."

She nods firmly, determination shining in her eyes.

As we dive into our work, I struggle to keep my thoughts on the task at hand, rather than the tantalizing image of Isabella laid bare before me. I much preferred the idea of her being my plaything and not my lawyer. But with every word she speaks, every idea she challenges, I can't help but be drawn deeper into her spell.

Isabella's fingers tap rhythmically on the polished

mahogany desk, her eyes locked onto mine as she leans in. "Tell me about the night you were arrested, Primo."

The memory hits me like a bullet to the chest, distracting my from my lewder thoughts. The sting of betrayal still lingers, even now. "I was outside New York City," I begin, my voice low and cold. "Dealing with an agent who'd gone rogue. He worked for the family, but he crossed us. We planned to take him out at a safe house."

Isabella's brow furrows, concern etching delicate lines across her forehead. "His name?"

"Acksel Michselson," I say, the words feeling bitter in my mouth.

"And that's when everything went to hell?"

"Exactly." My hands clench into fists, the fury still fresh. "Axe expected us. It was a setup. The plan was to lure him to this safehouse where he'd be killed and disposed of."

I can hear Isabella's breath hitch at my words, but if she wants to work on this case, she needs to get used to this sort of thing.

"I don't know who tipped him off, because he managed to get out of there alive. And the first thing he did was go to the Feds."

"I don't understand," Isabella says, writing down notes on her legal pad. "You were arrested for killing a man named Beau Bennett."

"Exactly," I say. "Beau was his old partner and was at the safehouse that night with me. When I left him that night, he was alive and well. Next morning, I'm being arrested for his murder."

As I lay bare the painful truth, I search Isabella's face for any sign of disbelief or doubt. Normally, I don't give a damn what people think of me, but somehow, her opinion matters. I want her to believe in my innocence.

"Primo," she says softly, her dark eyes filled with empathy, "I know you've done bad things. But you shouldn't go to prison for a crime you didn't commit. It sounds more and more like a set up to me."

I try and hide the shock I feel inside that she doesn't question my story. I told her the entire truth, but still, almost everyone in my life was questioning me right now. The fact that she believes me—*fuck*, it makes me feel something right in the middle of my chest. "Damn right." I lean back in my chair, the familiar weight of guilt bearing down on me. "If I could just tell my story to the jury, make them see the truth—"

"Absolutely not," she cuts in sharply, her gaze steely. "You are not taking the stand."

"Excuse me?" I bristle at her interruption, anger flaring. Who does she think she is, telling me what I can and cannot do?

"Listen to me," she says firmly, her voice commanding. "Taking the stand would be a mistake. The prosecution would tear you apart. We need a solid defense, not just your word against theirs."

Her words sting, but there's truth in them too. And beneath the indignation, I can't help but feel a twisted sense of admiration for her tenacity. This woman stands toe-to-toe with me, unafraid to challenge my every decision, and it sends a shiver of desire down my spine.

My pulse races with frustration and something more primal. "Isabella, I'm telling you, it's important for the jury to hear my side of the story," I insist, my voice rough with frustration. "I've been in this world long enough to know that perception is everything."

"Primo," she sighs, pinching the bridge of her nose as if she's trying to ward off a headache. "You don't understand. The moment you take the stand, you're giving the prosecution an open invitation to tear into every dark corner of your life. And trust me, they won't hold back."

"Are you saying I should just sit here and let them paint whatever picture they want?" I challenge, my gaze locked onto her steely eyes.

"Of course not." Isabella shakes her head, her red hair cascading over her shoulders. "But as your attorney, I'm in charge of our defense strategy, and there's well-established caselaw supporting that. You need to trust me, Primo."

My blood boils at her stubbornness. It only fuels my desire for her. But I push those thoughts aside, focusing on the matter at hand.

"Maybe I should get another lawyer," I snap, hoping the threat will be enough to make her reconsider.

"Fine," she retorts, her chin raised defiantly. "If you think you can find someone who'll put up with your stubbornness better than I can, go right ahead. Just remember, the prosecution is moving fast, and they're already trying to set a trial date within the next few weeks. But I'm sure you'll have no problem getting a new lawyer up to speed during that time. Or better yet, just represent yourself."

Her voice drips with sarcasm. She's resilient despite my mounting anger. She's not backing down, and my desire for her is almost overwhelming at this point.

"Alright," I grit out, clenching my fists at my sides in an effort to keep my composure. I realize that she won't be the one to handle my trial, anyways. For now, I just need to keep her placated so she does good work until I can find her replacement. "I'll trust you, Isabella. But I swear, if things don't go our way, I'm holding you responsible."

"Fair enough," she replies coolly, her eyes never leaving mine. "But trust me, Primo, when all is said and done, you'll be glad you listened to me."

As we continue to strategize and plan our defense, I'm forced to admit that there's something intoxicating about this woman who challenges me at every turn. She's stubborn, intelligent, and unrelenting, and as much as it infuriates me, it also ignites a fire within me that I've never experienced before.

The moment we agree I won't take the stand, Isabella's eyes gleam with determination. She leans forward in her chair, her fingers tapping on the table as if orchestrating our next move.

"Alright, now that we've settled that, let's talk about slowing down the trial." Her voice is steady and commanding, leaving no room for argument.

"Slowing it down?" I scoff, crossing my arms over my chest. "I want this over with as fast as possible."

"Primo, we need time to develop a solid defense strategy and look through all the evidence," she argues, her dark eyes locking onto mine with unyielding intensity.

"Listen, Isabella, I don't need—"

"Actually, you do." She cuts me off, her voice rising like a tide. "You're not an expert in legal strategy. This isn't a game of chess; your life is at stake here."

As she speaks, the fire in her eyes burns brighter. The way she challenges me, the way she refuses to back down—fuck, I want to bend her to my will and over several pieces of furniture, until she submits completely.

"Is that so?" I retort, my voice heavy with desire. I can barely concentrate on the words coming out of my mouth as I imagine her on her knees, doing everything I tell her to do. A vivid image flashes before my eyes: Isabella with a gag in her mouth, silencing her protests as she surrenders to me.

A small voice in the back of my mind says that I should start to take things more seriously, given that Charlie hasn't found a replacement for her. But then another voice counters and says that he's confident that he will and I'll be bribing my way out of these charges within a week's time. So, I allow myself to indulge. I lean into the daydream, thinking about how good it would feel to sit back and command her and then watch her do everything I tell her to.

"Strip," I say to her and she complies immediately. She doesn't argue, she doesn't talk back. She just slowly removes her clothes so that I can see her nakedness and then make use of it.

"Spread those beautiful thick thighs for me and show me everything you've been hiding," I say and she immediately opens her legs for me.

I hum in approval. "Already wet for me, huh?"

"Yes, Sir," she replies immediately.

"Why are you so wet, pretty girl?" I ask her.

"I'm always wet for you, Sir."

Her answer is like music to my ears. "I want to taste your wetness for myself," I say to her. "Come here."

She doesn't hesitate. Within seconds she's taking graceful steps until she's kneeling in front of me, her eyes cast downward in a sign of complete obedience.

"You're such a good pet," I say to her. "I'd like to taste you now."

She lays down on the floor and spreads herself bare for me.

"Please," she begs as she begins to finger herself. Her fingers slide in and out of her pussy, the juices dripping down onto the wood beneath her.

I stand over her and put my foot on her hand, just hard enough to stop her movements.

"Did I give you permission to touch yourself?"

"No, Sir."

"Then why are you touching yourself?"

*"Because I'm so desperate for your cock, Sir," she replies.*

*"You will stop now," I say to her. "Otherwise I will correct you."*

*I can see the fear in her eyes as she removes her fingers from her pussy.*

*"Such a good, obedient girl," I say to her. I lean down in front of her, wrapping my arms around her thick thighs. I bring her sweet cunt to my mouth and inhale deeply. "You smell divine," I say and she moans. "I bet you taste just as good."*

"Did you hear anything I just said?" Isabella snaps, her eyebrows furrowing in frustration.

I'm pulled out of my lust fueled thinking. "Of course," I reply, giving her a wry smile. "I was just imagining what I could do to keep you quiet and tamed."

Her cheeks flush with a mix of anger and something else, and for a moment, I think she'll lash out. But instead, she regains her composure, her eyes narrowing as she leans in, the scent of her perfume enveloping me like a sensual cloud.

"Let's get one thing straight, Primo," she says, her voice low and cold. "I am the attorney and you are the client. If you want any chance at winning this case, you'll listen to me."

As she speaks, I admire her strength and determination. She may be challenging my authority, but I know deep down that she has my best interests at heart. If she didn't, she could have already sabotaged my case in a number of ways, starting with making sure I wasn't released on bail. It seems that with the sea of treachery I've found myself in, she's the one lifejacket that's been thrown to me.

With her every word, my desire grows stronger, more intense... and more dangerous. It's too much and I find myself taking slow, measured steps toward her. Isabella's cheeks burn a deep shade of crimson, her eyes wide with shock and disbelief. Her chest heaves with each breath as she backs up, the outline of her breasts barely concealed beneath her thin blouse.

"Isabella," I murmur, my voice low and seductive as my hands find their way to her hips. "Don't you think it would be interesting to give in... just once?" I move her against the wall, trapping her between my body and the cold paneling. The scent of her arousal is intoxicating, and I can practically taste the desire that lingers on her lips.

"Primo," she stammers, her voice quivering with every syllable. "We shouldn't do this." But her body betrays her, leaning into me as if seeking solace from her own weakness.

"Maybe you're right," I concede, feigning thoughtfulness. "But maybe, just for a moment, you should let yourself be more...*submissive*."

Her pupils dilate as she struggles to process my words, her breath coming in short, ragged gasps. For a heartbeat, I believe she might succumb to my advances, but then her eyes blaze with indignant fire. She shoves me away with a surprising strength, her expression one of anger and defiance.

"Primo!" she snaps, her voice shaking with fury. "I am not some plaything for you to dominate! This is a serious case! You are on trial for murder!"

"Isabella, I–" I attempt to interject, but she cuts me off with a harsh wave of her hand.

"No!" she seethes, her eyes filled with tears of rage. "If you want to mess around, find someone else! I will not put my reputation on the line just for a good orgasm!"

With those final, biting words, she storms out of the mansion, slamming the door behind her. I watch her go from my office window, captivated by the sway of her hips as she stomps away. Even in anger, she is breathtakingly beautiful.

My cock aches with unfulfilled longing, and my thoughts are consumed by the memory of Isabella's flushed skin and trembling breaths. As I close my eyes, I can't help but surrender to my desires. I unzip my pants and my hand wraps around my throbbing length as I imagine thrusting into her warm, wet tightness, forcing her to submit to me.

"Isabella," I groan, my voice barely more than a whisper as I succumb to the fantasy, lost in the dangerous allure of a woman who refuses to bend to my will.

# Chapter Eight

## Isabella

The nerve of that man. I can't believe Primo thinks it's okay to treat me like that. I've told him countless times that I'm his attorney, not his little toy or whatever he called me. Rage bubbles up within me as I slam the door to my apartment, dropping my things inside the threshold. The sound rings through the empty space, but it does nothing to quell the fire burning in my chest.

I decide I don't want to work on his case for the rest of the day. Instead, I'm going to do things for myself since all I've been doing lately is bending over backward for other people. I make my way into the kitchen, the tempo of my thoughts frenzied.

I pour myself a drink and try and quell the anger still coursing through me. With a sigh, I glance over at the stack of documents on my small work desk, each page filled with Primo's case. It has consumed all of my time, leaving me barely able to work on the pro bono cases that once brought me a sense of fulfillment and purpose.

Just as I bring the glass to my lips, something chirps on my phone. My fingers shake slightly as I open up my messages and look through my spam filter.

> I hope you're enjoying the calm while it lasts, because the storm is coming. Pay your debt, or I'll make your life a living hell.

> I see you've been living the good life while owing me money. That ends now. Pay up, or I'll start taking things away, one by one.

> You've been playing games for too long. The interest on your debt is growing, just like your problems. Pay now, or things will get ugly.

My heart rate spikes as I read the threatening messages. I send each of them into the trash immediately, knowing that if I don't, I'll end up reading them over and over again. I'm doing all I can to get the money back, so worrying more isn't going to help anything.

I pull down my notifications and see that it wasn't these messages that pinged my phone. I look down, irritation flaring as I see a calendar reminder informing me there's a bar association meeting in 30 minutes. Crap, I totally forgot about that. My eyes flicker between the full glass of wine and the words on the screen. I guess taking the day for myself will have to wait.

With a resigned sigh, I set the glass down and quickly change into something more professional looking: a crisp white blouse tucked into a black pencil skirt, paired with a matching blazer. As I fix my hair and apply a touch of makeup, I steel myself for the meeting ahead, knowing it'll be filled with meaningless small talk and insincere smiles.

"Time to face the sharks," I mutter to myself, grabbing my keys and heading out the door.

The drive to the hotel is a blur, my mind already anticipating the conversations and connections waiting for me within its walls. As I park and exit my car, I notice the parade of stuffy suits filing into the hotel lobby - other lawyers, each one projecting an air of self-importance. I swallow down my apprehension; this is where I need to be if I want to succeed in this city.

Entering the hotel, I fill out a nametag, affixing it to my blazer. My last name stands out boldly against the fabric, a declaration of my presence. I really don't enjoy going to these meetings, but building a client base and making connections in the city are essential for my career. The Boston Bar Association represents both opportunity and challenge – a world of power players and legal minds that could make or break me.

As I step into the bustling conference room, I take a moment to survey the scene from my perspective. The space is filled with the low hum of conversation, punctuated by laughter and the clink of glasses. Crystal chandeliers cast a warm glow over linen-covered tables adorned with floral centerpieces. A lavish buffet lines one wall, an array of tempting dishes sending wafts of delicious scents toward me.

"Isabella! Long time no see!" A familiar voice draws my attention away from the surroundings. It's Janet, a colleague from law school who now works at a prestigious firm downtown.

"Janet, it's great to see you," I say, embracing her warmly. "How have you been?"

"Busy as always," she replies, rolling her eyes playfully. "But enough about me! I heard you're working on the Maldonado case. How's that going?"

I hesitate, not wanting to divulge too much. "It's complicated," I admit, my voice low, as if sharing a secret. "Primo is...a challenging client."

"Ooh, mysterious," she teases, raising an eyebrow. "Well, good luck with that. Say, have you met Daniel? He just joined our firm last month."

Janet introduces me to the eager young lawyer beside her. I shake his hand and exchange pleasantries. I feel a mix of pride and frustration at the meeting. I know where Janet works. Her firm pays what's known as Cravath scale salaries. Even a first-year associate like Daniel makes far more money than I do, and the most he's tasked with is creating meaningless checklists or pulling together signature pages.

I try and remind myself that I didn't choose to become

a lawyer for the money. That's what landed my father in an early grave. No, I chose to become a lawyer to redeem my family name and try and do good in the world. Money be damned. Even if I can barely afford my rent, I think to myself sadly.

"Let's grab coffee when things calm down, okay?" Janet asks. I nod and smile at her, and Daniel continues on their way.

"Isabella Moretti, right?" A voice interrupts my reverie, and I turn to see a young man extending his hand. His confident grin is more suited to a used car salesman than a lawyer. "I've heard about you. Greg's been talking."

"Ah," I smile tightly, taking his hand and giving it a quick shake. "You must be from his office. I can't quite recall your name..."

"Andrew," he supplies, not missing a beat. "And yeah, I work with Greg. So, how's it feel knowing you're gonna lose the Maldonado case?"

"Excuse me?" I bristle, clenching my fists at my sides. The audacity of this man – this child – is infuriating.

"Relax, sweetheart," he chuckles, leaning in closer. "Just having a little fun. Besides, it's not your fault you got stuck with a losing case."

"Isabella!" Greg's voice booms across the room as he strides toward us, a predatory grin on his face. "We were just discussing your inevitable defeat."

"Greg," I say through gritted teeth, attempting to maintain my composure. "Always a pleasure."

"Come on, Isabella, don't be so serious," he mocks, placing a patronizing hand on my shoulder. "We both know you've got no chance in hell of winning this one."

"Is that so?" I retort, trying to keep my voice steady despite the rage boiling inside me. "Well, I guess we'll just have to see how it plays out in court, won't we?"

Overhearing our conversation, a woman appears at my side, her eyes narrowed, and her lips pressed into a thin line. She gives me an encouraging nod before turning her icy gaze to Greg and Andrew.

I breathe a sigh of relief as I realize who it is. Tammy was one of my favorite professors in law school. I met her my first semester, and we developed a quick friendship. Since that time, she's remained a faithful mentor to me, always there for me in my times of need.

"Perhaps you gentlemen should focus on your cases instead of harassing my protégée," she says coolly, her tone as sharp as a freshly-honed blade. "I'm sure you have plenty of work to do."

"Tammy, always such a pleasure," Greg replies with a forced smile, the tension between them palpable.

"Likewise." Tammy's eyes never leave his, the air thick with unspoken animosity. "Now, if you'll excuse us, we have more important things to discuss."

As if on cue, the room falls quiet, and the meeting is called to order. The relief that I feel is palpable; I can finally breathe again. Tammy squeezes my shoulder reassuringly, her touch a comforting anchor amidst this sea of hostility.

"Give me a call later, Isabella," she whispers, her eyes warm and sincere. "We'll catch up properly soon."

"Thank you, Tammy," I murmur, my gratitude evident in my voice. With a final nod, she takes her seat, leaving me to find my own amongst the crowd.

The clink of silverware and the murmur of conversation fill the air as I make my way to my assigned table. The scent of roasted chicken and garlic-infused vegetables wafts from the nearby buffet, tempting my stomach even as my mind races with thoughts of Primo's case and my encounter with Greg. Every polished surface shimmers under the golden glow of the chandeliers, casting kaleidoscopic patterns on the crisp white tablecloths.

As I slide into my chair, I replay Tammy's words in my head, her fierce defense of me against Greg's barbs. Her confidence and unwavering determination are qualities I've always admired, and I'm grateful to have her in my corner.

"Isabella Moretti, right?" A woman seated across from me inquires, her smile friendly and inviting. She extends a manicured hand, her nails painted a deep, rich burgundy. "I'm Lila, I've heard great things about you."

"Nice to meet you, Lila," I reply, offering my own smile as I shake her hand. The conversation flows easily between us, a welcome distraction from the lingering sting of Greg's words. Our laughter mingles with the clattering of plates and the gentle hum of conversation around us, creating a symphony of camaraderie that soothes my frayed nerves.

Throughout the meeting, I steal glances at Tammy, sitting tall and confident amidst this den of legal lions. In her, I find solace and strength, a reminder that I am not alone in this fight.

## Chapter Nine

### Primo

"Something's off," I growl into the phone, my voice a mix of frustration and anger. The cold metal of the device presses against my cheek as I pace the length of my office. "I don't have time for amateurs messing up a simple gun shipment."

"Primo, we're doin' our best here. It ain't easy without you around," comes the reply from one of my guys on the other end. He sounds tired, worn out, but that isn't enough to stifle my irritation.

"Get it done, or heads will roll." I end the call abruptly, taking a deep breath to try and clear my mind. There's an itch in my gut that tells me something isn't right, but I can't pinpoint what exactly it is. House arrest is taking its toll on me; I feel like a caged animal, unable to oversee my family's business in person. Without me there, it's no wonder things are falling apart.

My thoughts veer toward loyalty, both within and outside of the family. I'm paranoid, I know, but I can't shake the feeling that something is amiss. How can I possibly solve these issues while trapped inside this gilded prison? I run a hand through my hair, trying to focus on the problem at hand, but instead, my mind drifts back to Isabella.

Ah, sweet Isabella. Her body pressed against mine in my office yesterday, her soft curves and the way she moved when I touched her... I crave more of her, yet it frustrates me that I cannot maintain my control around her. She's a distraction, but one I can't seem to resist. I can practically feel her warm breath on my neck, the hint of her perfume lingering in the air.

"Damn it," I mutter under my breath, shaking my head in an attempt to clear the vivid images from my mind. I can't afford to be distracted by lust, not when there's so much at stake. With a frustrated sigh, I close my eyes and try to focus on the matters that truly need my attention.

I try to refocus my thoughts on the trial, imagining the courtroom, the judge, and the jury. But as I envision the proceedings, Isabella's image overtakes my senses. Her beautiful figure, the way she leaned over the table in my office, examining the files with such concentration. I remember the curve of her breasts, just barely visible through the fabric of her blouse, and I can't help but think how they would feel in my hands.

My mind drifts further, imagining the satisfying sting of my palm against her round ass, the delectable sensation of reprimanding her for perceived disobedience. My body responds, arousal pooling in my abdomen, and I grit my teeth in frustration. I don't want to give in to these fantasies again, not when she's already tested my control so thoroughly.

"Enough," I mutter under my breath, standing up abruptly and heading toward the gym. The heavy door swings open, revealing a sanctuary of iron and sweat. I need to clear my head, to regain control over my desires and refocus on the tasks at hand. But even as I pick up a pair of dumbbells, Isabella lingers in my thoughts like a persistent phantom.

"Damn it," I curse, pushing myself through a set of bicep curls with more force than necessary. The burn in my muscles is a welcome distraction, but it's not enough to entirely banish her from my mind. I switch exercises, working my way through an intense workout, but still she remains, taunting me with the knowledge that my resolve is slipping.

"Primo," a familiar voice calls out behind me, snapping me back to reality. It's Teddy, smirking at my obvious frustration. "You look like you've got a lot on your mind, brother."

"More than you know, Teddy," I reply, forcing a smile and wiping the sweat from my brow. "More than you know."

As we continue our workout, I engage in small talk with Teddy, but it's only half-hearted.

"See dad lately?" he asks.

I shake my head and look down at my ankle monitor. "No. You?"

He shrugs. "Once or twice. Certainly not as much as Constantino, but hey, still more than Giovanni!" he laughs.

I nod.

"Yeah," he continues. "Although, it's not like you can really see him for all that long. Last time they limited visits to thirty minutes."

"I doubt I could even hold a conversation with our father for ten," I muse.

"Well, you know me," he says. "I'm pretty much able to hold a conversation with a brick wall. Sort of like yourself today."

"Yeah," I say absentmindedly.

I'm trying to pay attention but my thoughts are elsewhere, consumed by Isabella's presence and the ever-growing desire that threatens to overtake me. And as much as I try to refocus on the matters of the mafia and my trial, I'm starting to realize that I'm fighting a losing battle against the allure of the woman who seems to have entangled herself so completely within my mind.

As I struggle to shake off the persistent image of Isabella's curves, Teddy's voice cuts through my haze. "So, Primo," he continues with a chuckle. "Business has been slow for me lately. Not many murders to clean up this fall season. I know you're on trial for murder and all, but did that really mean you had to stop completely?"

His dark humor might have made me grin on any other day, but at the moment, it barely registers. Instead, I focus on the rhythm of my breathing and the strain of my muscles as I push through another rep.

"Alright, what's going on?" Teddy asks, concern etched across his face. He leans against a nearby bench press, his eyes locked onto mine as if trying to read my thoughts.

I hesitate for a moment before releasing a heavy exhale, allowing myself to admit what has been troubling me. "It's Isabella. I respect her intelligence, her passion, but—

Teddy cuts me off. "But, she makes little Primo a little bigger? Is that it?" He's got a grin a mile wide plastered on his face.

I inhale and exhale dramatically. "I'll never understand why women like you so much, Teddy," I say to him.

"It's because I make them laugh. Either that or I have a massive cock." He pauses and then adds, "It's both."

I shake my head but I can't stop the small smile that creeps onto my lips. "Well, if you must know, yes. I'm quite aware of the fact that Isabella is a beautiful woman."

"You guys are gonna do it," Teddy smirks. "I can feel the sexual tension from here."

I clear my throat. "Thank you for your predictions," I say. "What I was going to add was that I can't help but doubt her ability to handle this trial. She's young, inexperienced, and the stakes are so damn high. Charlie thinks he can find someone else, but I'm starting to lose faith that he can."

Teddy's expression shifts into one of understanding, his eyes softening with empathy. "Yeah, I get that. But from what you've told me about her, she seems like a fighter. And sometimes, that's exactly what you need in a situation like this."

"Maybe," I say, unconvinced. I return to my workout, the relentless pull of the weights mirroring the heaviness in my chest. My mind drifts back to Isabella, her fierce determination, the fire in her eyes. But it's not enough to quell my fears.

"Primo," Teddy interjects, "you know as well as I do that nothing is guaranteed in this life. You've taken risks before, and they've paid off. Give her a chance. Trust her to fight for you like she's already shown she will."

As I consider his words, I realize that my doubts have little to do with Isabella's abilities. It's my own vulnerability, the raw exposure of entrusting someone else with my fate, that terrifies me. But as I look at Teddy, my loyal brother, I know he's right.

"Yeah," I say, my voice barely audible above the hum of the gym equipment. "Maybe." I'm still not convinced and internally, holding out hope that Charlie will come through with someone we've worked with before.

As my eyes lock onto the sweat pooling on the cold floor beneath me, I feel Teddy's gaze grow heavy with concern. He knows me well enough to sense when I'm not sharing everything that's on my mind.

"Primo," Teddy says, his voice stern yet gentle. "Is there something else bothering you? Is it just that she's young and a woman that's making you doubt her abilities?"

I pause, considering his words. The truth is, the thought had crossed my mind. Would I be questioning her competence if she were an older man with a similar background? My gut tells me no, but admitting that aloud feels like exposing a weakness.

"Maybe," I confess, my voice barely audible. "But it's more than just that. I know she's smart and driven... but this trial could make or break our family name."

"Then judge her by what she's done so far," Teddy suggests as he wipes the sweat off his brow. "Has she shown any signs of incompetence? Or is it your own insecurities fueling these doubts?"

His words sting, but they ring true. Isabella has been nothing short of impressive in her dedication to my case. The more I think about it, the more I realize that it's my own vulnerability that's clouding my judgment.

"Thanks, Teddy," I tell him, clapping him on the back. "Sometimes I forget how wise you can be, despite all the jokes."

"Hey, don't go spreading that around," he chuckles, feigning offense. "I have a reputation to maintain."

As we continue working out, our conversation shifts to more pressing matters within the family. "Have you noticed anything strange going on with Constantino?" I ask, trying to keep my voice casual.

"Strange? Like what?" Teddy inquires, his eyes narrowing in suspicion.

"Like... I don't know. Meetings with other families that I'm only hearing about after the fact," I confess, my frustration mounting. "It feels like the family is starting to take sides, and I can't do anything about it from here."

"Constantino has always had a mind of his own," Teddy replies, thoughtfully. "But if he's forming alliances behind your back, that's something we need to address."

"Exactly," I agree, feeling responsibility settle onto my shoulders once more. "But what can I do? I'm stuck in this mansion, trying to lead from a goddamn phone."

The overwhelming scent of sweat and iron fills my nostrils as I glance down at the heavy shackles keeping me bound to this gilded prison. The ankle monitor is a constant reminder of my limitations and vulnerability, a weight that I can't seem to shake. Teddy's eyes follow mine, settling on the oppressive device.

"Y'know, Primo," he says, his voice low and conspiratorial, "I'm pretty familiar with that model you've got there. If you want it off, I could have it done in no time."

"Really?" I ask, feeling a flicker of hope ignite within me. My heart races at the thought of being unencumbered, free to move as I please and take control of my family's affairs once more.

"Of course," Teddy grins, his confidence contagious. "But can you put it back on when I need to go to trial? I don't want to get Isabella in trouble. She fought hard to convince them I wasn't a flight risk."

Teddy chuckles softly, clearly amused by my concern for the young lawyer. "Shouldn't be a problem, brother. Just give me a few minutes to grab the right tools and we'll have you out of those chains."

"Thanks, Teddy," I murmur, my gratitude genuine but tempered by the knowledge of the risks we're taking. As Teddy disappears into the shadows of the gym, I find myself lost in thought, contemplating the tasks ahead of me. There's so much work to be done, so many loose threads to tie up, and the thought of tackling them head-on fills me with a sense of purpose I've been sorely missing.

The metallic clink of tools against the concrete floor snaps me back to reality, and I watch as Teddy expertly dismantles the ankle monitor. My body tenses with anticipation, ready to burst into action once I'm finally free.

"Alright, Primo," Teddy says, looking up at me with a grin. "You're good to go."

"Thank you," I breathe, the weight lifting from my chest as I take my first unrestricted step in months, feeling like a man reborn.

# Chapter Ten

## Isabella

I'm hunched over my cluttered desk, buried in files and briefs from cases I've neglected since Primo's case took center stage. My fingers trace the edge of a manila folder, itching to delve into the details of another case when the shrill ring of my phone startles me.

"Moretti speaking," I answer curtly, my pen poised above the legal pad in front of me.

"Ms. Moretti, this is Janet from the clerk's office." The woman on the other end sounds almost apologetic. "I'm calling about the Maldonado case – the prosecution has requested an emergency hearing for Monday."

"Monday?" I balk, my grip tightening around the pen. "That's far too soon; there's no need to rush something like this."

"Sorry, Ms. Moretti, but the judge has already decided. This call is just a courtesy."

"Fine." I sigh, tossing the pen onto the desk. There really is no point in arguing with the clerks. They just deliver the messages. "Thank you for letting me know."

I hang up and slide back from the desk, my legs feeling weak. Primo needs to know about this hearing, and he needs to know now. Pushing aside the other cases, I grab my purse and head for the door.

The familiar creak of my beat-up car's door greets me as I climb inside. As I navigate the winding roads toward Primo's mansion, my thoughts return to him. Our last meeting had been tense, but he'd ultimately agreed to follow my strategy. And then there was the way he'd pressed me against the wall, his body so close, his eyes burning into mine. A shiver runs down my spine as my cheeks flush with desire. But he's still so arrogant, so insufferable – how can I want someone like that?

My car coughs and sputters, drawing me out of my thoughts. A loud bang slices through the air, and I grip the steering wheel tighter, praying I can make it to the mansion. But as I turn into the long driveway, my car gives up the ghost.

"Damn it!" I curse, slamming my hand against the dashboard before stepping out of the vehicle.

The gravel crunches beneath my shoes as I trudge toward the mansion, a mixture of frustration and anticipation swirling within me.

Sweat trickles down my back from the effort despite

the cooler fall temperatures as I finally reach the imposing front doors of the mansion. My legs ache, and my once-pristine clothes are now coated in a fine layer of dust kicked up from the long walk up the driveway. I take a deep breath to steady myself before knocking on the door.

"Isabella!" Teddy exclaims, opening the door with a guilty smile that doesn't quite reach his eyes. "You look exhausted. What happened?"

"Car troubles," I reply, trying to brush the dust off my clothing. "I need to speak with Primo – it's urgent."

"Ah, about that..." Teddy hesitates, scratching his head. "He's not available right now."

"Teddy, this is important. I'll wait." I step inside, glancing around at the expensive furnishings and lavish decorations adorning the entryway.

"Suit yourself, but you might be waiting for a while," he warns, leading me to a plush sitting area.

We sit on opposite ends of a luxurious couch, the silence between us growing heavy. To break the tension, I ask Teddy about his day, and we fall into an easy conversation about mundane topics – anything but the real reason I'm here.

Despite the small talk, I sense unease in Teddy. His eyes dart around the room, and he fidgets with the buttons on his shirt. He's hiding something, and my impatience grows with each passing minute.

"Teddy," I interrupt, no longer able to contain myself. "Where is Primo? This can't wait any longer."

"Uh, well, he's not here, Isabella," Teddy admits reluctantly. "He left earlier."

"Left?" I repeat incredulously. "How is that possible? He's supposed to be under house arrest!"

"Um..." Teddy rubs the back of his neck, avoiding eye contact. "I removed his bracelet... out of love."

"Teddy!" I snap, rising from the couch. "Do you realize how much trouble that could cause?"

"Hey, hey! Calm down, scary lawyer lady," he stammers, backing away with a nervous laugh. "I was just trying to help!"

"But you're not helping! You obviously knew that because you were trying to hide it from me!"

"Okay," he says, backing away further, his features still lighthearted like he's not taking this matter seriously. "I can tell you're angry, but if you just let me explain."

I cross my arms and wait for his words, but they never come. Instead, he turns on his heel and bolts down the hallway, legitimately running away from me.

"You can run but you can't hide!" I call after him. He laughs in response and then I'm left alone in the foyer.

As I stand in the silence of the mansion, the seriousness of the emergency hearing and Primo's reckless actions presses down on me. My mind races, trying to reconcile my desire for him with the mounting legal challenges we face. The stakes are higher than ever, and I can't afford to lose focus – not now, not when everything hangs in the balance.

I try his cell phone but it goes right to a voicemail box

that hasn't been set up yet. I resist the urge to scream in frustration.

I eventually make my way upstairs to Primo's office. Time seems to move slower than normal, and I lose myself in my thoughts as I wait for him to arrive.

Past midnight, shadows dance on the walls of the dimly lit room, casting eerie patterns in their wake. The grandfather clock in the corner ticks away the seconds, each one dragging on longer than the last. I sit in a plush armchair, unable to sleep, my thoughts consumed by Primo and the emergency hearing that looms over us.

The door creaks open, and Primo steps into the room, his tall, imposing figure silhouetted against the darkness. I can tell from the way he moves that he's exhausted, drained from whatever business matters pulled him away earlier. His voice is thick with fatigue as he speaks.

"Isabella...you're here?"

"Yes, and waiting for you," I reply, my tone sharp. "We have an emergency hearing on Monday, and we need to prepare."

"Ah, yes," he sighs, rubbing his temples. "I don't have the energy for this right now, Isabella. Can't it wait until morning?"

"No, it can't," I insist, rising from the armchair to face him. "I've been waiting here for hours, Primo. This is important."

"Fine," he grumbles, clearly not interested in discussing the matter further. He glances out the window and notices something. "Whose car is at the base of the driveway?"

"Mine," I admit, my cheeks flushing with embarrassment. "It broke down on my way here."

Primo seems lost in thought for a moment, his brow furrowed, before shaking his head and making his way toward the staircase. "I'm going to bed, Isabella. We'll talk about this in the morning."

"Primo, you're not going to bed," I declare, planting myself in the doorway. My heart races as I stand my ground, determined not to let him slip away without discussing the hearing. His dark eyes lock onto mine, a mixture of amusement and irritation dancing across his features.

"Isabella, don't play this game with me. You'll lose," he warns, leaning in close enough for me to feel the heat radiating from his body. The intoxicating scent of his cologne fills my nostrils, and I find myself momentarily distracted by the rippling muscles beneath his shirt. He catches my lingering gaze and smirks, attempting to lean in for a kiss.

"Get off me!" I snap, raising my hand to slap him, but Primo's reflexes are too quick. He catches my blow effortlessly, laughing softly before bringing my fingers to his lips. His warm breath sends a shiver down my spine as he murmurs, "Such hands could be put to good use doing other things."

"Infuriating," I hiss, wrenching my hand free from his grasp.

"You may say that, but your body cannot deny that it wants me," he retorts with a devilish grin. I glare at him, my frustration boiling over.

"Why aren't you more concerned about the emergency hearing coming up?"

"Because I trust you," Primo confesses, his tone shifting to one of sincerity. "I believe you can handle it."

My breath catches in my throat, taken aback by his words. This is the first time he's shown faith in my abilities, and it both warms and unnerves me.

"Now," he says, his tone still somewhat amused. "I'm going to bed, and I wouldn't object to you joining me."

"Go to hell," I immediately snap back.

"Oh, sweet girl," he drawls. "I've already built my forever home there."

"I'm going home," I say to him.

"Oh, are you?" he asks, amusement dripping off his words. "And, how do you expect to get there with a broken-down car?"

"I'll walk," I say, gathering my things and heading for the door.

He blocks my path. I look up to fight him, but his features tell me it's not a good time to argue. His eyes are dark, and he looks downright angry.

"You will do no such thing, and you will not argue with me about this," he says. "You're so smart at what you do but so foolish other times." I open my mouth to say something, but he cups his fingers over my mouth. My eyes go wide, but he doesn't flinch. "Do you not realize who your client is? There are forces outside of this family who would happily kill you on the off chance that it hurts my chances at trial. And you think you're just going to walk home in the dark? That I would let you do so?"

"Fine," I relent, my anger dissipating at his unexpected concern. "But I'm not sleeping anywhere near you."

"Of course," Primo chuckles darkly, his eyes never leaving mine as he leads me to a lavish guest room. The room is furnished with luxurious decor and furnishings. The walls are painted a warm gold, and the floor is covered in plush carpeting. A large four-poster bed sits in the center of the room, draped with soft sheets and fluffy pillows. There is an antique armoire in one corner, and a large vanity table with an ornate mirror in the other. I take a few steps in and peer into the bathroom.

A luxurious spa tub sits in the corner, begging to be used. The moment I see it, I can't help but feel a pang of longing – it's been ages since I've enjoyed a nice soak, and my small apartment doesn't offer such indulgences.

Primo catches my gaze lingering on the tub and smirks. "Allow me." He strides over to the faucet and turns it on, filling the room with the sound of rushing water and the scent of lavender. My eyes follow him as he makes his way to the door, and I reluctantly admit to myself that there's something irresistible about this infuriating man.

Just as he's about to leave, I blurt out, "Wait, you're leaving?" The words leave my lips and I know that the shock is written all over my face.

He turns and stands at the threshold. He raises an eyebrow as he looks at me, his eyes moving up and down my body. "Just a moment ago you were going to slap me, and now you want me to stay? Which is it, Isabella?"

I stand there, trying to think of a way to recover. I shake my head. "No, you can leave," I say, tripping over my words.

His lips lift into the smallest of smiles as he turns back towards the hallway. "As you wish, Isabella," and then he disappears into the shadows.

Morning comes, and I wake to find a set of keys on my nightstand. Confusion washes over me; I hadn't heard anyone enter the room while I slept. Picking up the keys, I notice the Lamborghini emblem and feel a surge of unease. What is Primo playing at?

I get dressed and head to his office, but it's empty. Descending the grand staircase, I'm greeted by Charlie, who introduces himself with a warm smile. He doesn't say much about himself other than the fact that he's known Primo and the family for a long time. I imagine that's mafia talk for him being a high-up mobster.

"Primo asked me to give you a message," he says, handing me a folded note.

"Thank you, Charlie," I reply, trying to mask my curiosity. Unfolding the paper, I read Primo's words:

*Isabella, I trust you'll take good care of the car - and yourself. You deserve nothing less.*

The words leap off the page in Primo's unmistakable scrawl, and I can't help but feel a mixture of gratitude and annoyance. He just couldn't leave well enough alone, could he? My old car, deemed unsafe, and now replaced by a sleek, black Lamborghini Urus waiting outside like a mechanical guardian angel. The note continues, assuring me that Primo is confident in my ability to prepare for Monday's hearing. It's both infuriating and flattering that he believes in me so much, even as he disregards his own safety by removing his ankle monitor.

"Charlie," I say, turning to face him, "what do you know about this?"

"Primo has always been one to... manage things," he explains with a shrug. "It's easier on everyone if he thinks he's still in control."

"Is that supposed to make me feel better?" I demand, gripping the letter tightly in my hand.

"Perhaps not," he concedes, "but it might help you understand him better."

With a sigh, I step over to the window and press the keys. The lights of the Lamborghini flash in response, confirming its existence as more than just a figment of my imagination. The sight of it sends a shiver down my spine;

it's hard to deny the allure of such power, the promise of protection it represents.

"Fine," I relent, looking back at Charlie. "I'll learn to play his game." But inside, my thoughts race - can I truly let Primo believe he's in control when I'm walking such a dangerous tightrope?

"Good," Charlie nods, seeming satisfied with my answer. "Now, if you don't mind, I've got things to attend to."

"Of course," I reply, watching as he disappears down the hallway. Left alone, I take a deep breath and brace myself for the task ahead. Returning to the upstairs office, I immerse myself in preparing for the hearing - because no matter how I feel about Primo's actions or my new car, there's one truth I can't escape: this case is the most important thing.

As the hours wear on, my frustration with Primo's recklessness only grows. But beneath it all, I feel a strange sense of gratitude for his belief in me. It's a twisted bond we share – and as much as I hate to admit it, I'm beginning to crave it more than ever.

## Chapter Eleven

## Isabella

Driving the sleek new Lamborghini to the courthouse, I can't help but admit to myself that I'm reveling in the feel of this luxurious machine. The purr of the engine sends vibrations through my body, making me feel powerful and alive. The car is fast, undeniably sexy, and, above all, it feels safe – like an iron cage surrounding me in a world that has become dangerous and unpredictable.

But despite the thrill of driving such a magnificent vehicle, anger simmers beneath the surface. Primo never showed up over the weekend to work on his case with me, and as the trial looms closer, I have no guarantee he'll even appear at the hearing today. I grit my teeth, resenting how much control he seems to have over me, both professionally and emotionally.

Pulling into the courthouse garage, I park the

Lamborghini next to a row of more modest cars. As I step out, the prosecutor - Greg - notices me, his eyes narrowing as they take in the gleaming SUV.

"Nice ride," he sneers, leaning against his own sensible sedan. "I guess selling your soul," he eyes me up and down, "or maybe more," he adds, "to the mob really does pay off."

His comment stings, but I refuse to let him see it. Instead, I toss my hair over my shoulder and stride past him, chin held high. "Good morning, Greg," I say coolly, not giving him the satisfaction of a reaction.

Entering the courtroom, anxiety begins to gnaw at my insides. Primo still hasn't arrived, and I glance around the room, searching for any sign of his tall, imposing figure. Greg sidles up to me, his voice dripping with false concern.

"Your client's cutting it a little close, don't you think?" he taunts. "Or maybe he finally realized he doesn't stand a chance in court."

I clench my fists, on the verge of snapping back at him when a deep voice makes me shiver. "I'd be careful about the way you speak to my counsel if I were you."

Primo appears seemingly out of nowhere, dressed impeccably in a tailored suit that accentuates his broad shoulders and narrow waist. He exudes an air of calm confidence, and for a moment, I find myself captivated by the sheer force of his presence.

"Ah, Mr. Maldonado," Greg says, unable to hide his surprise. "Glad you could make it."

"Wouldn't miss it," Primo replies, his eyes never leaving

mine. "Now, if you'll excuse us, we have matters to discuss before the hearing begins."

With that, he takes a seat next to me, leaving Greg sputtering in his wake. As much as I hate to admit it, seeing Primo come to my defense makes my heart pound with both gratitude and desire. But I can't afford to let him distract me – not now, when so much is at stake.

"Hello, Isabella," Primo says with a smile, his eyes locked on mine. I refuse to return the greeting, my jaw clenched in frustration at his weekend-long absence. He doesn't seem bothered by my silence, casually adjusting his cufflinks as he sinks into the seat beside me.

"Come now, Isabella. I made it on time, didn't I?" he teases, trying to coax a response from me. I bite my tongue, refusing to give him the satisfaction of knowing just how much his cavalier attitude has gotten under my skin.

"Primo, I—" I start, finally ready to let him know exactly what I think of his antics, but I'm cut off by the sudden entrance of the judge.

"All rise," the bailiff announces, and we do.

"Please be seated," the judge commands, and we follow suit. With an air of gravity, Judge Dolan launches into the proceedings.

"Ms. Moretti, Mr. Daniels," he addresses us both, "I understand there's a matter of witness credibility to discuss before we move forward."

"Your Honor," Greg begins, his voice dripping with disdain, "the defense has listed several witnesses whose connections to organized crime are well-documented. We believe their testimony should be disallowed due to the inherent unreliability of such individuals."

"Does the prosecution have a list of such witnesses?" the judge asks.

"Yes," Greg says. The clerk walks over to his table and grabs his copies. She hands one to me and then walks one back to the judge. I look over the list and my mind races. If the judge rules that these witnesses should be disallowed, we might as well just put Primo back into a jail cell ourselves. It would completely gut our case.

Judge Dolan looks over the list pensively. "Defense?"

"Your Honor," I respond, my mind racing for a solid counterargument, "the prosecution is attempting to introduce character evidence that has no bearing on the facts of this case. To strike our witnesses without consideration would be prejudicial to my client."

The judge narrows his eyes, weighing my argument carefully.

"Ms. Moretti, the prosecution brings up a good point as to the credibility of these witnesses. Do you have anything to say to that? I'm sure you're aware that as the judge I have the ability to keep this all out of evidence."

"I am aware, your Honor," I reply. "But, if the issue with the witnesses is the truth of their statements, then the jury should be the one to decide who is more credible. If the prosecution is so certain that these witnesses can be impeached, then they should feel free to do so at trial, rather than trying to hide behind the bench and risk creating an appealable issue for the Court."

I throw that last statement in as a subtle indication to the judge that I am not going to be a thorn in his side if he rules against me on this. The tension in the room is palpable, and I can feel beads of sweat forming along my hairline. Finally, he speaks, his voice firm and decisive.

"Ms. Moretti is correct. Unless the prosecution has evidence directly relating to the witnesses' credibility on the specific matters at hand, their character and personal associations are not grounds for dismissal and are matters for the jury to consider. The witnesses will be allowed to testify. The prosecution's motion is denied."

"Thank you, Your Honor," I say, relief washing over me like a cool wave.

"Very well, if there's nothing further," the judge looks between the two of us, neither of us getting up to speak, "This court is adjourned."

As everyone shuffles out, I steal a glance at Greg's scowling face. His frustration is evident, and a small, wicked part of me revels in his defeat. But I know that even with this victory, the battle ahead is far from won.

As the courtroom empties, I gather my papers and make my way toward the exit. Primo's presence lingers like a dark cloud, but I refuse to acknowledge him. Before I can slip away, his hand wraps around mine, stopping me in my tracks.

"Isabella," he says, his voice low and commanding. I grit my teeth, suppressing the urge to lash out at him.

"Let go of me," I demand, my tone icy. But Primo only laughs, pulling me into a small, windowless side room. He shuts the door behind us with a decisive click, leaving us alone in the dimly lit space. The air is heavy with tension, and I can feel the heat radiating off his body.

"Come on, Isabella," he chides, his grip still firm on my wrist. "You should know by now that such demands never work with me."

"Primo, this is not the time," I snap, irritation and exhaustion warring within me. "We have more important things to worry about."

"Exactly," he agrees, releasing my hand as he leans against the table. "Like Greg, for instance. Did you see the way he looked at you? Like he wanted to tear you apart."

"Greg's always been like that," I argue, rubbing my wrist where his grip had been. "It's nothing new, and it's not something we need to focus on right now."

"Isabella, listen to me," Primo insists, his dark eyes locking onto mine with an intensity that sends shivers down my spine. "I've seen men like him before. They're unpredictable, dangerous when they feel cornered. And believe me, he looks like he's about to do something foolish."

"Instead of obsessing over Greg, consider your own actions," I say, my voice edged with irritation. "You removed your monitor and put us all at risk. Besides, as far as dangerous men go, Greg's the least of my worries right now," I say, thinking about the messages I keep getting from the loan sharks. I push against his chest, trying to create distance between us. But he grabs my wrists, easily overpowering me, and pins me against the door.

"Seems we always end up like this," he murmurs, a wicked grin playing on his lips. My pulse races as I struggle to reconcile my attraction to him with my annoyance at his cavalier attitude.

"Let me go," I demand, my breath hitching.

"Isabella," he says, his voice low and husky. His lips barely brush mine as he adds, "You were fantastic in court today. I was particularly impressed with your oral skills." He smirks at his double entendre, and my cheeks burn with indignation.

"Primo, you need to stop—" but my words are swallowed by his sudden kiss, his mouth hot and insistent on mine. For a fleeting moment, I give in to the desire that's been simmering beneath the surface. His lips move against mine. I open my mouth and his tongue invades me greedily. I can feel myself falling into him as arousal courses through me. But then reality crashes in, and I remember that this is just another one of his games.

I bite down hard on his lip, a metallic taste flooding my mouth. He yelps and pulls away, freeing me from his grip. I take advantage of his momentary shock and wrench open the door.

"Isabella!" he calls after me, but I don't look back. Fear and adrenaline propel me through the courthouse, each step pounding out a frantic rhythm in time with my heart. When I finally reach my car, I fumble with the keys, my hands shaking.

As I slide into the driver's seat, the seriousness of what just happened begins to settle on my shoulders. Primo

Maldonado, the man I'm supposed to be defending, has once again left me breathless and conflicted. And as much as I want to deny it, I can't help but feel that I'm in way over my head.

My heart hammers against my ribcage as I merge into traffic, the sleek purr of the Lamborghini a stark contrast to the thunderous chaos inside me. I grip the wheel tightly, trying to steady my trembling hands and regain control of my breathing. The memory of Primo's lips on mine, the taste of his blood, refuses to dissipate, leaving me unnerved and disoriented.

"Get a hold of yourself, Isabella," I mutter, swallowing hard. I know I need help, someone to talk to about this tangled web I've found myself caught in. My thoughts turn to Tammy, my mentor and confidante from law school – she has always been there for me, offering guidance and support without judgment.

I reach for my phone and dial her number, praying that she'll pick up. "Tammy? It's Isabella. I... I need your advice."

"Isabella! How are you?" Her warm voice washes over me like a balm, soothing the frayed edges of my nerves.

"Can we meet for lunch today? There's something important I need to discuss with you."

"Of course, sweetheart. You know I'm always here for you. How about that little Italian place we used to go to during our study breaks?"

It's ironic, but fitting.

"Perfect," I say. "See you at one?"

"See you then. Take care, dear."

"Thank you, Tammy." As I slip my phone back into my purse, relief blooms in my chest, a fragile blossom of hope amid the thorny brambles of doubt and fear.

I focus on the road ahead, the sleek lines of the Lamborghini hugging the curves like a lover, the powerful engine humming beneath me. Stray sunbeams filter through the canopy of trees, dappling the asphalt with gold and casting intricate patterns on my skin. It's a beautiful day, and yet I can't shake the dark cloud of unease that clings to me, the sense of impending danger that prickles at the nape of my neck.

"Get it together, Isabella," I admonish myself, fighting against the treacherous currents of desire and dread that threaten to overwhelm me. "You are strong, capable, and smart. You can handle this."

With each mile that passes beneath the Lamborghini's tires, I try to steady my resolve, to shore up my defenses against the tempestuous storm of emotions that Primo has stirred within me. But as I navigate the twists and turns of the road, I start to wonder if I'm losing myself to something far more dangerous than mere lust – something that could shatter my world beyond repair.

# Chapter Twelve

## Isabella

A shrill ring pierces the air, pulling me from my thoughts. I glance down at my phone and see Primo's name flashing on the screen for the third time in less than an hour. My heart races, but I press the reject button with a shaky finger. *"Not now, Primo. I can't deal with you right now."*

Stepping out of my car, I take a deep breath, inhaling the intoxicating scent of garlic and fresh bread that wafts from the little Italian restaurant in front of me. The warm glow emanating from its windows promises solace, a brief respite from the chaos swirling around me. I'm excited to reconnect with Tammy, who has been my mentor and friend through thick and thin.

I tug on the heavy wooden door, and it creaks open to reveal a cozy, dimly lit room filled with laughter and clinking glasses. My eyes scan the familiar faces of couples sharing intimate moments, friends celebrating life, and then they land on her – Tammy. She's already waiting for me, her vibrant smile lighting up the room like a beacon. Her slightly graying blonde hair is tied up in a neat bun and she's impeccably dressed in a tailored skirt suit, as always. I wave, feeling a warmth spread through me as I think about what this woman means to me.

Tammy was more than just a professor during my first semester of law school; she became a confidante, someone I could turn to when things got overwhelming. She never judged me based on my father's mob connections, instead seeing me for who I truly was: a passionate, ambitious young lawyer determined to make a difference. As I moved into private practice and eventually took over my father's firm, our bond only grew stronger.

"Isabella! Over here!" Tammy calls, beckoning me toward her table nestled in the corner. Her voice soothes away the rough edges of my day as I weave my way through the crowded room.

"Tammy, it's so good to see you," I say, enveloping her in a tight hug. Her arms wrap around me, and for a moment, I allow myself to sink into the comfort of her embrace.

"Sit down, sit down," she insists, gesturing to the empty chair across from her. "I've been dying to hear all about what's going on with you."

As I settle into my seat, I notice the curious glint in her eye and I smile. This is what I've always loved about Tammy – her genuine interest in my life and well-being. It was a rarity in a world where people were often too consumed with their own problems to truly care about anyone else.

"Where do I even begin?" I sigh, running a hand through my hair.

A young waitress with a pixie cut approaches us several times, her pen poised over her notepad, ready to take our orders. But each time, we're too engrossed in our discussions to even glance at the menu. Eventually, we decide to order cappuccinos, providing us with the perfect excuse to continue talking without the interruption of food.

"So, how have things been?" Tammy asks, her blue eyes filled with genuine concern. She has this uncanny ability to sense when something's off, which is why I'm not surprised when she adds, "I could tell you were stressed out when I saw you at the Bar Association meeting, and I could hear it in your voice over the phone."

"Can't hide anything from you, can I?" I say, chuckling softly. My laughter fades as I think about Primo and the challenges his case presents. "Primo's case is more complicated than I anticipated. And, his compliance has been... difficult. He's stubborn and secretive, making it hard for me to build a strong defense for him. We've had frequent disagreements, and even though he's generally agreed to everything I've suggested, his compliance never comes easily."

Tammy listens attentively, nodding every so often. Our cappuccinos arrive, and I wrap my hands around the warm ceramic, eager for the soothing effect of the steaming beverage.

Taking a deep breath, I let the rich scent of my cappuccino wash over me. Tammy leans in closer, her kind eyes twinkling with the wisdom and experience etched in the fine lines around them. "Isabella, let me tell you about a case I had when I was working as a public defender. It might offer some perspective."

I nod, eager to hear her story, hoping it will provide solace amidst the chaos of Primo's trial.

"Years ago," she begins, "I had a client who was accused of recruiting high school boys into a gang. He was a teacher at their school, and he believed he could sway the jury with his charisma and lies." She shakes her head, her blond hair catching the warm glow of the restaurant's dim lighting. "This man was adamant about taking the stand, and despite my best efforts, I couldn't convince him otherwise."

My heart sinks as I imagine that responsibility on Tammy's shoulders, the same weight I now bear defending Primo. My fingers tighten around the ceramic cup.

"And what happened?" I ask, my voice barely above a whisper.

"Of course, it didn't go well," she sighs. "The jury saw right through him, and he was ultimately convicted and sentenced to life in prison."

"Tammy, I'm not sure this is helping me feel any better," I admit, my stomach churning with anxiety.

She reaches out and places her hand on mine, her

touch grounding me in the present moment. "Isabella, the point of my story isn't to scare you. It's to remind you that even I struggled with controlling clients back then. And look at you – you've already got someone like Primo Maldonado to comply with your strategy."

Her words weave a blanket of reassurance around me, her faith in my abilities helping calm my frayed nerves. I let out a shaky breath, trying to absorb the truth in her words.

"Thank you, Tammy," I say, feeling the ghost of a smile on my lips. "You always know what to say to make me feel better."

"Of course, dear," she says, her eyes crinkling with amusement. "Now go on and show them what a brilliant lawyer you are."

The confidence Tammy infuses into me blooms like a rose, petals unfolding to reveal its beauty. I take a deep breath, feeling the air fill my lungs and rejuvenate me from within.

"Isabella," she says, her voice warm, "have you come up with any theories about the evidence?"

I ponder for a moment, swirling the last drops of my cappuccino in the cup. "There's something lurking behind the scenes, but I can't quite pinpoint it yet," I admit, my words tinted with frustration. "It feels like a setup, and I need to determine who's behind it. That should be enough to clear Primo's name."

"Ah," Tammy murmurs, her eyes gleaming in the dim light of the restaurant. "You're on the right path, Isabella.

Just keep going." The certainty in her voice helps steady me against my own storm of doubts.

"Trust your instincts," she continues. "When you suspect something is going on, it usually is. You've always had good instincts."

Before I can respond, her phone trills with an incoming call. She glances at the screen and sighs, the corners of her mouth turning downward ever so slightly. "I'm sorry, dear, I have to take this. Duty calls."

We rise from our seats, our footsteps sounding softly on the checkered floor as we make our way toward the door. In the fading sunlight, her golden hair seems to shimmer, haloing her kind face. We embrace, the warmth of her body seeping into me, filling me with renewed strength.

"Take care, Isabella," she whispers into my ear before pulling away. "And remember – trust yourself."

As she walks away, I feel her words settle on my shoulders. Trust myself. It's a simple phrase, but one that has often eluded me in times of doubt.

The evening air kisses my cheeks with a gentle caress as I step outside. I marvel at how much time has passed, but it's always like this with Tammy. Hours feel like minutes.

As I walk up to my car, my thoughts are consumed by the trial and Primo and I momentarily lose track of my surroundings. I imagine Primo's dark eyes watching me, their depths hiding a secret longing for release, for the freedom to indulge in our shared desires without judgment or fear.

"Isabella," a voice rasps, as rough hands seize my arms, wrenching me from my reverie. A strange man's twisted visage leers into mine as he spins me around, his grip on my arms like a vice. His eyes are bloodshot and wild, glinting with maliciousness in the dim light of the evening. I can sense his rage and desperation in equal measure.

"You thought you could just walk away from your family's debts?" he growls, his voice barely recognizable through clenched teeth.

I try to shake him off, but it's no use; his grip is too strong. Fear clenches my chest as I realize I'm completely helpless against him.

"Your time is up and you've failed to pay. So, we'll find another way you can pay off your debt." He runs his hands down my body and I try and fight against him. "I think there's plenty of men who will pay a few hundred dollars to play with you. You'll get your balance paid off in no time."

My mind races as I frantically try to figure out a way out of this situation. Nothing seems to work – he's stronger than me and has the upper hand.

"Let go of me!" I struggle against his hold, but his strength is unyielding. As he attempts to drag me toward his car, a dark voice pierces the night, freezing us both in place.

"I've already got one murder charge to my name, ragazzo." The word drips from Primo's lips like venom, his tall figure emerging from the shadows, an avenging angel bathed in moonlight. "Adding another wouldn't really be that big of a deal."

"Fuck off," the stranger spits, trying to maintain some semblance of control, but I can see the flicker of fear dance across his features.

"Watch your language," Primo warns, his tone cold and calm, a stark contrast to the rage simmering beneath the surface. "Let Isabella go."

The man's grip falters for a moment but he refuses to release me, fueling Primo's anger. "Wrong choice," Primo says. In an instant, Primo's fist connects with his jaw, the sickening crunch breaking through the night like a gunshot.

As the man crumples to the ground, Primo turns to face me then, his features composed but his gaze still smoldering with barely contained rage. He reaches out and takes my hand gently, slowly drawing me closer until I can feel his warmth radiating off of him like a beacon of comfort and protection. The scent of his cologne envelopes me, a heady mixture of leather and spices that ignites a fire within me.

"Are you okay?" he murmurs, his breath warm against my ear, my body responding.

"Yes," I whisper, pressing myself closer to him, seeking solace in his embrace. Primo reaches down and cups my face in his hands, finally giving me the permission I seek. As our eyes meet, I see the raw desire flickering there, a reflection of my own yearning to surrender to the darkness we share.

"Thank you, Primo," I murmur, and his lips curl into a ghost of a smile, both tender and fierce.

"I can't have my lawyer go missing on me, can I?" he breathes out.

"You'd definitely lose without me," I say, looking into his eyes.

"I would be lost without you," he murmurs.

Then, as if on cue, our mouths meet, sealing our unspoken fate.

## Chapter Thirteen

### Isabella

Primo's lips break away from mine, leaving me breathless and burning with unbridled desire. His stormy eyes lock onto the loan shark as he tries to scramble to his feet. In an instant, Primo's suede loafer is planted firmly on the man's neck, pinning him down like a trapped animal.

"Touch her again," Primo snarls, "and it'll be the last thing you ever do."

My heart races as I watch the scene unfold, my body quivering with a mixture of fear and exhilaration. Primo pulls out his phone, and I clutch at his shirt, the desperation in my voice evident as I beg him not to put himself at risk.

"Primo, you can't do this. You're already on trial for murder – don't make things worse for yourself."

He looks at me, his gaze softening for a moment. "I

won't let anything happen to me, Isabella," he reassures me, before dialing 911. "There's been an attack on West Main Street. A woman needs assistance."

"Primo, you can't stay here. You're under house arrest," I remind him, the urgency in my voice rising.

"Trust me," he says, and I'm struck by the intensity of his gaze. He reaches into his pocket and pulls out zip ties, securing my assailant to a nearby street sign. As the man starts to protest, Primo lands one more punch to his face, knocking him out cold.

"Come on," he murmurs, taking my hand and leading me away from the scene. The world seems to blur around us as we rush to my car, my thoughts consumed by the violence and passion that just unfolded before me.

As Primo slides behind the wheel, the silence in the car is deafening. My pulse quickens with every mile that passes on our way back to the mansion, my body aching to be close to him. I know it's wrong – he's my client, and I should maintain a professional distance. But the way he defended me... I can't help but feel drawn to him.

As we drive through the night, the darkness outside mirrors the forbidden desires that swirl within me. I steal glances at Primo, watching his strong hands grip the steering wheel, and I long to feel those hands on my body. His actions were violent and reckless, and yet, they ignited a fire within me that I cannot ignore.

"Isabella," Primo whispers, his voice like velvet. "I promise you, everything will be alright."

But as our journey continues, I wonder if giving in to these feelings will be our undoing.

The moment Primo pulls the Lamborghini into the cavernous garage of the mansion, my heart races in anticipation. The dim lighting casts a seductive glow over us, heightening the tension that's been building between us since the incident. Primo turns to me, his dark eyes piercing through the night as he assesses my condition.

"Did he touch you? Hurt you in any way?" His voice is laced with concern and an underlying rage. It's intoxicating.

"Primo, I'm fine," I assure him, my voice trembling slightly. "You saved me before anything could happen."

He studies my face intently, gently turning it this way and that, searching for any signs of injury. Once satisfied, he leans back in his seat, his intense gaze still locked onto mine. "Is this the first time something like this has happened?" he asks.

I'm surprised by his question. Primo didn't really seem like the sort of man to be interested in my personal life.

"No," I admit. "It's the second."

"You're a lawyer. Why didn't you get a restraining order?"

"It's not as simple as you think," I reply to him. "Everyone thinks it's so easy to get a restraining order against someone else, but it's actually a really high standard to meet. Courts see it as restricting someone's freedom before they've been on trial."

Primo chuckles darkly. "I can't imagine what that feels like."

"Yes, well. Things had been quiet for a while. I sort of thought that maybe they'd just given up."

Primo turns to me and looks murderous. "You should have told me it had gotten to this point."

"Why? So you could end up with a second murder charge and I'd have to live with that guilt for the rest of my life? I'm not from your world, Primo. I couldn't handle something like that."

"Why go into the law if you knew this was waiting for you?" he asks.

I find myself admitting a vulnerability to him against my better judgment. "Because, when you don't love yourself, you end up doing what people tell you to do, even if they don't have your best interests at heart."

He leans toward me. "Isabella, what are you saying?"

He swipes a tear away from my cheek. "I'm just saying that there have been times when I've struggled against myself."

"Nonsense," he says immediately. "You're the perfect blend of beauty and brains. Who ever made you feel like less?"

I shrug. "My father demanded a lot of us growing up."

"Ah," Primo says with understanding. "Well, good thing he's dead."

I smile at his attempt at humor. It's dark, but that fits him.

"You shouldn't doubt yourself, Isabella," he says.

"You doubted me," I mumble back weakly.

He pauses, his brows furrowing as he considers my words. "Before I knew you, yes," he finally admits. "And that was my error."

I'm shocked by his words. It's not an apology, but in some ways, it's validation from him that he might think I truly am capable of winning this for him.

"Thank you," I reply, unsure of what else to say.

"But, from now on, you need to be more careful," he warns, the authority in his voice making me shiver.

I nod in silent agreement, feeling myself submit to his command for the first time.

A part of me knows I should maintain some semblance of professionalism, but the allure of relinquishing control to him is too strong to resist.

"Promise me," he murmurs, cupping my cheek with his warm hand.

"I promise."

Then, without warning, he closes the gap between us and captures my lips in a searing kiss. I willingly surrender to his imposing presence, allowing the heat of our passion to consume us both.

"God, Isabella," he breathes against my mouth, his hands roaming my body with a possessiveness that only serves to stoke the flames of desire within me. "The things I want to do to you..."

"Tell me," I plead, desperate to hear the sinful words escape his lips. "Tell me what you want."

His fingers trace the curve of my waist, the warmth of

his touch sending a shudder through me. "I want to explore every inch of you," he confesses, his voice low and dangerous. "To make you feel things you've never felt before."

As his hands continue their slow, deliberate journey over my body, I find myself becoming more and more aroused, craving everything he has to offer. My logical mind warns me of the consequences of giving in to this forbidden passion, but the relentless pounding of my heart drowns out its protests.

"Please," I whisper, arching into his touch. "Show me. Show me how it feels to be truly alive."

"Isabella," he murmurs, his eyes dark with desire as he leans in for another heated kiss.

Primo's hands, strong and demanding, slide under my shirt, pushing the fabric up over my breasts. I gasp at the sudden exposure, but his mouth is on mine, stealing my breath as he kisses me deeply. My bra follows suit, unhooked with an ease that speaks of experience, leaving my sensitive flesh bared to his hungry gaze.

"Such perfect tits," Primo murmurs against my lips, his voice rough with desire. "I need to taste them." And before I can respond, his mouth descends upon one nipple, sucking it forcefully into his mouth. The mix of pain and pleasure has me crying out, my back arching, desperate for more of his touch.

"Primo," I moan, my hands tangled in his dark hair, urging him closer. He obeys, switching to my other breast as his free hand grips my skirt, hiking it up around my hips. His fingers find their way beneath the lace of my panties, rubbing roughly over my aching center. I can feel the heat building within me, threatening to consume me completely, and just as I think I might come from the friction alone, Primo stops.

"Wait," I gasp, disoriented by the sudden loss of contact. He responds with a wicked grin, gripping the waistband of my panties and yanking hard, ripping the delicate fabric in two. I stare at him wide-eyed, my breath coming in ragged pants.

"Are these your favorite panties, Isabella?" he asks holding them in the air, his tone teasing. I try to form a coherent response, but all I can manage is a strangled sound. "They are now," he tells me, smirking as if he's just given me the greatest gift. "Because I made them better with my touch."

His hand traces the mark left on my hip from the force of his grip, and my body shivers. "You're welcome for the mark," he adds, his dark eyes locked onto mine. The roughness of his touch, the intensity of his gaze – it's unlike anything I've ever experienced. It should frighten me, but instead, I find myself craving more.

"Primo," I whisper, my voice heavy with need. "Please... I want more."

"Is that so?" he purrs, his fingers teasingly close to where I ache for him most. "Tell me, Isabella. What do you want me to do?"

"Touch me," I beg, the words spilling from my lips without thought. "Make me feel alive. Please, Primo," I plead, my voice quivering with desperation. "Touch me again."

I lie exposed before him in the car, my breasts bared and panties shredded, my neediness laid bare for him to see. And he revels in it, his dark eyes dancing with wicked delight.

"Tell me what you really want, Isabella," he urges, a predatory grin spreading across his face.

My heart pounds wildly in my chest as I give voice to my desires. "Everything," I plead, blushing.

His hand shoots out to grip my face roughly, his fingers digging into my skin. "I do love it when you beg me." He leans in close, our breaths mingling in the charged air between us. "Open your mouth."

I obey without hesitation, my heart skipping a beat at the command. He grins savagely before spitting into my open mouth. The shock of it sends a shiver down my spine, but the boldness of his action only serves to stoke the fire within me. My mind swirls with lustful thoughts, too hazy to process anything else.

"Taking it all in so well," he murmurs, his satisfied smile sending another current of desire through me. My body trembles with anticipation, my hips bucking upward in silent supplication.

"Where's my prim and proper lawyer now?" he taunts, his fingers hovering agonizingly close to where I crave his touch the most. But he refuses to grant me that pleasure, teasing me mercilessly instead.

"Primo," I whimper, unable to contain my impatience

any longer. He doesn't respond kindly to my protests, seizing my face once more and puckering my lips with force.

"Keep quiet and wait for me to give you pleasure on my terms," he growls, the low timbre of his voice sending me into overdrive.

I bite back a moan, acquiescing to his demand with a breathless nod. As I surrender myself to his control, I marvel at how this man – my client – has set me ablaze in ways I never thought possible. But right now, all that matters is the intoxicating dance of power and desire that binds us together in this moment, as I willingly submit to his every whim.

My body aches with need, the anticipation of Primo's touch making me feel as if I'm about to shatter. His fingers finally enter me, and it feels like an answered prayer. The pressure, the sensation, it's all nearly enough to make me come just from that first thrust.

"God, Primo," I gasp, my head falling back against the car seat as he fills me in all the right ways. He leans over, his mouth capturing one of my nipples, sucking on it with a ferocity that borders on pain—but only serves to heighten my pleasure.

"Look at you," he growls between licks, "so wet for your client, someone who represents everything you hate. But you can't help but make a mess over this brand new leather. Just how far will you go for me, Isabella?" His words should embarrass me, but instead, they ignite something deep within, a desire to submit fully to him. My mind lets go, surrendering to whatever he wants.

"Anything," I breathe, "I'll do anything you want."

His teeth graze my neck, biting down gently but firmly, while his fingers curl inside of me. The dual sensations hit my g-spot, sending waves of ecstasy crashing through me. I scream out his name, my orgasm overwhelming and consuming every inch of me.

As I come down from the high, Primo removes his hand, his fingers glistening with my arousal. He holds them up to my lips, commanding me to taste myself. I obediently stick out my tongue, eager to sample my own essence, but he gives me only a teasing taste before pulling away.

"So greedy," he chides, his eyes dark and smoldering. "Your pussy juices are mine now." The possessiveness in his voice causes a thrill to run down my spine.

"Get on your knees and clean up your mess," he orders, nodding toward the leather seat below me. I give him a hazy smile, realizing that I want nothing more than to obey his command, to please him in any way I can.

I move into the footwell of the car, kneeling before the evidence of my pleasure. As I lick the glistening liquid from the leather, savoring the taste and the submission, I hear Primo's ragged breaths above me. I glance up and see him watching me intently, stroking himself to the sight of my obedience.

"Good girl," he murmurs, approval lacing his voice. "You're learning so well."

The praise sends a shiver through me. I don't even recognize myself in this moment. Primo is my client. Someone I'm representing to get money so I can get away from mobsters like him. And yet, here I am, exploring fantasies I never even knew I had with him.

"Primo," I whisper as I crawl up toward him, my eyes locked on his swollen, throbbing cock. He catches me by the cheeks, a firm grip that forces me to look into his eyes.

"Isabella, what do you think you're doing?"

"Please," I reply meekly, "I want to taste you."

His wicked grin spreads across his face. "That is an honor, and you need permission first." He releases my face and pinches my nipples between his fingers, making me squirm in response.

"Please, Primo, let me make you feel good."

"Filthy girl, needing it so bad," he says, his voice dark and intoxicating. "Tell me what you are."

"Your filthy, needy slut," I confess, my cheeks flushing with both arousal and embarrassment. Only then does he nod his consent, his eyes never leaving mine as I lower my mouth to his erection.

My lips wrap around his thick shaft, and he places a hand at the back of my head, controlling my movements. His hips thrust upward, forcing his cock deeper into my mouth than I've ever taken before. Normally, this sort of thing would make me uncomfortable, but with Primo, I find myself relishing every moment of submission.

As I struggle to accommodate his size, I wish for a taste of his cum. But with his cock filling my mouth, I'm unable to communicate my desire. Instead, I glance up at him through my lashes, hoping he understands my silent plea.

"Ah, Isabella," he taunts, "you want something, don't you? Too bad you can't tell me, and you won't be able to when your pretty little mouth is dripping with my cum." The thought sends a fresh wave of anticipation through me, and I redouble my efforts, desperate to please him.

Finally, after endless moments of thrusting and teasing, Primo's grip tightens in my hair, and he groans as his cum floods my mouth. I swallow it greedily, savoring the taste and texture, a testament to our dark and twisted connection.

"Drink it down like the beautiful, needy slut you are," he commands, his voice thick with approval. "What a good girl you are, sucking me dry," he moans. "You look so gorgeous like this: on your knees, swallowing every last drop of my cum."

My heart swells with pride and satisfaction, knowing that I've pleased him. As I sit back on my heels, my chest heaving, I realize that this is only the beginning of our dangerous liaison.

## Chapter Fourteen

*Primo*

As the haze of adrenaline begins to clear, I watch Isabella's chest heave with each breath she takes. Her body glistens with the remnants of our passionate encounter, and for a moment, satisfaction courses through me like a wave. I had longed for this moment, for her submission, but now that it has come to pass, I find myself holding back from sharing my darkest secret.

"Isabella," I say, my voice low and hesitant. "I would like you to stay here at the mansion tonight instead of going home."

She looks up at me, her dark eyes shimmering with an emotion I can't quite place. To my relief, she nods, not arguing or questioning my request. As she regains her composure and begins to right her clothing, I steal one last longing look at her exquisite form before it is hidden beneath the layers of fabric.

"Alright," she agrees softly, her lips curling into a gentle smile that tugs at something deep within me. The sensation is both intoxicating and terrifying, as it threatens to unravel the walls I've built around my own heart.

"Thank you," I murmur, struggling to maintain the facade of control that I pride myself on. The truth is, I'm terrified of allowing anyone to get too close – especially someone as trustworthy and captivating as Isabella. And yet, in this moment, I find myself craving her presence.

"Are you alright?" she asks, her concern palpable as she places a hand on my arm. The warmth of her touch sends shivers down my spine, and I fight the urge to pull her into my arms once more.

"I am," I reassure her, though my voice trembles ever so slightly. "It's just... It's been a long time since I've felt this way."

She gives me a reassuring look. "I understand."

Her words bring a small measure of comfort, but the fear still lingers in the shadows of my heart. As we sit there, our bodies mere inches apart, I wonder if I am making a mistake by letting her get so close. But despite my reservations, I know that I cannot resist the tension between us any longer.

"Come," I say, extending my hand to her. "Let's go inside."

As Isabella takes my hand and follows me into the

mansion, I cannot shake the feeling that something has irrevocably changed between us. And as much as it terrifies me, I find myself wanting to embrace the vulnerability that comes with trusting another person – even if it means risking my own carefully constructed walls.

As we step into the grand entrance of my mansion, the intricate chandelier above casts a warm glow upon Isabella's delicate features. My heart beats faster, knowing that I should say goodnight and let her rest, but the thought of parting from her presence brings an unexpected emptiness within me.

"Isabella," I begin hesitantly, "I know it's late, but would you mind working on the case with me for a little longer?"

Her eyes brighten as she smiles softly, nodding in agreement. "Of course. I'm always up for late-night strategizing."

Together, we make our way to my dimly lit office, where the scent of aged leather and rich mahogany fills the air. Isabella immediately sets to work, pulling out the discovery documents and organizing them meticulously on the large oak table. Her focus is resolute, her movements deliberate, and I'm completely captivated by the sight before me.

As I watch her work, guilt gnaws at my chest, reminding me of my initial skepticism toward her abilities. The memory feels like a distant echo, drowned out by the vivid proof of her dedication and skill. I can still see the way she looked at me in the car when she pointed out that I doubted her.

I realize now that I was foolish to think I needed another attorney. It's time to set things right.

"Isabella," I say, my voice low and sincere, "I want to apologize for doubting you in the beginning. You've proven yourself to be a formidable attorney, and your performance during this morning's hearing was nothing short of impressive."

She pauses, her cheeks flushing a lovely shade of pink as she meets my gaze. "Thank you. That means a lot coming from you."

A warmth spreads through my chest, and I find myself longing to share more about my past with this woman who has already seen the darkest parts of me. It is a new sensation, one that both exhilarates and terrifies me.

"Isabella," I confess, my voice barely above a whisper, "I think I know why I was so hard on you to begin with."

Her eyes widen with curiosity, but she remains silent, giving me the space to continue.

I take a deep breath and let it out slowly, trying to steady my nerves. "I've always had self-doubts about whether I'm truly fit to lead the family. My father... our relationship has been complicated, to say the least."

"You know you can talk to me about your father and your childhood," Isabella urges gently, her gaze never leaving mine.

"Growing up, it was clear that my father favored

Constantino over me," I admit, feeling a mixture of bitterness and vulnerability as I speak the words aloud. "You see, while I am the oldest, our father had a penchant for marrying and divorcing. Each of us sons are technically a firstborn from each of his marriages."

"Ah, I see," Isabella murmurs, nodding in understanding.

"Constantino has always been the one to side with our father when it comes to how the family business should be run," I continue. "Unlike Giovanni, I never felt we should leave the crime world entirely. However, I did believe there was merit in expanding our family into more legitimate holdings to secure our future."

"And your father disagreed with you?" Isabella asks, her brow furrowing in concern.

"Strongly," I confirm. "He could never see the wisdom in my ideas, and Constantino was always there to back him up. It wouldn't surprise me if my father actually wants Constantino to lead the family instead of me."

"Primo," Isabella says softly, reaching out to touch my hand. "You cannot let your father's favoritism dictate your worth as a leader. You have proven yourself time and again in your own unique way."

Her words wash over me, and for a moment, I feel the crushing weight of my self-doubt lift from my shoulders. But then, the reality of my situation comes crashing back down.

"Thank you," I murmur, struggling to keep my

emotions in check. "But no matter how much I might wish to change the course of our family, I fear that it may be too late."

"Don't give up on yourself or your vision for the future," she pleads, her eyes shining with determination. "I can relate to your struggles. I had a difficult relationship with my own father. My father wanted me to continue running the law firm in his shadow, working for the mob. But I never wanted that life for myself, or for a family I might have someday."

I watch as she absently traces patterns on the table, and I'm struck by the vulnerability in her eyes. It's a side of Isabella I've never seen before, and it only makes me feel more connected to her.

"Frankie Moretti..." I murmur, reflecting on her father. "I knew him, but not well. He was a shrewd businessman and a loyal friend to my father."

"Despite our differences, I loved my father," she admits, lifting her gaze to meet mine. "But I couldn't bear the thought of perpetuating the cycle of violence and crime that had defined his life."

"I can relate to that more than you know," I confess, feeling an unexpected surge of emotion. "I... actually have a son."

"Really?" Her eyes widen in surprise, and I can see the curiosity dancing in their depths. "What's his name?"

"Lucas," I say, the name feeling like both a comfort and a burden on my tongue. "He lives with his mother outside of Washington, D.C. I try to stay out of his life because I don't want him to be sucked into this way of life."

"Tell me about him?" she asks gently.

I shake my head. "I wish I could. I wish I could tell you his favorite sport, TV show, or color, even. But, I've not been in his life enough to know."

"I'm so sorry," he says, her eyes kind. "That must be really difficult."

I look off to the side. "It is what it is."

"What about his mother?" she urges, her hand resting lightly on my forearm.

"Her name is Leah," I explain, memories of our brief time together flooding back. "We met right after high school, and our relationship was passionate but short-lived. She didn't want to be with me because she knew what my life entailed. Leah comes from a family that owns an expensive clothing label, and being associated with me would have hurt her career."

"Primo," Isabella whispers, her eyes filled with empathy. "That must have been so difficult for you both."

"More for her than me," I admit, guilt gnawing at the edges of my heart. "I've always felt torn between my duty to my family and my love for them. My son deserves better than a life mired in darkness."

As the silence stretches between us, heavy with unspoken thoughts and emotions, I realize just how much Isabella truly understands me.

A single tear rolls down Isabella's cheek as she looks at me with a mixture of understanding and sadness. "It must be so difficult for you not to have a relationship with Lucas," she says softly.

"Perhaps it's for the best," I reply, my voice cracking with emotion. "Lucas has already shown an interest in our business, trying to weave his way in. I do my best to keep him out, but I fear I may not be successful. He's stubborn and hard-headed, just like his father."

"You can only do your best. One day he'll realize how much you sacrificed to keep him safe," Isabella reassures me, her hand finding mine and giving it a gentle squeeze. I look into her eyes, finding solace in their depths.

I realize that if I don't change the subject, I'm going to spill all of my secrets to this woman. "Let's talk about the case," I say gruffly.

"Oh, okay," she replies, a bit of shock in her eyes at my sudden mood shift. "Well, I've been reviewing the evidence and the chain of events you've given me many times. I think our best strategy is to pin Beau's killing on someone else, but not the agent, Axe— he's working with the Feds."

"Do you really believe there was someone else behind all this? I was assuming it was just Axe." My heart pounds with a mix of hope and dread.

"Absolutely," she nods confidently. "Axe wouldn't have gone rogue without a reason. There must be someone pulling the strings, but I can't figure out who yet. And, I bet that they're the one that killed Beau and had it pinned on you."

I glance at the clock, noting that it's midnight. "You've

done more than enough for today, Isabella. You should get some rest."

"Alright," she concedes, releasing my hand and standing up.

Escorting Isabella to her bedroom, the tension between us is palpable. Our connection has deepened tonight, and I can feel the magnetic pull of her presence, urging me closer.

"Goodnight, Isabella," I murmur, my voice thick with unspoken desire.

"Goodnight, Primo," she replies, her eyes searching mine for a moment before they flicker away.

I find myself drawn to her, desperate to taste the sweetness of her lips. She seems to anticipate my intentions, her breath hitching ever so slightly. But as my face hovers inches from hers, doubt seizes me. The uncertainty of my fate looms over us, casting a shadow on the fragile bond we've formed. It would be selfish to let her get attached, only to leave her heartbroken if this trial costs me my freedom.

"Sleep well," I manage, forcing myself to step back.

"Thanks, you too," Isabella whispers, her gaze now fixated on the floor.

Turning away, I retreat to my bedroom, my chest heavy with regret and longing. As I climb into bed, the silky sheets offer little comfort against the turmoil raging within me. My thoughts drift back to Isabella's conviction that someone had orchestrated the setup, manipulating events from the shadows. Who could it be? What twisted motive lies at the heart of this conspiracy?

The possibilities swim through my mind, each more sinister than the last. Sleep eludes me as I grapple with the mounting questions, but eventually, the darkness claims me. Even in slumber, my restless thoughts continue to churn, seeking answers that remain shrouded in mystery.

# Chapter Fifteen

## Isabella

My eyelids flutter open, the faintest hint of dawn's light seeping through the heavy curtains. Despite how late I slept, my body protests its early awakening. As I tiptoe to the door, the mansion remains eerily silent, as if everyone is still asleep, held captive by the night's velvet embrace. My stomach rumbles with hunger, a gnawing sensation that drives me to explore the somewhat unfamiliar halls in search of sustenance.

I glide through the corridors, my bare feet whispering against the cold marble floor. Primo's silk dress shirt clings to my form like a second skin, a thin veil between me and the world around me. The grand walls of the Maldonado mansion are adorned with photos, each frame cradling a moment frozen in time. As I walk, I feel the eyes of history bearing down on me, the specters of the past watching from their gilded perches.

"Is this really where I belong?" I murmur, an uneasy sensation settling into the pit of my stomach.

A particular photo catches my attention, and I pause, my breath hitching in my throat. My father stands among a group of men, their eyes sharp and calculating. There, among them, is Primo's father, Johnny Maldonado, his dark gaze piercing through the photograph and straight into my soul. My heart twists, caught between loyalty to my family and the undeniable pull I feel toward Primo.

As a lawyer, I'm well-versed in the art of negotiation and manipulation, but the Mafia world is a different beast altogether. The Maldonado family, with their complex web of alliances and betrayals, embodies everything I've tried to distance myself from. And yet, here I am, representing them in a trial that could change the very course of their criminal empire.

Shaking off the tendrils of doubt that threaten to ensnare me, I continue onward, finally reaching the haven of the kitchen.

I step inside, and the aroma of coffee beans envelops me like a warm embrace. My stomach growls impatiently, urging me to hasten my breakfast preparations. I busy myself with grinding the beans and setting up the coffee maker, the familiar motions soothing my frazzled nerves.

"Are you one of Giovanni's whores?" a cold voice cuts through the silence, startling me.

I look toward the entrance to find Constantino

leaning against the doorway, his dark hair disheveled, and his piercing green eyes fixed on me with an air of disdain. The sharp angles of his face and the predatory gleam in his gaze make him appear as though he's been plucked from the pages of a Gothic novel.

"I'm Primo's lawyer," I reply tersely, bristling at his crude remark. "Isabella Moretti. We've met."

"Oh, right. I remember now," he drawls dismissively, pushing himself off the doorframe and sauntering over to the kitchen island. He slides onto a stool with an air of entitlement that rankles me. "Make another pot of coffee for me, will you?"

I grit my teeth, torn between acquiescing to maintain a polite façade and snapping back at him for treating me like a servant. Reluctantly, I set about making another pot, my hands trembling slightly with indignation.

"Tell me, Ms. Moretti," Constantino begins, drumming his fingers on the countertop, "How is Primo's trial coming along?"

"Fine," I say curtly, my senses prickling with unease. His questions feel like probing needles, digging beneath the surface to unearth our strategy.

"Really? Such detail. It must be riveting," he smirks, his emerald eyes gleaming with amusement and something darker – perhaps malice or curiosity. "What are your plans for the defense?"

"Constantino, why are you so curious?" I ask, unable to maintain my composure any longer.

He feigns a smile, his lips stretching into a chillingly

disingenuous grin. "Of course, I'm worried about my older brother. How could I not be?" Despite his words, my intuition screams that there's more to his interest than just fraternal concern.

My thoughts whirl with confusion and frustration, my heart thumping wildly in my chest as I try to decipher the enigma that is Constantino Maldonado. I pour out the coffee, the dark liquid swirling in my cup.

"Perhaps if you're so worried about your older brother, you can help shed some light on what was going on that night," I suggest, my voice wavering slightly under his scrutiny. The kitchen seems to shrink around us, and I feel as though I'm suffocating.

Constantino waves his hand dismissively, his eyes narrowing. "I don't know anything, and I wouldn't be of any help. If you were doing your job and looking through all the evidence, you would already know that." His words sting like a slap across my face, and I struggle to maintain my composure.

I watch in disbelief as he saunters over to the freshly brewed coffee, his movements both fluid and predatory. He grabs a cup and takes a sip, his lips curling in distaste. "This is very bad," he sneers, dumping the contents into the sink with a clatter that lingers in the cavernous room.

Constantino smirks at me, his mockery palpable. "Good luck with the trial," he drawls, his gaze raking me up and down as if I'm merely an object for his amusement. "Even if Primo goes to prison for the rest of his life, at least he can say he got to fuck his lawyer. We should all be so lucky."

My cheeks burn with humiliation, and I fight the urge to scream or sob – or both. But before I can even think of a response, he's gone, leaving me alone in the cold, sterile kitchen.

***

"Is something wrong?" Primo asks, his voice a whisper of concern as I sit next to him in the dimly lit office. His dark eyes linger on me, scrutinizing my every move. For the last ten minutes, I've been staring at the same document, unable to focus.

I shake my head and apologize, murmuring, "No, nothing's wrong." But even as the words leave my lips, I know he sees through me. Primo has always been perceptive, a trait that serves him well in his precarious world.

He arches an eyebrow, and there's a hint of ice in his tone when he speaks. "You're clearly lying, Isabella. And I don't like the thought of you lying to me."

The words hangs heavy between us, and I sigh, finally admitting, "I ran into Constantino this morning in the kitchen."

His eyes narrow, and he leans forward in his chair, elbows resting on the desk. "What happened?"

"Other than being exceedingly rude," I start, picking at

the frayed edge of the document to avoid meeting his gaze, "he was asking for details about our strategy."

"Ah." Primo's expression hardens, and the atmosphere in the room thickens with tension. "I'm sure you didn't give him any."

"Of course not," I say quickly, my fingers clenching the paper. "But I don't like that he was asking, and the way he was asking. There's one thing to be supportive, but there's another thing to be nosy. And he's shown no signs of being supportive."

"Constantino is dangerous," Primo warns. "You would do well to avoid him in the future. Perhaps reconsider walking around the mansion alone so that you don't run into any of my brothers."

I sigh, frustrated, and confess, "I get it, but it's just another reason why I don't want to live here full time. I don't feel comfortable in a place where I can't even walk around by myself."

For a moment, Primo looks offended, and his words are tinged with bitterness. "Better that than raped or worse by some loan shark."

I blink in surprise, not sure if I should be hurt or angry at what he just said to me. My mixed emotions must show on my face because, in a rare move, he apologizes.

"Isabella, I'm sorry," he says softly, reaching across the desk to touch my hand. "Your safety is paramount to me, and I don't want you feeling uncomfortable."

"Thanks," I reply, offering him a small smile. We turn our attention back to the work at hand, preparing for an upcoming and very public hearing ahead of the trial itself. I try and put thoughts of Constantino out of my mind for the meantime. Even still, there's a nagging feeling in the back of my head that says there's more to our morning conversation than face value.

## Chapter Sixteen

### Isabella

I stand outside of Judge Dolan's chambers, my heart pounding in my chest as I try to quell the tremors running through my fingertips. He's called a meeting with just the attorneys so that he can discuss some things with us. It's a little unusual to have something like this, but then again, this is a pretty unusual case. I decided against telling Primo; he would try and demand he come with me, and I know that I'd be helpless to tell him no, which would only get him and me in trouble. I wish I knew what this meeting was about so I could prepare. I try not to be anxious, but it's hard not to be.

The courthouse looms around me, its grand architecture casting long shadows over the polished marble floor. The walls are adorned with paintings of stern-faced judges and somber lawyers – their eyes seem to follow me, silently judging my every move. A low murmur of conversation buzzes through the vast halls, barely audible above the clicking of heels on stone. As I look around, the scent of old books and stale air fills my nostrils, adding to the already oppressive atmosphere.

My heartbeat quickens, each thud resounding in my ears like the strike of a gavel. The responsibility weighs heavy on my shoulders as I think of Primo, his fate resting in my hands. I take a deep breath and remind myself that I am strong, determined, and fiercely dedicated to this case.

The sounds of footsteps break the tense silence, drawing my attention down the hallway. Greg approaches, his smug grin plastered across his face like a grotesque mask. He exudes entitlement with every step, his tailored suit and polished shoes screaming of a man who's never known struggle.

"Isabella," he says, his voice dripping with insincerity as he stops before me. "Fancy seeing you here. Can't say I'm surprised though – seems like Judge Dolan's finally realized that you're in over your head."

I clench my fists, my nails biting into my palms as I force a smile onto my lips. "Nice to see you too, Greg. Always a pleasure." I can't help but roll my eyes at his bravado, remembering how he never managed to get hired by anyone in private practice after law school. Instead, he ended up stuck working a government job, trying to hide his shortcomings behind arrogance. But then again, who am I to judge? After all, I took over my father's law firm, even if it was by choice.

Greg chuckles, a condescending sound that grates on my nerves. "You really think you have a chance in this trial, don't you? Bless your heart. Quite brave of you to defend a monster like Primo."

"Everyone deserves a fair trial," I retort, my voice firm. The memory of Primo's touch weaves through my thoughts, igniting a fire within me that drives away any lingering doubts. "And I intend to give him one."

"Brave or foolish, I suppose we'll find out soon enough," Greg counters, his smirk widening. "But let's not mince words, Isabella. We both know why Judge Dolan called this meeting. It's clearly to chastise you for your... unconventional methods."

"Careful, Greg," I warn, my voice low and fierce. "Your jealousy is showing."

His laughter rings out, a hollow sound that fills the stale air of the hallway. "Jealousy? Oh, Isabella, you give yourself too much credit. I simply can't wait to see the look on your face when I tear your case to shreds."

"Keep dreaming," I shoot back, refusing to let him shake my resolve.

The door to Judge Dolan's chambers swings open, revealing a mousy girl with wide eyes and a nervous smile. She clutches a stack of papers in her trembling hands as if they're the only thing keeping her grounded. I recognize the look all too well – fresh out of law school and eager for experience, only to be met with the harsh reality of low pay and thankless work.

"Judge Dolan is ready for you," she announces, her

voice wavering slightly under Greg's condescending gaze. A pang of sympathy strikes me, but I know better than to show it. The legal world is cruel to those who display weakness.

"Thank you," I say, offering her an encouraging smile as I follow Greg into the judge's chambers. The room feels stuffy and oppressive, the air thick with the scent of old leather. Dark wood paneling lines the walls, adorned with countless framed accolades and photographs of Judge Dolan shaking hands with politicians and celebrities alike. The pretentious atmosphere is suffocating, reminding me that in this room, we are mere pawns in a game played by those who wield true power.

I slide into one of the leather seats, feeling the cool material press against my back as I face Judge Dolan behind his imposing mahogany desk. Greg takes the seat beside me, his smug demeanor replaced by a veneer of obsequiousness, his eyes gleaming with something akin to hunger.

"Miss Moretti, Mr. Daniels," Judge Dolan drones on, his voice monotonous and heavy, "I presume you are well aware that this case is bound to be high profile." His fingers tap rhythmically on the polished surface of his desk, betraying a hint of impatience. "Given its nature, I've decided to authorize that this trial be filmed and broadcast."

Greg's response is immediate and enthusiastic. "That's perfect, Your Honor! We welcome the media's presence."

My heart tightens in my chest, and my nerves flare, an

involuntary shiver racing down my spine at the thought of cameras capturing every moment of the trial. My mind races, assessing the potential consequences for Primo and myself. Yet, defiance surges through me, and I know I cannot give in now. With a forced smile, I muster the courage to speak. "If it's Your Honor's decision, I will respect it." My voice is steady, but the knot of anxiety in my stomach remains.

"Excellent," Judge Dolan says, his eyes scanning both our faces. "I expect a clean and professional trial from both parties. You're dismissed."

Greg rises from his seat with nauseating enthusiasm, already agreeing with the judge even before we exit the chambers.

As soon as the heavy oak door closes behind us, Greg's facade crumbles, and he sneers at me. "You look pretty nervous, Isabella. Not sure you can handle everyone watching when I get your client convicted for all those murders he committed?"

My jaw clenches, and I force myself to remain composed. "Why don't you focus on what Primo is actually on trial for, and remember that everyone is innocent until proven guilty?" I retort, refusing to let him intimidate me.

"Believe me, I intend to prove just that," Greg smirks, his words dripping with arrogance. "And you won't get in my way." With that, he strides away.

I make my way back to the entrance of the courthouse, Greg's words ringing in my mind. What does he mean by not letting me get in his way? I can feel the uncertainty settle upon my shoulders as I make my way through the bustling crowd, their voices blending into a cacophony that only heightens my anxiety.

As I push open the heavy glass doors and step outside, the sunlight is almost blinding, casting sharp shadows across the courthouse steps. The air is thick with anticipation, and I feel as though everyone is watching me, scrutinizing my every move as if they already know the outcome of Primo's trial.

"Isabella!" A voice calls out from somewhere behind me. I turn to find no one, only the whisper of the wind carrying the sound away. Shaking off the eerie sensation, I focus on the task at hand - defending Primo. My heels click against the pavement as I cross the parking lot, the sun now a comforting warmth on my skin. Settling into the driver's seat, I take a deep breath and start the engine. The hum of the car feels like an anchor, grounding me amidst the storm of emotions that threatens to consume me.

As I drive, I let my thoughts drift back to Greg's blatant arrogance. It must be nothing more than the bravado of a desperate man, I tell myself. But a nagging voice in the back of my mind whispers, what if it's not? I remember what Primo told me about men like Greg. About how they can be dangerous when cornered. I grip the steering wheel tighter.

Approaching my apartment building, the familiar sight offers some semblance of solace. I park the car and gather my things, my mind already racing with strategies and counterarguments, legal precedents and case studies. The door to my apartment creaks open, revealing the chaotic sanctuary that is my home.

"Focus, Isabella," I tell myself, dropping my bag on the cluttered kitchen counter. "You can do this."

# Chapter Seventeen

## Isabella

The heavy oak doors of the courtroom creak open, and I step inside, Primo's reassuring presence by my side. The anticipation of the first major pre-trial hearing hums in the air as murmurs from the gathered crowd buzzes through the gilded chamber. Reporters jostle for space, their cameras flashing like lightning. A shiver runs down my spine, but it's not fear – it's excitement.

"Here we go," I whisper to Primo, feeling the warmth of his hand on the small of my back. He gives me a nod and a half-smile, his eyes filled with determination and something else - desire.

"Isabella Moretti, late as always," Greg sneers from across the room, his voice dripping with condescension. "And still without a second chair, I see."

"Someone like Isabella doesn't need a second chair

when facing such a weak opponent," Primo interjects, his voice cool and steady.

Greg's face flushes with anger, his lips pressed into a thin line. He casts an irritated glare at Primo before turning away.

"Thank you," I murmur, leaning close to Primo's ear. His scent, a mix of sandalwood and leather, fills my senses. "But don't rile him up too much. It'll only make things worse."

"Understood," he replies, his breath warm against my skin.

As we settle into our seats, I can feel the expectation pressing down on us. The whispers and stares from the gallery are like tendrils wrapping around my throat.

"Order in the court!" the bailiff bellows, and the room falls silent. With a steadying breath, I straighten my spine and fix my gaze on the judge's bench, ready for battle.

"Judge Dolan presiding!" the bailiff announces, and the courtroom rises as one. The air crackles with anticipation, a living thing that wraps around me like a snake.

"Please be seated," Judge Dolan says, his voice stern but fair. I glance down at my notes, my fingers itching to turn the thin pages of the legal pad. But then, it happens - a sudden sensation of being watched, a prickling at the nape of my neck. My gaze lifts, scanning the crowd until it locks onto him.

He is an imposing man, broad shouldered and muscular, his dark suit straining against the flex of his biceps. His face is all sharp angles and deep-set lines, with eyes so blue they're almost ice-cold, and a contemptuous sneer curling his lips. He exudes danger, menace radiating from his very pores, and even though the room is packed with people, there's no doubt in my mind that his attention is focused solely on Primo and me.

"Miss Moretti," the clerk calls, and I jerk my gaze away, heat flooding my cheeks. "The dates for expert witness designation?"

"Ah, yes," I stammer, flipping through my calendar. "April 17th."

"Very well," the clerk replies, making a note on his own schedule. I steal another glance at the brooding stranger, curiosity gnawing at my insides like a ravenous beast.

We continue to go through the dates, finally leading up to setting the trial date itself in just one week.

"Court adjourned," Judge Dolan finally declares, and the room erupts into a cacophony of voices. As we gather our things, I can feel the stranger's cold eyes still boring into us, sending shivers skittering down my spine.

"Who is he?" I ask Primo once we step outside, casting a surreptitious glance over my shoulder. The man approaches, his strides confident and predatory.

"Doesn't concern you," Primo replies tersely, but I can see the muscle in his jaw twitching, betraying his unease. The stranger stops in front of him, their eyes locked in a silent battle of wills.

"Primo," the man grunts, a hint of an Irish brogue coloring his voice. Their exchange is curt, clipped, and as they part ways, Primo's hand falls to my elbow, steering me toward the car.

"Who was that?" I demand once we're safely inside, the doors locked and the engine purring beneath us. "And don't give me that 'it doesn't concern you' crap."

"Isabella, please," he murmurs, but there's a pleading note in his voice that makes my heart ache.

"Did our time together mean nothing to you?" I snap, tears pricking at the corners of my eyes. "How can you still not trust me?"

"Fine." He exhales heavily, running a hand through his hair. "His name is Declan O'Leary. Second in command of the Irish mob, also known as the Westies."

My heart skips a beat as I process this information, a cold knot of fear forming in my stomach. But I swallow it down, steeling myself for whatever comes next.

The car hums beneath us as Primo navigates the congested city streets as we make our way out to his mansion. Tension hangs heavy in the air, a palpable presence between us. I feel a tinge of fear mixed with curiosity as he begins to speak.

"Declan O'Leary..." he murmurs, his grip on the steering wheel tightening. "The Westies...they've been hungry for power and control for a long time, always looking for ways to undermine us."

"Undermine you how?" I ask, trying to keep my voice steady.

"By questioning our legitimacy," he replies, his jaw set

and eyes focused on the road ahead. "Have you ever wondered why our name isn't the most Italian sounding?"

I shake my head. "I never really thought about it."

"During the unification of Italy, my ancestors changed their surname to escape persecution," Primo explains, a hint of bitterness creeping into his voice. "At least, that's always been the excuse. I don't know whether it's actually true or if something more sinister happened with our lineage. But with my father now in prison, others have taken the opportunity to question our place at the head of the New England crime syndicate."

My pulse quickens as the implications of his words sink in. "Do you think Declan will make a move against you?"

He shakes his head. "Not directly. He'll likely try something more insidious, like influencing the trial."

"His name isn't on the witness list," I point out, my mind racing.

"Doesn't matter," Primo says dismissively. "He might try to influence the witnesses in other ways, without having to take the stand himself."

"Good point," I concede, my thoughts turning to the upcoming trial. "We should discuss who will testify."

Primo's silence is deafening as he navigates the car through the cityscape, the tall buildings casting dark shadows over us. Our situation feels heavy on my chest, but I refuse to let fear consume me.

The mansion looms ahead, a symbol of the power and control that has been challenged by those who dare to question the Maldonado name. As we pull into the driveway, Primo takes a deep breath and turns to face me, his eyes filled with determination.

"I've already taken care of the witnesses," he says coolly. "The family has always had witnesses lined up for these sorts of matters."

"Are you telling me that you have bribed witnesses?" The words taste like bile in my mouth as I spit them out.

"Look, this is just how it's done, all right?" Primo says defensively, his dark eyes now locked onto mine. "We need to be prepared for anything."

"Absolutely not," I reply, my voice shaking with anger. "As an attorney, I have a duty of candor toward the court. I will not work with bribed witnesses, Primo. I won't compromise my integrity."

Primo brushes off my concerns with a dismissive wave of his hand. "This is the way it's always been done, Isabella. You're new to this world, so trust me when I say it's necessary."

Primo turns off the car, but I'm already out, slamming the door behind me. I storm around to his side, flinging open the door with a huff.

"Primo Maldonado!" I yell, my face flushed with fury. "After everything we've shared, after the trust we've built, you still don't believe that I can handle this case without resorting to criminal tricks?"

He looks at me, his eyes filled with a mixture of frustration and something else – is it fear? "Isabella, I'm not questioning your abilities," he says, his voice softening. "But there's more at stake here than just a trial. This is about my family's future, our legacy. I need to know that everything has been taken care of."

"By resorting to the same tactics that put your father in prison?" I counter, my voice breaking. "No, Primo. There has to be another way. Let me do my job – let me prove to you that there's a better path for us."

He hesitates, his dark eyes searching mine for any hint of doubt. But all he finds is determination, the fierce fire that burns within me.

# Chapter Eighteen

## Isabella

"Ah, Isabella," he smirks, the corners of his eyes crinkling with amusement. "I must admit, I do love it when you argue with me now."

My heart flutters in my chest, momentarily taken aback by his words. "What?" I scoff, trying to maintain my focus on our current argument. But the intensity in Primo's gaze tells me he has other intentions.

"Every time you challenge me, it's another chance to make you submit to me, which I relish, cara mia," he whispers, causing a shiver to run down my spine.

"Primo, we're talking about the trial here, not..." My voice trails off as I struggle to find the right words. Slowly, he stands, exiting the car and taking a step closer, his dark eyes never leaving mine. The fire inside me begins to burn hotter, my desire to argue with him slipping away. I feel my resolve weakening under his presence and I take an involuntary step back.

"Alright," he says, closing the car door. "Let's make a deal." He grabs me suddenly and circles me around, pushing me against the door. The cold metal presses against my back, but the heat emanating from Primo's body overshadows it. "I might let you have your way with the witnesses, but you need to earn it from me first."

I swallow hard, feeling the heat rise in my cheeks. "And what would you have me do?"

"Remove your clothing, one piece at a time," he commands, his voice low and firm.

My heart races as I hesitantly reach for the buttons of my shirt, my fingers fumbling with each one. The logical part of my brain wonders why I'm just giving in to him and so easily, but it's mostly drowned out by the torrent of desire washing through me. With every button undone, I reveal more of my flushed skin to him. The shirt falls to the ground, followed by my skirt, leaving me standing in just my bra and panties.

"Continue," Primo says, his voice barely audible, as he watches me with a predatory gaze. I can feel the heat radiating off him, making my arousal even more potent.

I reach behind me, unhooking the clasp of my bra and letting it fall to the ground. My hands tremble as I slide my panties down my legs, stepping out of them. Standing completely naked before Primo, I am consumed by the desire to please him, to submit to his every whim.

"Good girl," he murmurs, his eyes never straying from

my exposed body. "Now, let's see how far you're willing to go for your precious witnesses." He walks around me, opening the back door to the car and then steps back. "Turn around, Isabella," Primo commands, his voice a low growl that has me immediately acquiescing.

I obey, feeling the cool air on my bare skin as I face the open back seat of the car. "Bend over for me and show me that pretty ass and those sweet pussy lips I've been craving to taste."

I comply, bending at the waist and presenting myself to him. My heart races as I feel his eyes drinking in the sight of my exposed flesh. I can't help but wonder when he'll finally touch me.

"Look at you," Primo muses, his voice thick with desire. "So wet and dripping down your thighs for me. Have you ever squirted before, Isabella?"

"Never," I admit, heat flooding my cheeks.

"Then I'll claim that first from you soon enough." His tone is possessive, sending a thrill through me. He begins trailing his fingers against my skin, starting low at my ankles and slowly moving up my legs. The anticipation of his touch is maddening, and I stifle a moan as he caresses every part of me. When I try to move closer to him, seeking more contact, he tugs my hair back forcefully, making me gasp.

"Did I give you permission to move?" he asks, his voice sharp and dangerous. He squeezes one of my breasts until I yelp in pain and pleasure. "If you move again without my permission, I will correct you."

"Sorry," I whisper, trying to catch my breath.

"Good girl," he says, though there's no warmth in his voice. "Now, let's start over, since you misbehaved."

"Please... just touch me," I beg, desperate for his fingers on my clit. But he ignores my plea, starting once more at my ankles and moving even slower this time. The seconds stretch into minutes, my arousal building as his touch teases and torments me. I can feel my juices rolling down my thighs, dripping onto the floor.

"Are you ready for more?" Primo asks, his voice husky with lust.

"No," I answer, trying to deny my need for him.

He smacks my ass hard, sending a jolt of pain through me. "That's not the right answer, Isabella. You should be ready to receive whatever I choose to give you, whenever I'm ready to give it."

His fierceness, his control over me – it's intoxicating, stirring something primal within me. When he asks again if I'm ready for more, I know what to say.

"Please, Primo. Give me whatever you want, whenever you're ready."

"Good," he says.

The slightest graze of his fingers over my nipples sends a shockwave through me, and my entire body convulses from the simple touch. Primo scolds me, his voice low and menacing. "If you come without my permission, Isabella, I will punish you in a way you won't enjoy."

"What would you do to me?" I ask breathlessly, unable to hide the curiosity and fear that mingle within me.

He chuckles darkly, and I shiver. "I'd bind your ankles and wrists, spread you out on a bed, completely exposed and helpless. I'd take my time exploring every inch of your body, marking it as mine while you beg for more. But I wouldn't give it to you." His words paint a vivid picture in my mind, and despite the threat of punishment, I can't help but feel a thrill at the thought of being so utterly at his mercy. "Only when you're crying, begging me to fuck you so you can come, then – maybe – I'll consider it."

The image he paints for me has me going crazy with desire, my body aching for his touch. It's shocking how much I want this – to be tied up and completely under his control. As if sensing my thoughts, Primo starts degrading me.

"Awe, such a pitiful little slut," he goads. "Begging me for more because she needs her wet pussy touched."

"Yes, please," I whimper, desperate for him to relieve the tension building inside me.

Finally giving in to my pleas, he moves between my legs, pressing his lips against my clit. He licks and teases me mercilessly, making me squirm and moan. His fingers pump inside me, hitting all the right spots as I feel myself getting closer and closer to the edge.

"Can I come, please?" I beg him, feeling like I'm about to explode.

"Not yet," he orders, and I whimper in frustration. But I obey, holding back my orgasm with every ounce of willpower I possess.

"Please, Primo. Let me come," I cry out after what feels like an eternity, desperate for release.

"Alright, Isabella. You may come."

His permission is all I need, and he presses hard on my g-spot as an intense orgasm rocks through my body. I gasp and moan, feeling a gush of fluid leaving me, completely losing myself in the moment.

The euphoria of my climax gradually fades, and Primo's voice cuts through the haze. "I knew I could make you squirt, Isabella. It was truly a beautiful sight." I can feel the heat still coursing through my veins. My body craves more, yearns to serve him in any way possible.

"Get on your knees," he commands, his tone firm yet seductive. Without hesitation, I drop onto the cold cement floor of the garage. He gazes at me with dark, hungry eyes. "You're such a good girl."

I swallow hard, my voice barely a whisper as I respond, "Yes, I am."

"Then you'll do this for me," he says, his voice like velvet. "I want to see you lick your juices off the garage floor, just like you did from the leather seat the other day. It would please me greatly."

My heart races at his command, and I lean forward, ready to obey. But his hand on my shoulder stops me. "Not like that," he murmurs. "I want to degrade you further."

"Please," I beg, breathless with anticipation. "I want it."

"Then lie down on this filthy garage floor, where you belong. Press your breasts against the dirt and grime. Put your hands behind your back and lick your juices off the floor like the needy little slut you are."

With trembling limbs, I lower myself onto the cold, dirty floor, feeling the grit press into my skin. My hands clasped behind my back, I begin to lap up the remnants of my pleasure from the concrete. Primo growls his approval, and I can hear the sound of his belt unbuckling as he begins to stroke himself while watching me.

As I continue to clean the floor with my tongue, he walks around me, his footsteps echoing in the space. His touch alternates between gentle caresses and stinging smacks on my ass and body. I can feel myself falling further under his spell, lost to his domination.

"Such a good job," he praises, his voice thick with desire. "You deserve a reward." He motions for me to sit up on my knees, and I eagerly comply. Primo stands before me, his cock hard and glistening. He moves it closer to my face, but as I lean in to take it into my mouth, he grabs me by the chin, stopping me abruptly.

"Did I give you permission?" he asks, his voice stern.

I shake my head, chastened, and sit back on my heels. He continues to hold his cock in front of me, teasing me by slapping my face with it. "You're so fucking naughty," he taunts. "Don't you want this cock so bad?"

In that moment, I have never wanted anything more. His gaze and his words wrap around me like silk and steel, binding me to him completely. And as I surrender to his control, I know I would do anything for Primo Maldonado – anything at all to please him.

"Open that pretty mouth of yours," Primo commands. I obey immediately, feeling the head of his cock press against my lips. A surge of desire courses through me as he grants me permission to take him in. He slides into my eager mouth, and I wrap my tongue around him, savoring the taste and feel of him.

"Such a good girl," he growls in approval, gripping my hair and guiding my head as he begins to face fuck me. The intensity of the act only heightens my arousal, and I can't help but love every second of it. His filthy words punctuate the air with each thrust, spurring me on to please him further.

"Tell me you want this cock in your wet pussy," he demands, his grip tightening in my hair. I can barely nod, unable to speak with my mouth full of his delicious length. He chuckles darkly at my response. "Pitiful little slut, can't even talk because her mouth is always so full with my dick."

My cheeks burn with humiliation and unexpected pleasure, feeling both degraded and desired in equal measure. He continues to ravage my mouth, his pace relentless and unforgiving.

"Since you didn't tell me you want your pussy fucked, I'll just have to finish down your throat again," he sneers, his tone dripping with derision. "Perhaps you're not quite worthy to receive my cock in that way yet. You'll need to prove yourself before I give you that gift."

As he utters those words, I'm consumed by the need to earn his approval, to show him that I am deserving of the pleasure he could bestow upon me. But for now, I continue to submit to his rough treatment, taking him deeper with each forceful thrust.

Finally, with a guttural moan, Primo reaches his climax, releasing hot streams of cum down my throat. I struggle to swallow it all, choking and gasping as he fills me. He looks down at me with a wicked grin, clearly enjoying my desperate attempts to accommodate him.

"Such a good girl for drinking it all down," he praises, pulling his cock out of my mouth. "Now clean the rest of my cum off."

Eagerly, I lick him clean, savoring the taste of his essence, even as I mourn the end of our illicit encounter. He gives me a mocking pout as he holds my chin between his fingers, forcing me to meet his gaze.

"You know, I adore it when you're my filthy toy," he says, his voice low and dangerous. "You'd look so good doused in my cum." His free hand moves to caress my breasts, his touch both possessive and teasing. "Next time," he continues, kneeling down to capture one nipple between his teeth before biting down, marking me as his, "I'm going to leave my cum all over these perky tits of yours and forbid you from washing it off until it's well and soaked into your skin."

The promise of his words sends another wave of desire crashing through me, my body yearning for the next time we give in to our darkest desires. As I kneel before him, marked and claimed by Primo Maldonado, I start to wonder if this man is truly my new vice.

My body trembles in the aftermath of our dark dalliance, and Primo's lips gently press against mine. His tender kiss is a stark contrast to the raw passion that had consumed us moments before.

"Come back to me, Isabella," he murmurs, his breath warm on my cheek as I struggle to find my bearings.

We sit on the cold, unforgiving floor of the garage, my back leaning against Primo's chest, his arms encircling me protectively. With deliberate care, he removes his suit jacket and drapes it around my naked, dirty form, shielding me from the chill in the air.

"Primo, I... I don't know what came over me," I stammer, suddenly feeling ashamed of my lascivious actions. "I've never..."

"Shh," he hushes me, running his fingers through my disheveled hair. "There's no need for apologies, Isabella. You're never more beautiful than when you submit yourself to me like that."

His words soothe the storm of self-recrimination swirling within me, and a newfound sense of trust and intimacy blossoms between us. Primo's hold on me tightens, and I can feel his heart beating steadily against my back.

"About the trial," he begins, his voice low and serious. "You were right. I won't bribe the witnesses. I trust you to handle it the right way."

The admission takes me by surprise, and my heart swells with something more profound than mere lust:

respect, perhaps even admiration, for the man who has just bared his darkest desires to me.

"Thank you, Primo," I whisper, reaching up to touch his face. "That means everything to me."

He grunts softly, his thumb tracing the curve of my jaw. "Now, let's get you cleaned up, shall we?"

Primo stands, his strong arms lifting me with ease. He carries me out of the garage and into the lavish bathroom inside his mansion, the scent of expensive soap and warm water filling my nostrils.

"Close your eyes," he instructs as he lowers me into the steaming bath, the water enveloping me like a comforting embrace.

"Primo," I murmur, feeling vulnerable yet cherished in this moment. "What are we becoming?"

He gazes down at me, his dark eyes reflecting a world of possibility. "Something beautiful, Isabella. Something neither of us can deny."

Primo's hands are gentle, his touch like a whisper on my skin. His movements are slow and deliberate, as if he is savoring each moment of our shared intimacy. His fingertips brush over me in a soothing caress, and I feel myself begin to relax and let go. His touch speaks of a deep tenderness that I have never felt before.

"Is this alright?" he asks.

"Yes," I moan my response, leaning into him further.

He washes away the remnants of our sinful encounter, and I find myself yearning for more than just the touch of his body against mine.

His hand caresses my face and I can feel the intensity of our desire for one another still. He pulls me closer to him and his lips ghost over the back of my neck. The whole experience leaves me relaxed and at peace. And though I dare not voice it aloud, I know that the seeds of love have taken root within my heart.

## Chapter Nineteen

*Primo*

The aroma of leather and old books fills my nostrils as I sit at my desk with Isabella. Her fiery red locks cascade in delicate waves past her shoulders, her eyes as green as emeralds, seeming to pierce through your very soul. We meticulously go through the list of legitimate witnesses for my upcoming trial.

"Vinny Martini," I suggest, recalling his potential knowledge of the events that fateful night. "He might be able to vouch for my innocence."

Isabella scribbles the name on her legal pad, nodding thoughtfully. As she does so, my mind drifts back to the previous evening when she had so intriguingly submitted to my darkest desires. A dangerous addiction is forming between us, a vice that threatens to consume me whole.

Our intimate reverie is shattered by a knock on the

office door. Charlie, one of the most trusted members of my family, enters, his salt-and-pepper hair slicked back in its usual style. I beckon him forward, feeling guilty for not having made more time for him lately.

"Charlie, I apologize for not seeing you sooner," I say as he waves off my apology.

"Primo, it's obvious you've been busy," he replies, his gaze shifting between Isabella and me.

I'm about to introduce Isabella to Charlie, but he smiles knowingly and says, "No need for introductions, Primo. We've met." His eyes linger on Isabella for a moment before turning back to me. "How are preparations for the trial coming along?"

"We're going over the witness list right now," I explain, gesturing to the legal pad on the desk.

"Ah, I see," Charlie nods, his eyes scanning the names we've compiled thus far. It feels like a test, not only of our strategy but also of my trust in Isabella.

"Charlie," I say, swallowing the knot in my throat, "we're trying something different this time. We want to build a case with legitimate witnesses."

"Legitimate?" Charlie raises an eyebrow, clearly confused. "Why deviate from our established methods? You know the family always has reliable witnesses ready to testify."

The authority in his voice makes me uneasy, but before I can respond, Isabella interjects, her tone firm and resolute. "We won't be bribing witnesses, Charlie. This case will be won on its merits, not through manipulation."

He regards her with a hint of skepticism, replying with a patronizing air, "With all due respect, Ms. Moretti, you should use the tools that have been provided to you. It's for Primo's benefit, after all."

I'm about to stand up to Charlie, defend Isabella's choices, but she beats me to it. Her eyes narrow as she speaks with absolute determination. "I am more than capable of managing the strategy for this case, and when we win, not if, when, it will be by honorable means."

My heart swells with admiration and attraction as I watch her stand her ground. She is vibrant and passionate in her convictions, unafraid of challenging even the most authoritative figures within my family.

"Alright then," Charlie concedes, thoughtfully stroking his chin. "What about your plan for cross-examination? How do you intend to discredit the prosecution's key witnesses?"

"By exposing inconsistencies in their testimonies and presenting irrefutable evidence," she replies without hesitation. "We'll leave no room for doubt about Primo's innocence."

Charlie's gaze narrows as he studies Isabella, a calculating glint in his eyes. "You know, Primo," he says, his voice dripping with skepticism, "I think the way she's handling this is risky." He leans against the doorframe, arms crossed over his chest. "Wouldn't it be better to go the route we always go? Try and get the case transferred to another judge who is bribe-able?"

My heart skips a beat at his words, but I refuse to let

my fear show. Instead, I push back from the desk, standing tall and defiant. "We don't need to do that, Charlie," I say, my voice steady and strong. "I have every confidence in Isabella's skills to handle this trial."

"Really?" Charlie sneers, raising an eyebrow. "And what if she fails? What then, Primo?"

"Failure is not an option," I reply, my gaze never leaving his. I can feel the embers of my desire for Isabella ignite within me, fueled by the sight of her fiery determination and resolve.

Charlie continues to antagonize me, probing for weaknesses and questioning my faith in Isabella. But my resolve does not waver, and I continue to defend her, each rebuttal increasing my admiration and trust in her abilities.

Finally, Charlie's facade breaks, and a wide grin splits his face. "Alright, alright!" he exclaims, clapping me on the shoulder. "You've got one hell of a lawyer there, Primo. I'll admit, I have every confidence she'll win this case for you. I just wanted to be sure."

A wave of relief moves through me, knowing that I have Charlie's blessing. His approval means everything to both my family's reputation and my own sense of security.

"However," he continues, his tone growing serious once more, "there are a few matters of business I need to discuss with you." He glances at Isabella before looking back at me, his eyes filled with a mix of urgency and caution.

"Of course," I reply, nodding in understanding.

Turning to Isabella, I offer her a reassuring smile. "I'll be right back."

As Charlie and I step out into the dimly lit hallway, I steal one last glance at Isabella. The image of her standing there - fierce, defiant, and unyielding - sears itself into my mind. I long to have her.

Charlie leads me down the shadowy hallway, his polished shoes clicking against the marble floor. The air is heavy with tension that clings to my skin, and the darkness seems to swallow us as we move further away from Isabella's comforting presence.

"Primo," Charlie begins, his voice low and urgent, "there are problems on the ground with gun shipments."

I furrow my brow, my stomach tightening with unease. "What do you mean?"

He leans closer, the scent of his cologne mingling with the dampness of the hall. "The Irish usually move the gun shipments for a certain price, right? They've always been reliable."

I nod impatiently, eager for him to get to the point. "Yeah, I know all that. What's the problem?"

"Word is, they want more money now, or they're not moving the shipment." He straightens up, his eyes searching mine for understanding. "And we both know we can't afford any delays."

My heart clenches at the thought of yet another obstacle in our path, but I force myself to remain calm. "Constantino has always handled the Irish, and things have always been smooth. Now suddenly there are problems?"

The mention of Constantino's name leaves a bitter taste in my mouth, but I swallow it down, focusing on the matter at hand.

Charlie nods solemnly. "Something needs to be done about it, Primo. We can't let this jeopardize our operation."

"Of course," I agree, my mind racing with potential solutions. In the midst of my legal troubles and growing infatuation with Isabella, I'd nearly forgotten how high the stakes truly were.

"Listen, I'll handle it," Charlie offers, placing a reassuring hand on my shoulder. "You focus on your trial. I'm still looking for someone who can take over when the time comes."

I give him a confused look. After the song and dance he just went through in my office, I thought he understood that I didn't intend to switch lawyers. "Charlie," I say to him. "I've decided to continue through to the trial with Isabella. I thought that was clear."

Charlie looks shocked at my words. "Are you sure that's the right decision?"

"Let me ask you this, Charlie," I say to him, "even if I did doubt her abilities—which I do not—were you able to find anyone anyways?"

"Well, no," Charlie admits.

"Then, the decision is made," I say. "And, I'm happy with it."

"She certainly seems like she believes in you, Primo," Charlie says.

"Yes," I reply immediately.

"Good," he says. "So do I."

"Thank you, Charlie," I reply, my voice thick with gratitude. "I appreciate your help, but I can't rely on you to do everything."

"Not everything, but some things are okay," he says.

He gives me a curt nod before departing, leaving me alone in the darkened hallway. As I make my way back to the office, my thoughts are a swirling maelstrom of concern for the family business and the alluring pull of Isabella's fiery spirit. It is a dangerous balancing act - and I'm tipping dangerously over the edge.

## Chapter Twenty

*Primo*

I return to my desk with a heavy sigh, feeling the weight of the world on my shoulders. My eyes drift to Isabella, and I see the concern etched on her beautiful features. A swell of gratitude fills me that she is here, standing by me despite the darkness that surrounds us both.

"Primo," she says softly, and as if drawn to me by an invisible force, she moves closer. Her eyes search mine, and I can almost feel her trying to read my thoughts. Seemingly sensing that I'm holding something back, she sits on the edge of my desk, directly in front of me. I place my hands on her waist, and she doesn't resist. The warmth of her body seeping into me is a comfort that I didn't realize I needed.

"Whatever you need to tell me, it's protected under attorney-client privilege," she tells me, her voice steady and reassuring. "You don't have to worry about me sharing anything with anyone else."

I shake my head, a wistful smile tugging at the corners of my mouth. "It's not that I don't trust you, Isabella. I just... I don't want you to become a target because of what I share with you."

"Primo," she says patiently, her dark eyes holding mine captive. "I'm already a target simply by being your attorney. So why not tell me what's on your mind? Let me help you any way I can."

Her fierce dedication and bravery stir something deep within me, and I find myself unable to hold back any longer.

"Our family's power is waning further, and there are problems with the Irish," I admit, feeling as though a weight has been lifted off my chest.

"Is there anything I can do to help?" she asks, her voice laced with concern.

"Unfortunately, no," I sigh. "But I appreciate the offer." Running my fingers through my hair, I continue, "The issue is that Constantino is obviously making moves behind my back. It's threatening my control and status, opening doors for other families. Plus, I haven't even seen Giovanni lately. I'm not sure what he's been up to since he got back from Miami."

"Tell me about Miami," Isabella says, her eyes searching mine for answers.

"Okay," I concede, knowing that she deserves the truth. "It was the first time I tried to handle the situation with

Axe. But then Giovanni showed up at the scene, which was completely unexpected." As I recount the events, Isabella listens intently, her eyes never leaving mine. "The leader of the main Cuban gang was there, and he brought his daughter along. The whole situation was...odd."

"Odd how?" she asks, curiosity piqued.

"Things went south quickly. The cops appeared, and during the chaos, the girl got shot. Giovanni ended up taking her under his protection because her father was arrested."

"Where are they now?" Isabella wonders aloud.

"I thought they were living here at the mansion," I say, glancing around the room. "But I haven't seen either of them since that first day you met my brothers. Come to think of it, I haven't seen Constantino, either."

A heavy silence falls over us, punctuated only by the ticking of an ornate clock on the wall. Isabella's fingers absentmindedly trace patterns on the polished surface of the desk as she processes the information I've shared.

Isabella sighs, her breath warm and heavy against my skin. "This is a very difficult situation," she says, idly tracing the curve of my jaw with one delicate fingertip. "I know there's not much I can do to help you on the business side of things, but I want to be here for you. What helps you relax when you're so stressed?"

Her question catches me off guard, and I feel myself flush beneath her gentle touch. I think about my darkest sexual desires – the ones I've only ever allowed myself to explore with faceless, nameless submissives online. I've given Isabella a taste of what I'm capable of, but I worry that sharing the full extent of my desires might drive her away.

"Whatever you're thinking, Primo," she murmurs, her green eyes searching mine. "You should share it with me."

I swallow hard, my heart pounding in my chest. "I...I have deep, dark desires. Desires centered around domination." The words hang heavy in the air between us, and I brace myself for her reaction.

Isabella's gaze doesn't waver. "I suspected as much," she admits softly. "After the few times we've been intimate, I looked into it. I don't know much about it yet, and I never imagined that I would be into this sort of thing, but I really am intrigued. I'd be open to exploring it more with you."

"Really?" The relief that floods through me is palpable, and I struggle to keep my voice steady. "I never thought I could share this side of myself with anyone."

"Primo," she whispers, her fingers brushing against the nape of my neck. "I'm always expected to be in control, to be in charge. In my line of work, if I make a mistake, my clients pay the consequences. It's a lot of pressure. Not to mention the added responsibility of my father's debts on my head. With you, it feels nice to let go, to submit, to let you tell me exactly what you want. I...trust you."

Her words wrap around me like a warm embrace, and I marvel at the depth of our connection. The relief I feel is a tidal wave, crashing over me and leaving me breathless. Excitement mingles with the newfound hope inside of me, as I realize that Isabella is open to exploring this hidden part of myself with her.

"Isabella," I begin, my voice shaky yet laced with anticipation, "what we're talking about here is beginning a dynamic."

She tilts her head to the side, her curiosity piqued. "A dynamic? What does that mean?"

"It's a negotiated relationship between a dominant and a submissive," I explain, watching her eyes widen in understanding. "But we need to approach it slowly, so you don't experience something called 'sub frenzy.'"

"Sub frenzy?" she repeats, confusion etched on her delicate features.

"Yes," I nod, trying to find the right words to describe it. "It's when a new submissive becomes overwhelmed by the excitement of a new dynamic, and they might agree to do things they don't actually feel comfortable doing. It's important that we take our time and communicate openly."

Isabella nods thoughtfully, absorbing my words. "I understand. I promise I'll be careful, and we'll take it as slow as we need to."

Her sincerity warms my heart, and I reach out to take her hand, giving it a gentle squeeze. Satisfied with our conversation, I turn to my computer and print out a document, handing it over to her.

"This is an exhaustive list of sexual preferences," I inform her. "Fill it out, and tomorrow evening we can discuss it in more detail and negotiate a scene for us to explore together."

"Thank you," she says, clutching the papers to her chest. Her eyes sparkle with excitement, but she hesitates before continuing. "As much as I am eager to delve into this with you, I need to return home for the evening."

"Home?" I frown, disappointment settling in my chest. "Why? Are your accommodations here not adequate?"

"Of course they are," she reassures me. "But I haven't been home in several days, and I just... I miss my own bed."

I try to hide my discontent, but it's difficult. The thought of her presence filling the mansion has become a comfort to me. Reluctantly, I concede and walk her to her car.

The night air is cool on my skin as we step outside, the stars sparkling brightly above us. I open the car door for her, watching as she places her files and the list of preferences inside. She gives me a grateful smile before turning toward the driver's seat.

"So," I say, leaning against the car as she puts her things inside, "how do you like this new ride?"

She laughs, a melodious sound that dances through the air, and shakes her head. "I still haven't forgiven you for getting rid of my old one."

"Ah, bella," I reply playfully, placing a finger to her lips to shush her. "It was time for an upgrade. Must you really leave?" I ask, my voice softening with genuine concern.

"Yes," she answers, her eyes filled with warmth. "But I'll be back tomorrow, I promise."

My hand finds its way to her cheek, and without thinking, I pull her into a deep, passionate kiss. Surprised by my own boldness, I feel her return the intensity, our lips moving in sync as if they've known each other for years. We break apart, both breathless, and I look into her eyes, feeling a connection deeper than anything I've ever experienced.

"Text me when you get home safe," I tell her, my voice husky with emotion. "And remember, I expect you back here tomorrow. We have much to discuss – the trial, and our scene negotiation."

"Of course," she smiles, her eyes sparkling with anticipation. She slides into the driver's seat, her body bathed in the moonlight, and glances at me one last time before pulling away. I watch her disappear into the night, my chest swelling with a mix of longing and excitement.

As I make my way back into the mansion, its vast emptiness makes me realize how much Isabella's presence has come to mean to me. I climb the grand staircase, feeling my responsibilities on my shoulders, and head straight to my office to confront the issue at hand: the Irish.

I sink into my chair, the leather cool against my skin, and dial a trusted associate. "Find out who's in charge of gun shipments for the Irish," I command, my voice firm but quiet. "And report back to me as soon as you can."

"Understood, boss," they reply before hanging up.

I lean back in my chair, my thoughts consumed with the challenges that lie ahead – both in my business and my burgeoning relationship with Isabella. But beneath the uncertainty, there is an undeniable thrill, a sense of anticipation that keeps the darkness at bay.

I look at the time and realize that the best and only thing I can do now is to get some rest.

I make my way through the dimly lit corridors of the mansion, each step ringing with a sense of emptiness that was foreign to me until Isabella's departure. My nightly routine is set in motion: I pour myself a glass of aged whiskey, savoring its rich aroma as it fills my senses. I think of her, of the delicate scent that clings to her skin and the fire that burns within her eyes.

"Tomorrow," I murmur to the empty room, as if saying it aloud might will the hours away more quickly.

I take a sip of the whiskey, letting the liquid warmth soothe my throat before continuing on with my routine. The familiar motions of showering and changing into my nightclothes provide a brief respite from the thoughts that consume me. But as soon as I slide between the cool satin sheets, they return in full force.

Closing my eyes, I envision Isabella – her red hair framing her face like a fiery halo, her full lips parted in anticipation. The thought of her willingness to explore our deepest desires together sends a shiver down my spine, igniting a hunger within me that had long been dormant.

"Isabella," I whisper her name, and it feels like a spell, a sacred incantation that has the power to both save and damn me. My hands roam over my body, seeking the relief that only she seems capable of providing.

I imagine her kneeling before me, the look of complete submission in her eyes as she awaits my command. I consider all the things we'll do together in our exploration, the boundaries we'll push, and the trust we'll build. The fantasies grow darker, more intense, and with each passing moment, my arousal only deepens.

My hand wraps around my cock, stroking it in sync with the images that play behind my closed eyelids. I can almost feel her body against mine, the silkiness of her skin as it yields to my touch. I long to possess her, to claim her in a way that transcends the physical and seeps into the very core of our beings.

"Tomorrow," I repeat, the word a mantra that fuels my desire as I bring myself closer and closer to the edge. The thought of Isabella – of all we will share together – is enough to send me tumbling into the abyss of pleasure, my cries echoing through the otherwise silent mansion.

I lay there, breathless and spent, the taste of whiskey still clinging to my lips. My mind quiets for the first time in what feels like an eternity, and I am left with nothing but anticipation for what tomorrow holds.

"Tomorrow," I whisper once more before succumbing to the darkness, a single word that encapsulates both hope and desire – a promise of things to come.

# Chapter Twenty-One

*Isabella*

I step into my small apartment, the stale air settling around me like an old coat. It's been a few days since I've been here, and I'm not sure it even feels like home anymore. The dim light filtering through the windows casts a somber glow over the place, highlighting the dust that has settled in my absence.

"Home sweet home," I murmur to myself as I begin to unpack my things.

As I fold back the flap of my bag, a piece of paper flutters to the floor. It's the sexual preference list Primo gave me earlier. I pick it up and start to read it over, my heart quickening with each unfamiliar term.

"Edge play? Fire play?" I raise an eyebrow, curiosity piqued. "I need to do a bit of research."

Settling down at my computer, I open an incognito browser and tentatively type in the first term. I click on a link and watch as my screen fills with information I never knew existed.

"God, I didn't know there were so many different ways to spank someone," I mutter, shaking my head in disbelief. A few hours later, I've learned more about kinks than I ever thought possible. A few videos shock me, others leave me horrified, but a select few awaken an intrigue deep within me. I complete the list, feeling a mix of excitement and apprehension for my meeting with Primo tomorrow.

"Time to get back to work." I turn my attention back to the case files spread out across my desk, trying to focus on the upcoming trial. But no matter how hard I try, my thoughts keep drifting back to the list and the dark desires it represents - desires I now share with the enigmatic man I am defending.

"Damn you, Primo," I whisper, my pulse racing. "You're making it impossible to concentrate." The words hang in the air, a testament to the power he holds over me, both in and out of the courtroom.

I imagine submitting myself to him, and I shudder at the thought of what lies beneath the surface of his desires. My hand drifts lower as I sit at my computer desk, fingertips teasing the fabric of my panties. Just as sensation begins to build, a sudden chime pulls me back to reality. It's a text message from Primo.

> Isabella, why haven't you told me that you've arrived home safely?

> Sorry, I've been distracted.

> By what?

> Your list.

I hesitate for a moment before hitting send.

> I've been researching some of the things on it.

> Have you completed it?

> Yes, I have.

> Good. I'm pleased.

There's something in the brevity of his response that sends a thrill down my spine.

> Tell me, Isabella. Has your research had any... effects on you?

> Effects?

I pause, considering my answer.

> Yes, I suppose you could say that. Some of what I've learned has... turned me on.

> Interesting.

I can almost hear the smile in his words.

> Are you in need of release, Isabella?

My cheeks flush as I read his question. My fingers hover over the keyboard, debating whether or not to admit my desperation. Finally, I relent.

> Yes, I desperately am.

> Very well. I could use a release myself. If you assist me in this, then I will reward you and allow you to come.

> Assist you how?

My heart is pounding with anticipation.

> Let's engage in a little game. We can take turns describing our fantasies to one another. Each of us will offer a scenario, and the other will respond in kind. Let's see if we can push each other to the edge without ever touching one another.

It's a tantalizing proposition, one that makes my breath catch in my throat. I can't help but be seduced by the idea of building this intimate connection with Primo through words alone.

> I'm intrigued. Let's play.

> Excellent. Why don't you start?

I pause for a moment, considering the countless

fantasies that have been swirling through my mind since I began exploring his list. Finally, I settle on one that has been particularly haunting me.

> Imagine me, bound before you, completely at your mercy. You tease me with your touch, never quite giving me what I crave.

My fingers tremble as they tap out the words.

> Ah, Isabella. You have no idea how much I've thought about that very scenario. In return, picture me taking control of your body, guiding you through every sensation until you're begging for release.

My eyes flutter closed as I imagine it, my body responding to the mere idea of his touch.

> I'd like to see you enact my fantasies right now.

> Now? But, how?

> I will instruct you and you will film yourself and send me the video. Can you do this for me, sweet Isabella?

Eager to please Primo, I swallow the lump in my throat and agree to his instructions. I have never done anything like this before, but the thought of giving him control over my body, even from a distance, makes me shiver.

> Alright. I'll do it.

> Good girl.

I can almost hear the satisfaction in his voice.

> Start by stripping out of your clothes slowly. Make sure you capture every moment on video.

I prop my phone up on the nightstand, ensuring that the camera has a full view of me. The room feels heavy with anticipation as I begin to undress, each article of clothing sliding off my skin like silk. I am painfully aware of the camera's gaze; it is both unnerving and exhilarating.

As I shed my final garment, I stand completely naked before the lens. My heart pounds wildly in my chest, but I force myself to remain composed. I send the video to Primo, my fingers trembling slightly.

> Good.

I let out a breath I didn't realize I was holding.

> Now, I want you to trace your body with your fingertips, but don't touch yourself where you truly desire. I need to see the longing in your eyes.

I take a deep breath and follow his command, my fingers grazing across my collarbone, down my arms, and over my breasts, stopping just short of my nipples. As I continue to explore the contours of my body, the ache between my thighs grows more insistent. I can feel the wetness pooling there, slick and hot.

I send Primo the second video, my pulse racing. His approval comes swiftly.

> You're doing good work, Isabella. Now, lay back on the bed and spread your thighs. Show me that beautiful pussy, and remember, you are not to touch yourself.

My face flushes with a mixture of embarrassment and arousal as I comply, positioning myself on the bed with my most intimate parts exposed. The camera captures every detail, from the glistening wetness of my arousal to the delicate folds of my labia. As I send him the video, my body quivers with need.

> Your nipples look so hard, Isabella. They're begging for attention. Toy with them for me, and remember that next time, I'll be sending you home with nipple clamps.

I bite my lip, imagining the sensation of cold metal tightening around my sensitive flesh. Fingers trembling, I tease my nipples, tugging and pinching them just enough to elicit a moan. The camera captures it all, each gasp and shiver as I surrender myself to Primo's desires.

> Such an obedient girl you are.

I feel a swell of pride mingled with my mounting lust. His messages grow darker, more insistent.

> Now, I want you to take two fingers and slowly enter your pussy. Make sure the camera is very close.

I position my phone carefully, ensuring every detail will be captured. My fingers tremble with anticipation as they slip between my slick folds. It's torturous how slowly I must move, but I know that defying Primo isn't an option. At least, not yet.

> Good girl. Now, take those sweet juices and rub them into your nipples. You're not allowed to come, understand?

Every nerve in my body screams for release, but I nod obediently, even though he can't see me. Dipping my fingers back inside myself, I gather the evidence of my desire and bring it up to my swollen nipples. The sensation of my own wetness against them is electrifying, and I struggle to hold back my climax.

> Your obedience is tantalizing, Isabella. But I sense you're on the brink. Remember, you mustn't come.

I grit my teeth, determined to follow his command.

But as I continue to circle my slick fingertips around my nipples, the pleasure becomes unbearable. My inner muscles clench and unclench, aching for release. In a moment of rebellion – or perhaps simply weakness – I plunge my fingers deep inside myself, riding the wave of ecstasy that threatens to consume me.

"Primo," I gasp, filming my disobedience for him to see. "I can't... I can't hold back any longer."

And then, with a shuddering moan, I allow myself to come, my fingers coated in the evidence of my betrayal. I'm panting and my mind is reeling with the fact that I've just disobeyed him, but I send him the video still. Perhaps I still have a bit of fight left within me that is begging to be tamed.

> Isabella. You have defied my orders, and you will be punished for your disobedience. Prepare yourself for tomorrow evening.

His words are dark and full of promise.

I read his message over and over, a thrill of anticipation zipping through me. I should be frightened, or at least apprehensive about what he might do to me as punishment. But instead, a wicked smile curls my lips, and I can't help but feel aroused by this dangerous game we're playing.

> I'll be ready.

## Chapter Twenty-Two

*Isabella*

The steam dissipates, leaving a faint haze in the bathroom. I step out of the shower, feeling renewed. The warm water droplets embrace every curve of my body, making me shiver with delight. My release and Primo's words have left me invigorated, ready to tackle the challenges that his case presents.

"Isabella, focus," I whisper, gathering my thoughts that are still swirling around. A vivid memory of Primo's voice plays back in my mind, "It's the Irish and my own brothers who I fear may betray me." The words feel ominous, their weight bearing down on me. It's time to unravel this tangled web of deception.

I wrap myself in a plush towel and make my way to my desk. Documents are strewn about, a testament to my relentless pursuit of the truth. I begin to sift through the words on the pages, desperate to find something that might help point me in the right direction.

"Let's see what we have here," I murmur, poring over the documents in front of me. Accounts of the night in question are inconsistent, timelines are muddled. I can feel it in my bones – someone somewhere is hiding something. But what?

And, it's all mixed up with the situation in Miami. Why were the feds there in the first place? Someone tipped them off and they were clearly after Primo.

"Alright, according to Axe's deposition testimony, he was at the warehouse by 11:45 PM and he claims that Primo shot Beau just before midnight."

I turn to the coroner's report. "Beau Bennett was found dead from a gunshot wound to the head at a close distance through the left temple."

I recreate how something like that could happen, pretending to hold a gun up to my left temple.

"Someone was able to get right up next to him to shoot him. It had to be someone he trusted," I realize. "Otherwise it's unlikely that he would have allowed anyone that close."

Primo said that Teddy was there at the safehouse with them, but that he stepped outside and didn't see Beau leave.

I try and put the doubt out of my mind and trust Primo. He told me that he was innocent and I need to believe him, even if everything is pointing against it.

As I dig deeper into the documents, Primo's words

about being set up ring in my ears. He claimed he was trying to take care of Axe that night, but instead found himself arrested and accused of a murder he didn't commit the next day. The injustice fuels my determination, and I feel a fire ignite within me.

The room feels colder, the air heavy with revelations yet to be uncovered. My fingers tremble as I turn the pages, my mind racing, hungry for the truth.

The testimony of one witness seizes my attention – he claims to have spoken with a "CM" the night of the crime.

"Constantino," I murmur, the letters forming his name like a bitter taste on my tongue. His deposition sits before me, a cleverly crafted alibi nestled among the sea of documents. He says he was visiting their father at the prison at the time, but my gut twists and turns, urging me to look closer.

"Could it really be him?" I wonder aloud, my voice barely a whisper, swallowed by the darkness of my apartment.

I start taking a closer look at his alibi. "Visiting the prison," I say to myself, running my fingers through the logs that support his statement. I look at the time stamps and suddenly, things aren't adding up right.

"Fifteen minutes, twenty-three minutes, seventeen minutes, 4 hours," I say to myself, looking at the time stamps of his various visits.

"Primo, I think you were right," I say, as if he could somehow hear me through the walls that separate us. "Your brother...he set you up."

As I pore over the evidence, the pieces fall into place. Constantino's plan had been to frame Primo for the murder of Axe in Miami, but when things went awry, he had to readjust. The incident at the safehouse was arranged, but even still that went poorly, with Axe escaping with his life.

That left Constantino with the need for a dead body that he could pin on Primo. Who better than Beau, who continuously failed to set things up correctly so that Constantino could be rid of his brother and take control of the family.

Beau trusted Constantino. They were working together, so it wouldn't be hard for Constantino to deliver the fatal blow at close range.

And, it wasn't just Constantino that wanted Primo out of the way. The feds would be far too happy to see him gone. They'd just managed to get his father behind bars. They don't want him to pick up where he left off. So now, the feds are entangling themselves with Axe, weaving a web of deceit in an attempt to ensnare Primo once and for all.

"Two fronts," I sigh, rubbing my temples. "Primo, you're being attacked from every angle. No wonder your world is crumbling."

The more I delve into the case, the more apparent it becomes that what the feds are doing borders on criminal. Tampering with evidence, perhaps even entrapment – it's enough to make any jury question their motives.

And, Constantino's alibi raises so many questions when you look at it under heavy scrutiny. Surely the jury might see through his carefully constructed facade to see the monster beneath.

"Reasonable doubt," I say, clenching my fists. "That's all we need. Just enough to make them question everything they've been led to believe."

Shadows creep along the walls as I glance at the clock, its hands taunting me with the passing time. Three in the morning, far too late to share my discovery with Primo. Exhaustion pulls me toward my bed, and I surrender to its call, letting the soft sheets envelop me like a cocoon.

I wake up to the sound of my phone ringing, its shrill tone cutting through the silence of my apartment. Reluctantly, I reach over and grab it from the nightstand, squinting at the screen. "Eve" flashes on the display, and a small smile tugs at the corners of my mouth.

"Hey, sis," I answer, trying to sound more awake than I feel. "What's up?"

"Isabella!" her voice is bubbly and excited, a stark contrast to my grogginess. "I'm finally done with my string of shifts, and I'm starving! Want to grab breakfast together at our favorite spot?"

My stomach grumbles in agreement, but I hesitate, knowing Primo expects me back at the mansion early today. Yet, reconnecting with Eve feels important, almost necessary. "Sure," I say, "let's do it."

"Great, see you there!"

As I pull into the parking lot of the cozy little café that holds so many memories for us, I spot Eve leaning against the hood of her car, arms crossed, an amused grin plastered on her face. She waves me over with a flourish, and I can't help but roll my eyes at her dramatics.

"Wow, Isabella," she drawls as I step out of the sleek Lamborghini, her eyebrows rising incredulously. "You've certainly upgraded since the last time I saw you. Where did this beauty come from?"

"Primo bought it for me," I admit sheepishly, running my fingers along the smooth curve of the door. "I know I shouldn't be taking gifts from clients, but he didn't give me much choice."

Eve's eyes narrow, curiosity gleaming in their depths. "Oh really?" she teases, linking her arm through mine. "I want to hear all about it, but let's do it over food. I'm starving."

The warmth of the café envelops us like a comforting hug as we slide into our favorite red-vinyl booth. The sounds of busy waitstaff and clinking dishes create a familiar, soothing hum around us. I glance over at Eve, her eyes sparkling with anticipation, and take a deep breath, inhaling the rich aroma of coffee and buttery croissants.

Eve has strawberry blonde hair that falls to her shoulders, and her olive skin glows with warmth. Her lips are curved in a playful smirk, and her eyes are wide with curiosity. She wears a bright blue sundress and ivory sandals, and her delicate jewelry glitters in the light.

"Alright, spill," Eve demands, leaning in close as she stirs her steaming cup of coffee. "Tell me everything about this Primo guy since we last talked."

I open my mouth to speak, but she cuts me off, waving her hand dismissively.

"Actually, let's order first. I'm starving." She flags down a waitress, and we place our orders—omelets for both of us, just like old times.

As the waitress scurries away, I try to steer the conversation toward Eve, asking how she's been holding up after so many long shifts. But she fixes me with a knowing gaze, and I can tell there's no escaping her curiosity.

"Nice try, Isabella, but don't change the subject," she says firmly. "Why are you driving a Lamborghini? It's obvious he has a thing for you if he's buying you such expensive gifts."

"Primo's... complicated," I admit, stirring my own coffee nervously. "And that's the only thing he's purchased for me, but it still feels... excessive."

"Excessive?" Eve scoffs, her eyes wide. "That's a massive understatement. But go on, tell me more."

My cheeks grow hot as I confess how dangerously close Primo and I have become. "We've been crossing lines I never thought I'd cross with a client," I say, my voice barely above a whisper. "He's awakened something in me I didn't know was there."

Eve's interest is piqued, her eyes growing wider with

each word. "Like what? You can't just leave me hanging like that!"

"Alright," I relent, taking a deep breath. "He's been giving me the most mind-blowing orgasms I've ever had."

"Wow," Eve exclaims, her face lighting up with a devilish grin. "That's something to celebrate! It's about time you found someone who knows how to please you, especially after that ex of yours."

"Still," I murmur, my fingers tapping nervously on the table, "it feels like we're playing with fire."

My sister reaches across the table and squeezes my hand reassuringly. "Isabella, don't be ashamed. Live your life. If Primo is making you happy, then enjoy it while it lasts."

Our food arrives, creating a temporary lull in our conversation as we dive into the fluffy omelets before us. But as I savor each bite, I can't help but wonder if Eve's right. Maybe I should just embrace this whirlwind romance with Primo and see where it leads.

"Promise me one thing," Eve says suddenly, her voice serious. "If things get too intense or dangerous, walk away. There are some lines that shouldn't be crossed, even for great sex."

I nod solemnly, knowing she's right. Yet, as we chat and laugh together over breakfast, my thoughts keep drifting back to the mysterious man waiting for me at the mansion, and the dark passion that simmers between us.

"Speaking of dangerous," I blurt out, feeling the need to share the recent incident with Eve. She leans in, her eyes wide with curiosity. "One of the loan sharks showed up and tried to attack me."

"Attack you?" Eve gasps, her fork pausing mid-air. "What happened?"

"Primo stepped in and saved me." My voice is hushed, a shiver running down my spine as I recall the terrifying moment.

"Wow, that's seriously hot," Eve says with a wicked grin. "But how did he manage that? I thought he was under house arrest?"

"Primo has...ways," I admit, taking a sip of my coffee. "He's always pushing the boundaries, bending the rules. It's not what I'm used to, and it scares me sometimes. But there's something so alluring about it, too."

"Isabella," Eve says, her tone teasing, "are you falling for a bad boy?"

I laugh nervously, my cheeks flushing with heat. "Maybe. There's more, Eve. Things between us have taken a turn... Primo wants to take our relationship further."

"Further?" she raises an eyebrow. "As in...?"

"I can't go into details," I say, averting my gaze. "Some things are private, even for him. But yes, he wants more from me than just a professional arrangement."

"Girl, you're living the dream!" Eve exclaims, grabbing my hand. "You've got a sexy, powerful man who knows how to please you and protect you. What more could you want?"

"Are you sure it's worth the risk?" I ask, my heart

pounding in my chest. "Mixing business and pleasure like this?"

"Relax, Isabella," Eve reassures me. "You're an amazing lawyer and a smart woman. Trust yourself. You've got this."

I smile, touched by her words. Just then, my phone buzzes with a text message from Primo.

> Where are you?

> Meeting. Will be at the mansion soon.

His concern for me both irritating and endearing.

"Alright," Eve says as we finish our food. "Just remember what I said: if things get too intense or dangerous, walk away. There are some lines that shouldn't be crossed."

"Thank you, Eve," I say, hugging her tightly. We say our goodbyes, and I head to my car, my heart racing with anticipation for what awaits me at the mansion.

As I drive, the sun casts a golden glow on the city and the wind caresses my face. It feels like an omen of the unknown pleasures and dangers that lie ahead.

## Chapter Twenty-Three

*Primo*

I watch the sun as it dawns over the mansion, its golden rays gently brushing against the marble floors. I stand by the window, feeling restless and agitated, my thoughts entangled in knots. Isabella should have arrived by now. The empty halls are silent, and a growing sense of unease settles in.

I pull out my phone and type a terse message, each character punctuated by the drumming of my fingers on the screen:

Where are you?

Meeting. Be there soon.

Good.

My heart clenches at the reminder that she's not living here with me. She has her freedom, and yet, I long to know every detail of her life, to protect her from the darkness closing in around us. This distance between us feels unbearable; I resolve to change it.

But for now, I need something to occupy myself. Deciding to get something to eat while I wait, I head toward the kitchen.

As I enter the kitchen, I find Constantino already there, devouring breakfast and perusing the newspaper. Our eyes meet, and we exchange terse greetings, the tension thick and palpable.

"Good morning, Primo," he says, and I can't help but notice the sly glint in his eyes.

"Morning," I reply curtly, turning my attention to the cappuccino machine, hoping it will distract me from the gnawing suspicion that my brother is up to no good. The hum of the machine offers no solace.

Constantino puts down the paper, a wicked smile playing across his lips. "You seem tense, brother. Anything you want to talk about?"

"Nothing that concerns you," I snap, feeling the bitterness well up inside me. The urge to confront him about his actions grows stronger, but I fear what that might unleash.

"Really?" Constantino raises an eyebrow, leaning back in his chair, observing me like a predator stalking its prey. "Because it seems to me that you've been preoccupied lately."

"Like I said," I growl, pouring the steaming liquid into my cup, "it's none of your business."

"Of course," he says, smirking, and I can't shake the feeling that he knows more than he lets on.

Taking a sip of my cappuccino, I feel its bitterness spread across my tongue. My gaze flicks to Constantino as he leans forward in his chair, scrutinizing me with an intensity that makes my skin crawl.

"Primo," he begins, his voice dripping with feigned innocence, "how are our shipments coming along? You know, the times, amounts... and what about our people on the ground? How much money do we have floating around to keep the officials cooperative?"

My jaw clenches at his probing questions, the muscles in my neck tensing. The delicate china cup in my hand threatens to shatter under the strain of my grip. "I told you, it's none of your concern." Each word is a warning, a boundary drawn between us. "I am more than capable of handling things."

Constantino's lips curl into a smirk, and his eyes glint with something dark. "You may think so, brother, but these matters concern me more and more each day."

The anger within me flares, and I slam the cup down onto the countertop, deaf to the sound of shattering porcelain. The splatters of coffee on the pristine white marble mirror the chaos brewing inside me. "Enough!" I snarl, glaring at him. "I know you've been liaising with the Irish behind my back, Constantino. It needs to stop."

He remains unruffled, a picture of calm in contrast to

the storm raging within me. "I've always been in charge of our dealings with the Irish," he retorts coldly. "I will do as I please with that business relationship."

"Like hell you will!" I shout, my hands curled into fists at my sides. "I am in charge, Constantino. Me!"

His laughter cuts through the air, a razor-sharp reminder of the power struggle between us. "You think you're in charge, brother? You're not as in control as you believe."

With a final derisive glance, he rises from his chair and leaves the kitchen. My heart pounds like a war drum, and I'm left with the broken pieces of my cappuccino cup and the bitter taste of betrayal.

As I stand amidst the shattered remnants of my morning ritual, my mind races with thoughts of Isabella's impending arrival. The mansion feels colder, more treacherous, every corner tainted by Constantino's ominous presence. I know that I must protect her from this darkness, to shield her from the ever-growing shadows.

But for now, I am alone in the wreckage, struggling to hold on to the tenuous threads of control that bind me to this life. And as I stare at the broken porcelain, I start to wonder if these fragments are a reflection of my own fractured soul.

The rage within me still burns, a fire stoked by the lingering sounds of Constantino's laughter. I leave the kitchen and pace the mansion halls like a caged beast, my shoes striking the marble floor with a rhythmic cadence that does little to calm my frayed nerves. The lush surroundings that once brought me comfort now seem stifling, suffocating—a gilded cage forged from my own ambition and desire.

I round a corner, my heart hammering in my chest, and there she is. Isabella, a vision in her tailored suit, her bright hair cascading over her shoulders like a waterfall of ink. She stands before me, a defiant angel in this den of vipers, her eyes blazing with an intensity that rips through the veil of my fury.

"Where have you been?" I snarl, my anger momentarily taking hold as I close the distance between us. "You should have been here sooner."

"Primo," she retorts, the fire in her eyes never wavering, "you don't control my every move. You can't dictate where I go or who I see."

"Isabella, I need to know where you are," I argue, desperation seeping into my voice. "You're my attorney, and the trial is just around the corner."

"Your concern for the trial is understandable," she says, her tone measured, "but it doesn't give you license to control me."

The tension between us crackles like electricity, and in a sudden surge of emotion, I press her against the wall. My hands find purchase on her slender waist, and I lean in, my face mere inches from hers. "I thought you liked being controlled," I whisper, my breath hot against her skin. "I thought you enjoyed submitting to me."

My arousal surges at the feel of her against me, my cock stiffening as the urge to dominate her consumes my thoughts. I imagine turning her around, taking her right here in the hallway, driving into her with a primal intensity that leaves no doubt as to who is truly in control.

"Remember last night?" I murmur, my voice low and dangerous. "You disobeyed me, Isabella. You came without permission, and now I can't wait to punish you."

Her eyes darken, and for a moment, she seems to submit, her body yielding to the force of my desires. But then she speaks, her voice trembling with a quiet strength. "I need to be able to do things for myself outside of this mansion, Primo."

"Alright," I relent, releasing her. The heat of her body lingers on my skin as I lead her to my office, the memory of our recent exchange still smoldering within me.

"Constantino and I had a confrontation," I confess, my anger simmering beneath the surface. "I'm growing more concerned about his intentions."

My heart is still pounding from our earlier confrontation when Isabella speaks up, her voice soft but firm. "Primo, I need to tell you something. Late last night, I had a breakthrough in the case."

I raise an eyebrow, curious and wary. "Go on."

"From what I've found, I think... I think I can prove it was Constantino who set you up," she says, her eyes never leaving mine.

The air shifts around us, thick with tension. Shock courses through me as I struggle to process this accusation. "Are you certain?" I ask, my voice barely more than a whisper.

Isabella hesitates before answering. "The evidence is circumstantial, but it should be enough to create reasonable doubt in the jury's mind."

"Is that a wise strategy?" I question, my thoughts racing. "Accusing my own brother could cause a bigger divide within the family and further threaten our power."

"Is it a better option for you to go to prison for a crime you didn't commit?" she counters, her eyes flashing with determination. "Think about it, Primo. You don't have to make a decision right now, but you need to consider the possibility."

"Give me a few days," I say, my mind churning with conflicting emotions. "I need time to think about whether pinning this on Constantino is really the right move."

"Alright," she agrees reluctantly, and I nod my thanks. With so much at stake, I need to weigh my options carefully.

Eager to shift the conversation to less volatile territory, I clear my throat. "Now, about that sexual preference list you completed."

Isabella hands me the paper, her cheeks flushing pink. As I review her answers, a smile tugs at the corner of my mouth. "Interesting," I murmur, feeling my cock stiffen at the thought of the delicious things I plan to do to her body.

"Interesting?" she repeats, curiosity lacing her voice. "How so?"

"There are a number of things on this list that you said you'd like to try together," I explain, the anticipation and lust building within me. "I'm excited about the idea of teaching these things to you."

Unable to resist teasing her further, I add, "As for your punishment for coming without permission last night... I've decided on orgasm denial."

Her eyes widen, but I see a spark of desire flicker deep within them. This game we're playing, it's only just begun, and I can hardly wait to see where it leads us.

"Isabella, I'd like to negotiate a scene with you now," I say, my voice firm but gentle. She nods her agreement, and I continue, "I'm going to tell you everything I intend to do to you, and you may refuse anything I say."

As we sit in the dimly lit office, I notice her eyes flicker with curiosity and anticipation. "I want to tie you down on the bed, spank you, and touch you freely," I explain. "This being our first scene together, I plan to take things slow and make sure you respond well to it."

"Okay," she breathes out, her cheeks flushed with excitement. I can't help but feel the arousal building within me as I watch her squirm in her seat.

"Remember, Isabella, don't just agree because you're excited. Make sure you're truly comfortable with everything," I remind her with a stern gaze. She takes a few minutes, biting her lip and considering my words before finally nodding her understanding and agreement.

"Let's talk about safe words," I say, eager to establish clear boundaries for both of our sakes. "We'll use the stoplight system. If you're uncomfortable but don't want to stop, say 'yellow.' If you want the scene to stop immediately, say 'red.'"

"Should I ever use 'green'?" she asks, her voice quivering slightly.

"Only if I check in with you and ask how you're doing," I explain. "Otherwise, you'll wait to experience what I have planned when I decide it's time." The thrill of control courses through my veins, heightening my arousal even more.

"Understood," she whispers, her eyes wide and filled with trust.

"Follow me," I command as I stand and lead her from the office to my bedroom. With each step, I feel the intensity of my desire grow, fueled by the heady mix of power and vulnerability that our upcoming scene promises.

# Chapter Twenty-Four

## Isabella

As Primo leads me away from the office, I can't help but feel an anticipatory shiver run down my spine. My heart races with each step we take in tandem, and I begin to wonder where he plans to take me. The guest bedroom looms ahead, and I assume that's where he wants our illicit encounter to happen. But as we pass by the door, he doesn't hesitate, guiding me further down the hallway.

"Where are we going?" I ask, my voice barely above a whisper.

"Somewhere more... intimate," he replies cryptically, his eyes never leaving mine.

He stops before a heavy oak door, adorned with an intricate brass handle. With a subtle flourish, he opens it, revealing a room I've never seen before – Primo's master bedroom.

The moment I step inside, I'm enveloped by the scent of him – a heady mix of sandalwood and something uniquely masculine. This is obviously a space he has curated with great care. Every detail, from the dark wood paneling to the plush carpet beneath my feet, speaks of luxury and refinement.

My gaze is immediately drawn to the massive four-poster bed at the center of the room. It's draped in rich, burgundy velvet, giving it a regal appearance. A sense of vulnerability fills me as I imagine what might transpire between us in that very spot.

"Like what you see?" he teases, enjoying the look of awe on my face.

"It's... beautiful," I breathe, unsure of how else to articulate the grandeur of the room.

"After you," he says, his voice low and seductive.

As I take in the rest of the space, I notice a seating area near a grand fireplace. Two high-backed chairs sit opposite one another, a chessboard positioned between them as if waiting to be used. I can't help but think of the strategic games Primo and I have played with one another, both in court and behind closed doors.

"Are you a good chess player?" I inquire, genuinely curious.

"Very," he replies smugly. "But I'm even better at other... games."

My cheeks flush with heat as I consider the implications of his words. My gaze drifts to a nearby bookshelf, filled with leather-bound volumes that exude an air of mystery. I long to run my fingers over their spines, to learn more about the man who has captivated me so thoroughly.

"Perhaps you'll teach me those games," I suggest coyly.

"Maybe," he says, drawing closer. "But first, let's focus on the game we're playing right now."

Primo gestures for me to sit on the plush, velvet sofa near the fireplace. I comply, my heart pounding in anticipation as I watch him glide across the room and disappear into his walk-in closet. When he reemerges, he holds a variety of items that send a shiver down my spine. He carefully lays out ropes, paddles, and other implements I've never seen before on a nearby table.

"Come," he commands, his voice firm but gentle.

I obey, rising from the sofa and stepping toward him. My eyes linger on each item, curiosity mingling with apprehension. As my hand reaches out to touch one of the mysterious objects, Primo's fingers close around my cheeks, forcing me to look into his dark eyes.

"Isabella," he says, his voice low and stern, "you are not to touch these without my permission. The only time you will be allowed to touch them is when they are being smacked against your skin or when you are given the honor of cleaning my tools for me under my watchful eye. Do you understand?"

"I understand," I reply, my voice trembling with excitement and nerves.

"From now on, when I ask you a question or give an order, you will respond with 'Yes, Sir' or 'No, Sir,' as appropriate. Can you do that?" Primo asks, his eyes never leaving mine.

"Yes, Sir," I murmur, a hint of a smile playing on my lips. He returns the smile, clearly pleased with my quick adaptation.

"Good girl," he praises, releasing my cheeks.

Primo then leads me back to the sofa and instructs me to sit once more. Slowly, he starts to undress me, his fingers lingering on each piece of clothing as it's removed. With every revealed inch of skin, his gaze seems to grow hungrier, devouring me in a way that makes me feel both vulnerable and cherished.

Finally, I am completely naked before him, a shiver of anticipation running down my spine. "This is how I enjoy you the most," he whispers, his breath warm against my ear. "Naked and submitting to me. Now, "get on your knees," he orders.

Without hesitation, I drop to my knees before him. I remain silent, forgetting the protocol we've just established. Primo narrows his eyes at me, a dangerous glint flashing within them. He begins walking around me in slow circles, scrutinizing my every move. I can sense his thoughts - I defied him yesterday by coming without permission, and now I struggle to follow even the simplest instructions. Yet, this only serves to fuel my arousal, and I find myself falling deeper into the spell of Primo's domination.

As he continues to circle me, I wonder what he has

planned for me. How will he push my boundaries, and how far am I willing to go under his control?

"Sit up straight, pet," he commands, his voice a velvety growl that makes my spine tingle. "You should always strive to be the very best version of yourself when you're around me."

I comply immediately, sitting up as tall and proud as possible. His words resonate with me – I am a reflection on him. The idea of him owning me, of being his possession, sends a shudder of pleasure coursing through me.

"Does the thought of being my little fuck pet excite you?" Primo asks, leaning down so close that I can feel the heat radiating off his body.

"Yes, Sir," I breathe, my voice trembling with desire.

"Good girl," he praises, and I feel a rush of warmth at his approval. "A proper little fuck pet obeys her master's every command." With that, he gestures for me to open my mouth, and I do so without hesitation.

He spits in my mouth, and I suppress a gasp of shock. It's degrading, but it only serves to stoke the fire within me. I watch as his lips curve into a smile, clearly pleased with my submission.

"Ah, look at those nipples," he murmurs, reaching forward to tweak them between his fingers. "Hardening without permission. You're such a needy little slut for me, aren't you?"

I nod, unable to speak as my arousal builds, threatening to consume me. He leaves me kneeling there, my gaze locked on the bed before me. As much as I ache to watch him, I know better than to disobey.

When he returns, he's holding a pair of leather cuffs lined with rabbit fur. I shiver as he gently fastens one around each wrist, the soft fur caressing my skin like a whispered promise of pleasure to come. The anticipation is almost unbearable, and I can feel the heat pooling between my thighs.

"Are you ready for what comes next, pet?" Primo asks, his dark eyes searching mine for any sign of hesitation.

"Yes, Sir," I reply, my voice thick with desire. "I want to please you."

"Good," he purrs, drawing me further into the depths of his intoxicating dominance. "Because you have a lot to learn, and I'm going to enjoy teaching you every lesson."

"Green" is the word that slips from my lips when he asks how I'm feeling. My heart races with anticipation, but there's a sense of safety in our connection – a trust that has grown from our shared passions.

"Stand," Primo commands, and I obey without hesitation.

"Yes, Sir."

He guides me to the base of his bed, his hand warm and firm on the small of my back. "Lean forward, grasp the base of the bed, and spread your legs wide," he instructs, his voice low and authoritative. "I want your sopping pussy on display for me."

My cheeks flush with heat as I follow his command, my fingers gripping the edge of the bed while my legs part to reveal the evidence of my arousal. The air around us seems to grow thicker, charged with desire and unspoken promises.

Primo begins to trace his fingers along the curve of my legs, lingering on the sensitive skin behind my knees. "So fucking naughty," he murmurs, his breath hot against my ear. "Defying my orders yesterday. Do you plan on defying me again?"

I can't help the cheeky grin that crosses my lips as I look back at him, my eyes dancing with defiance. "Maybe, Sir."

His palm connects with my ass in a swift, unexpected motion, and I cry out, both startled and aroused by the sharp sting. "That," he warns, his voice dark and dangerous, "is just a taste of what you'll get for disobedience."

As the heat of his touch lingers on my skin, I find myself craving more. Primo caresses my legs once more, stirring a hunger within me that only he can satisfy. But he avoids touching my nipples or my cunt, and I know better than to ask for it.

The soft fur of the cuffs encircles my ankles, and I wonder what Primo has planned. When he connects a bar between the cuffs, I glance down and see his knowing smirk. "It's a spreader bar," he explains. "Be careful not to struggle, or I might just make it wider."

I shiver at the thought, feeling completely exposed – my body an open book for Primo to read and devour. As his hands roam over my skin, teasing but never quite satisfying my need, I find myself lost in the exquisite torment of his touch, surrendering willingly to his dark desires.

"Isabella," Primo says, his voice a low growl, "you disobeyed a direct order. You're going to be punished for it. Understand?"

"Yes, Sir," I reply, my heart racing with anticipation.

"Such a good girl," he praises, "even when you're being a brat." The word 'brat' piques my curiosity, but I have no time to ponder its meaning. His hand meets my ass with a forceful smack, and I yelp at the sudden jolt of pain. It sends a shockwave through me, mingling with the electric thrill of arousal.

Primo alternates between gentle caresses and hard smacks, showering my body with tender kisses before punishing me with sharp bites. "When you disobey me," he muses, "I can't help but wonder if you're asking for punishment. Don't worry, my pet, I'm more than happy to put you in your place."

My desire for release grows stronger with every touch, every word. Primo seems to sense my need, and he asks, "Do you need to come, Isabella?"

"Yes, Sir," I breathe out, desperate for any relief.

He chuckles darkly. "You should have thought about that yesterday when you defied me."

With that, Primo leaves me aching and wanting as he circles to the front of me and climbs onto the bed. He reclines against the headboard, making himself comfortable. "You look absolutely lovely like this," he tells me, his eyes raking over my exposed body. "Good enough for me to stroke myself to."

As Primo removes his shirt, I'm mesmerized by the rippling muscles I've never seen before. Intricate tattoos adorn his skin, and I yearn to explore them. Leaning back, he begins to stroke his cock, his gaze never leaving mine.

"I'm sure you'd like to help, taste me, touch me," he taunts. "But I won't allow it. You'll remain bent over in punishment, yearning for my touch while I bring myself pleasure. You owe me this orgasm."

The raw honesty of his words sends a shiver down my spine, and I stand there, bent over and vulnerable, as he takes his own satisfaction. All the while, I'm left to ache and wonder when, or if, he'll finally grant me release.

"Look at you, Isabella," Primo murmurs as he continues to stroke himself, his voice a sultry whisper. "Dripping for me like the desperate little slut you are."

I'm acutely aware of the wetness between my legs, the evidence of my desire for him gathering and running down my thighs. My body trembles with need, but I remain bent over, my wrists bound by the leather cuffs, the spreader bar holding my legs apart.

"Such a beautiful sight," he taunts, his breathing growing ragged as he nears completion. "You're lucky I'm even considering giving you relief."

The filthy words only serve to fan the flames of my desire, making me yearn for the moment when he'll finally grant me the release I crave. My heart races as I watch him reach climax, his grip tightening on his cock as he spills into his palm.

"Open your mouth," he commands, moving toward me on the bed. His cum-coated hand hovers above my open lips, and I know what's expected of me.

"Clean it," he tells me, his voice heavy with authority. As I obediently suck his fingers clean, tasting his essence, I feel a sense of pride at the praise he bestows upon me.

"So beautiful," he purrs, his eyes dark with lust. "Now that you've paid for your mistake, I may consider giving you a release. But you'll have to earn it, Isabella."

My entire being thrums with anticipation, and I find myself completely under his spell, ready and willing to do whatever he asks of me. "Yes, Sir," I breathe, my voice barely audible, yet filled with determination.

"Good girl," he says with a smile that holds equal parts menace and promise. "Let's see if you can truly prove yourself worthy of my touch."

As I stand there, bound and on display for Primo, I know that I will do whatever it takes to earn the pleasure he has the power to bestow upon me. His control over my body and mind is absolute, and I am more than willing to submit to his every desire.

Primo rises, his shirt discarded on the floor, revealing his sculpted chest and intricate tattoos. I ache to trace each line with my fingers, but he commands me with a stern voice. "Eyes forward." The unyielding authority in his tone leaves no room for objection.

"Yes, Sir," I murmur, swallowing my disobedience as I

fix my gaze on the wall before me. My legs tremble beneath me, a mixture of desire and exhaustion threatening to give way.

"Your composure is impressive, Isabella," he praises, his strong hand petting my hair tenderly. The contrast between his dominance and gentle touch sends shivers down my spine. "But I sense reluctance. Do you need another lesson in obedience?"

"No, Sir," I breathe out, hoping my voice doesn't betray the longing that has taken root deep within me.

"Good girl." His approval warms me like a sunbeam caressing my skin. He retreats from my side, leaving me momentarily bereft of his presence. But when he returns, something new shrouds his intentions – a blindfold. With practiced hands, he ties it securely over my eyes, plunging me into darkness.

"Still green?" he asks, checking in with our established safeword system.

"Green," I confirm, surrendering my sight to him, trusting him implicitly.

A sudden rush of air announces his movement, and before I can comprehend his intention, I feel his powerful arms lift me effortlessly, draping me over his shoulder. My heart races as I dangle helplessly, completely at his mercy.

"I love the feeling of you this way, Isabella," he confesses, his voice a low growl. "So vulnerable, so helpless. As much as I'd revel in watching your body succumb to exhaustion, I'll grant your muscles respite."

His words send a mixture of relief and anticipation

coursing through my veins. The gentle embrace of satin sheets greets me as he lays me on the bed, my body sinking into the luxurious fabric.

"Try to move," he orders, and I hear the unmistakable sound of chains rattling. My heart beats faster, knowing that I am now bound by both ankles and wrists to the bed, completely at his mercy. I squirm, testing the restraints, but they hold me fast.

"So needy," Primo chuckles affectionately, and I feel a flush spread across my cheeks. "I will enjoy bringing you to climax...on my own terms."

My breath hitches, and in the darkness of my blindfold, I surrender myself to him, ready for whatever comes next.

My body trembles with anticipation as Primo's hands begin to explore my flesh once more, deliberately avoiding the most sensitive places that crave his touch. My entire being screams for release, but I know better than to ask outright.

"Tell me what you want, Isabella," he murmurs, his breath hot against my ear. "Let me hear your desires."

"Please, Sir," I gasp, my voice strained with need. "I'm desperate for release."

"Ah, so you're a pitiful whore who can't think of anything else but coming?" The teasing edge to his question sends a shiver down my spine.

"Yes," I admit, shame mingling with arousal.

"I love it when you're like this." His words fan the flames within me, and I struggle not to beg for more.

Suddenly, I hear the faint hum of vibrations, and I feel something clipped onto each of my nipples. "It's such a shame you can't see how beautiful you are adorned with butterfly vibrators," he tells me, and I bite my lip, trying to suppress a moan.

He tortures me with the varying speed of the vibrations, never allowing my body to find its rhythm, leaving me teetering on the precipice of ecstasy time and time again. Each denied climax only serves to stoke my desire further, until I can no longer keep quiet.

"Speak freely, Isabella," he commands, and I seize the opportunity, spilling forth a torrent of pleas and longing. As my desperation grows, his touch becomes bolder, finally massaging my breasts and grazing my clit.

"I need to taste you again, my filthy little lawyer," he growls, and I whimper in response. The sensation of his tongue on me is so much more intense now that I am blindfolded, my nipples still throbbing under the relentless vibrations. I feel myself teetering on the edge, but just as I am about to tumble into bliss, he slaps my tender flesh, and the stinging shock wrenches me back from the brink.

"Did you not learn your lesson, Isabella?" His voice is stern, but not unkind. "You came without permission yesterday. Are you too much of a dirty whore to contain yourself?"

"Please," I sob, my body wracked with need. "I want -" The words catch in my throat, but he knows, he always knows. "Your cock, Sir?" I offer hesitantly, hoping against hope that he will grant my wish.

"Too bad," he says, his tone almost gentle. "You don't deserve it yet. But you do deserve a release."

I gasp as the cold, unyielding dildo penetrates me, my body clenching around the intrusion. It's not what I want - it's not him - but the disappointment fades quickly when he starts thrusting it in and out of me at a relentless pace. The vibrations from the butterfly clips on my nipples send shivers across my entire body, and I moan with each stroke.

"Can... can I come, Sir?" I whimper, feeling my orgasm building, my muscles tensing in anticipation. I need this release.

"Ah, so you want my permission to come, is that it?" His voice teases, a hint of amusement in his tone. God, how I love his voice.

"Please, Sir," I beg, clutching at the chains that bind me, desperation lacing my voice. "I need to come so badly."

"Good girl," he finally concedes, and the words are like a key unlocking my cage. "You may come for me now."

The orgasm rips through me, making me scream his name as waves of pleasure crash over me. He continues to work the dildo inside me, coaxing every last shudder from my trembling form. When my vision clears and my breath returns, he tells me in a gentle voice, "That was beautiful, Isabella. But we're not done yet."

"Yes, Sir," I reply obediently, my heart soaring at his praise. I've made him proud, and that means everything to me.

He removes my blindfold, and as my eyes adjust to the soft light, I see him straddling me, his throbbing erection just inches from my face. He slaps my cheek gently with his cock, and I wait, eager to please but knowing better than to act without instruction.

"Such a good, patient slut," he murmurs, and I preen under the praise. "You may take me in your mouth now."

I eagerly open my lips and encircle his length with my tongue, savoring his taste as he slides deeper into my throat. He leans back and reaches for the vibrator, pressing it against my clit once more.

"Come again for me, Isabella," he commands, turning the speed up to its highest setting.

My body convulses at the sudden onslaught of sensations, and I moan around his cock as another orgasm builds within me. He fucks my face in a steady rhythm, driving me further and further toward the edge. Just as I feel myself spiraling out of control, he groans and comes down my throat, filling me with his essence.

The taste of him combined with the relentless assault on my senses pushes me over the edge once more, and I shatter into a million pieces, my second orgasm washing over me like a tidal wave.

## Chapter Twenty-Five

*Isabella*

Breathing heavily, Primo gazes down at me with a dark intensity that makes me shiver, despite the heat still lingering in my flushed skin. "You did such a good job sucking my cock and coming for your Dominant," he praises, his voice a velvety blend of satisfaction and command. I smile, feeling at ease and relaxed, even as I remember the filthy things we just engaged in.

"Thank you, Sir," I whisper, basking in his approval.

With gentle hands, Primo carefully releases me from my cuffs. The contrast between his firm grip during our scene and the tenderness he shows now is astonishing – it makes me feel cared for, protected. I watch him methodically put away all of his tools back into his closet, each item meticulously placed in its designated spot. It's a side of him I've never seen before, and I find it oddly endearing.

"You were amazing," he murmurs, extending a hand to help me up. His touch sends a current through me, coaxing me back to him so that I can relax in his arms. As he holds me close, I breathe in his scent – now a mix of leather, cologne, and sweat – and relish in the warmth of his embrace.

"Come, let me take care of you," Primo suggests, his eyes softening as he guides me toward the bathroom. We step into the bath together, the water hot and soothing against our skin. I sigh in contentment, sinking into the luxurious embrace of the fragrant water.

In the dimly lit room, Primo begins massaging my shoulders, his strong hands working wonders on my tense muscles. I melt under his skilled touch, my body relaxing and opening up to him. Every stroke of his fingers feels like a balm to the aches left behind by our passionate encounter.

"Your touch is incredible," I admit, leaning into him and feeling his chest rise and fall with each breath. He chuckles, a low rumble that vibrates through me.

The warm water envelops me, soothing my tired muscles as Primo's strong hands glide across my body in the gentle massage. I close my eyes and let the fragrances of lavender and sandalwood intoxicate me, carrying me away to another plane of existence. A soft sigh escapes my lips, a testament to the tender care Primo is showering upon me.

"Tell me, Isabella," he murmurs in my ear, his breath hot against my skin, "what did you think of our scene tonight?"

I open my eyes, momentarily startled by the intimacy of the question. My heart races as I search for the right words, but honesty prevails. "It was wonderful," I confess, feeling my face flush with both pleasure and embarrassment. "I enjoyed myself very much."

"Is there anything you didn't like or would want to change?" Primo asks, his fingers continuing their sensual exploration of my body.

I shake my head, unable to think of anything that marred our delicious encounter. "Not that I can think of," I reply, then hesitate before adding, "But I do wonder... why didn't you fuck me?"

Primo chuckles softly, his warm breath tickling my ear. "I cannot wait to fuck you," he admits, his voice low and husky. As if to prove his point, his hand slips between my legs, his fingers sliding into my wetness. I gasp at the sudden intrusion, my body arching against his touch.

"Sex during our first scene together can overly complicate things," he explains, his fingers continuing their delicious invasion. But just as I feel myself succumbing to the waves of pleasure building within me, he slows his movements, leaving me wanting more.

"Always wanting and needy for me," he whispers, a wicked smile playing on his lips. "That's how I like you."

My body trembles with desire, my mind whirling at the implications of his words. "Open communication is important," he continues, his fingers still teasing me mercilessly. "We need to be honest about our wants and desires, and where they are or aren't being met."

"Did you have anything you'd like to change?" I ask, my voice breathy and pleading.

"You were marvelous," he replies, his tone sincere as he withdraws his fingers from my aching core. "All I want is to play with you more." His words ignite a fire within me, and despite the relaxation that fills me, I find myself hungering for him once more.

I take a deep breath, feeling the warmth of the bath water envelop me as Primo's strong arms support me. The sensation of his fingers still lingers within me, leaving me craving more. He massages my shoulders and I lean into him, seeking comfort and solace.

"Primo," I murmur, hesitating for a moment before continuing, "I'm curious about something else." His hands pause in their ministrations, and he regards me with that intense gaze of his.

"What is it?" he asks, encouraging me to speak my mind.

"During our scene," I begin, my cheeks flushing at the memory, "you called me a brat. What did you mean by that?"

"Ah," Primo chuckles softly, resuming his massage, "a brat is someone in the BDSM world who enjoys teasing and challenging their Dominant, often pushing boundaries to elicit reactions or punishments."

"And what are your thoughts on that?" I inquire, genuinely curious about his preferences.

He sighs thoughtfully, his fingers tracing circles along my spine. "I'm not particularly fond of bratting. I prefer a partner who willingly submits to me, without trying to test my resolve."

His words settle like a warm blanket around me, affirming our compatibility and shared desires. We seem to fit together like puzzle pieces, our edges aligning in ways I never imagined possible.

"Would you like to continue this exploration together?" he asks, his voice gentle yet commanding.

"Absolutely," I reply without hesitation, my heart swelling with excitement and anticipation.

"Good," he purrs, pulling me closer to his chest. "Now, let me tell you more about dynamics and how we can build ours together."

As Primo speaks, I drink in every word, eager to learn from him. He explains that our dynamic will be unlike any typical relationship, as it requires an extreme level of trust between us. While many people are content with surface-level connections, we will delve deeper, trusting each other implicitly during our most vulnerable moments.

"Sub space," he says, "is a state of mind where you feel incredibly relaxed and suggestible. You've likely already experienced it."

I nod in agreement, recalling the heady sensation that washed over me earlier, leaving me pliant and eager to please.

"However," Primo cautions, his voice growing serious, "we must be careful not to fall into the trap of sub frenzy. Honesty, both in and out of the bedroom, is key to maintaining a healthy dynamic."

The flickering candlelight casts shadows on the walls, setting the mood for an honest conversation.

"Primo," I begin hesitantly, feeling my pulse quicken in anticipation, "there's something I haven't been completely honest about."

His strong hands pause on my back, and he looks at me with genuine concern. "What is it?"

I swallow hard, struggling to put my fears into words. "Even though I've always said I'm confident in my strategy and skills for the trial, the truth is... I'm really nervous. I know I'm smarter than the people on the other side, but there's so much at stake, and it terrifies me."

As I confess my deepest insecurities, Primo listens intently, his eyes never leaving mine. When I finish speaking, he smiles softly, his fingers resuming their gentle movements on my body.

"I had a feeling you were holding back self-doubt," he admits, his voice soothing and reassuring. "But that's okay. It's natural to be nervous, especially when so much is on the line. I'm glad you shared your concerns with me, and I want you to know that I have complete faith in you."

His words wash over me, easing the tight knot of anxiety in my chest. As we continue to soak in the bathtub, our thoughts melding together, I realize how important honesty is in our newfound relationship.

Eventually, the water begins to cool, and we reluctantly leave the sanctuary of the bath. I reach for my clothes, eager to cover my nakedness, but Primo stops me with a gentle touch.

"Where are you going?" he asks, an amused glint in his eyes.

"Back to my room," I reply, confused by his question. "I wouldn't want anyone to see me like this."

"Isabella," he says firmly, capturing my gaze with his intense stare, "you will spend the night in my bed. I may have need of your body again."

My heart twists at his invitation, and I stammer, "Are you sure?" In some ways I feel as if we are growing too close too fast, and I worry whether it will cause problems. Deep down, I worry whether I am a fleeting fling for him despite the feelings that are starting to grow inside of me.

"Of course," he answers without hesitation, his voice laced with authority. "When I speak, it's because I've thought about what I'm going to say. I don't like to repeat myself."

The satin sheets feel cool and inviting as I slip into Primo's bed, my body still tingling from our earlier intimate encounter. The room is dimly lit by the soft glow of a single lamp on the nightstand, casting sensual shadows on the walls. I hesitate, unsure whether to inch closer to him or remain on my side of the bed. His dark eyes seem to sense my uncertainty, and with a knowing smile, he reaches out to grab my waist, pulling me against him.

"None of that," he murmurs, his voice deep and soothing. "You're mine tonight, Isabella."

The warmth of his naked body against mine sends a shiver down my spine, and I relax into his embrace, reveling in the contrast of his hard muscles pressed against my soft curves. As we lie together, I notice the intricate tattoos adorning his arms, their designs mysterious and captivating.

"Your tattoos," I say, tracing the inked lines with my fingertips. "They're beautiful. Will you tell me what they mean?"

"Perhaps another time," he replies, a hint of a smile playing on his lips. "For now, let's just rest. I'll need my energy for tomorrow."

"Of course," I sigh contentedly, feeling more at ease than ever before. But a sudden thought crosses my mind, and I add, "We also have to prepare for the trial, remember?"

He chuckles softly, the vibrations resonating through both our bodies. "Oh yes, that too."

As we lie there, wrapped in each other's arms, I find myself reflecting on how our relationship has evolved – from professional to personal, from colleagues to lovers. It's a thrilling transformation, one that has allowed us to shed our inhibitions and bare our souls, forging a connection more profound than I could have ever imagined.

"Primo," I whisper, my voice barely audible in the stillness of the room.

"Yes?"

"Thank you," I say, my heart swelling with gratitude. "For sharing this part of yourself with me... for trusting me."

He tightens his embrace, pressing his lips against my forehead in a tender kiss. "The pleasure is all mine, cara mia. I'd like to give you something."

I'm shocked by his words. "Oh, okay," I reply, stumbling over my answer.

He reaches into the nightstand next to him and pulls out a little velvet box. My breath hitches in my throat as I wonder what could be inside.

"Close your eyes," he instructs me and I smile but comply.

I feel his fingers brush against my neck as he gently moves my hair to the side. Then I feel the cold sting of metal against my throat. I shiver as his fingers clasp the necklace around my neck, his touch gentle and intimate.

"Keep those eyes closed," he says, almost as if he can sense that I'm about to open my eyes. His thick hand wraps around the front of my throat, toying with me gently before his fingers slide down the metal of the chain to the little token I can feel sitting on my chest. As his fingers move, I feel myself wanting him to touch me further and I'm amazed at how easily this man affects me.

"Okay," he says, and I open my eyes. I look down and see that I'm wearing a beautiful necklace with the sigil of St. Ives on it.

"The patron Saint of Lawyers," he says.

I smile and turn to him, our gazes meeting. "It's beautiful, thank you."

"It will help keep you safe," he says to me.

"You make me feel safe," I admit to him.

His gaze softens and then his fingers slide behind my neck and he's kissing me deeply again.

# Chapter Twenty-Six

*Primo*

I recline in my leather chair, the dimly lit room casting shadows on my brooding face. My thoughts presses down on me as I recall Isabella's request to work from her apartment for a few days. She needed time alone to prepare for the trial, to practice and rehearse. I reluctantly agreed, respecting her wishes but disliking the fact that she's not here with me. The memory of placing a delicate necklace around her neck before she left lingers in my mind. I had instructed her not to take it off; it symbolized a sense of safety for both of us.

The shrill ring of my phone yanks me out of my reverie. With a sigh, I answer, receiving updates from the person I'd tasked with looking into our current situation. My heart sinks as I hang up the call. Things are not going well in the business – relationships with the Irish have not improved. I know that my brother could fix this issue if he would just comply, but the information I've just learned tells me that's not going to happen.

"Primo," Charlie greets as he walks into my office, his brow furrowed. "You look worried."

"Charlie," I respond, rubbing my temples. "I'm struggling with thoughts of the upcoming trial and what to do about my brother."

"Ah," he says, nodding solemnly. He takes a seat across from me, concern etched on his face. "It's never easy dealing with family matters, especially when they're mixed with the business."

"True," I concede, leaning back in my chair. "But it's more than that. I find myself constantly thinking of Isabella and the trial. It's been a while since I felt this way about anyone."

"Love is a strange beast, Primo," Charlie muses, his eyes glinting with wisdom. "But in our world, it can be both a strength and a weakness."

"Perhaps," I reply, my gaze fixed on the dancing shadows in the room. "But for now, I must focus on keeping this family together and finding a way to run things."

The dim light of my office casts flickering shadows on the walls, a somber reflection of the turmoil within my heart.

"Charlie," I begin hesitantly, "Isabella has found... troubling evidence." My voice cracks as I struggle to find the right words. "It appears that Constantino was the one who set me up to take the fall for the murder at the safehouse."

The room seems to grow colder as Charlie absorbs the information. "You're sure about this?" he asks, his voice betraying a hint of disbelief.

"Isabella has been relentless in her trial preparations," I explain, running a hand through my hair in frustration. "She's certain of it. And what's worse, it may even be that Constantino was working with my father to orchestrate my arrest."

"Your father?" Charlie's face pales, and I can see the hurt etched in the lines around his mouth.

"Yes," I admit, my confession settling heavily on my shoulders. "I haven't visited him much in prison, but I never thought our relationship had deteriorated to such an extent that he would conspire against me like this."

"Primo, I'm so sorry," Charlie murmurs, genuine sympathy in his eyes. "What do you plan to do?"

"I don't know," I concede, the words heavy with uncertainty. "I don't want to take the fall for a crime I didn't commit. But implicating my brother... What kind of future will I have if I destroy my own family?"

As the silence settles between us, Charlie furrows his brow, deep in thought. "Tell me more about this rogue agent, the one working with the feds," he says after a moment.

"His name is Axe," I reply, the bitter taste of betrayal still fresh on my tongue. "He was close to my father growing up, saved him from the streets in New York."

"Ah, I remember him now," Charlie nods slowly. "It's a shame he turned against us. But Primo, have you considered that perhaps it's not your father and Constantino conspiring together, but rather Axe manipulating the situation?"

"Isabella's evidence is convincing," I say, my heart torn between loyalty and self-preservation. "But it's possible that Axe played a larger role in this than we initially thought."

I rub my temples, my family's betrayal pressing down upon me. I can't deny the evidence Isabella has shown me; it's as if Constantino and our father had tied the noose themselves.

Charlie's eyes reflect the same sadness that clouds my heart. "It's never easy to accept such things, Primo," he says gently. "But we cannot allow sentimentality to cloud our judgment. As much as it pains me to say it, you must do what is best for yourself."

"Even if it means turning against my own family?" I ask, the question heavy with the gravity of what it entails.

"Especially then," Charlie replies, his voice firm but compassionate. "I have a saying: 'Prima per me.' Loosely translated, it means 'First for me.' This seems quite fitting, given your name."

"*Prima per me*," I repeat, the words settling into the depths of my soul. My father knows he will die behind bars, and perhaps that knowledge has driven him to betray me, his firstborn son. If I don't act now, I risk losing everything – including Isabella, who has become more than just a trusted confidante, but a woman who has awakened desires within me I never thought I'd get the chance to explore.

"*Prima per me*," I say once more, steeling myself for the path ahead. I know I must make difficult choices, but survival demands nothing less. With a deep breath, I look Charlie square in the eye. "Thank you, Charlie. Your wisdom and loyalty mean more to me than you can ever know."

"*Sempre al tuo fianco*, Primo," Charlie answers with a nod. *Always at your side.* The fierce loyalty in his eyes enough to steady me for the storm to come.

"Charlie, tell me the truth," I begin, my voice steady despite the storm raging within. "Do you truly believe I'm fit to lead?"

He gazes at me with a mixture of surprise and contemplation, his eyes narrowing as he searches his memories. "Primo, I remember you as a boy – fierce, determined, and unyielding in your pursuit of what was right for our family. Over the years, I've watched you grow into a man who wields power with wisdom and cunning while maintaining an ironclad loyalty to those you care for."

"Is that enough, though?" I ask, my heart aching from Charlie's words.

"Perhaps this is the moment where you must decide for yourself," he answers thoughtfully. "Just because the position may be yours doesn't mean you need to take it. You must evaluate what you truly want in life and follow that path."

"Thank you, Charlie," I murmur, gratitude filling me for the wisdom he has shared.

As he leaves my office, I sink into my chair, lost in thought. I never considered a life outside of organized crime; it was always Giovanni who dared to dream of a different existence. My mind drifts to Isabella. I yearn for more with her, but I know all too well that a life of crime offers no future for someone like her.

Would she even consider exploring something deeper with me once this trial is over? If I manage to clear my name, could we forge a new path together? The uncertainty gnaws at me, but one thing remains clear: I cannot bear the thought of losing her.

"First for me," I whisper, repeating Charlie's earlier advice. Perhaps it's time I choose my own destiny, one that might bring me closer to a passionate, captivating woman.

"*Primo, non farti illusioni,*" I murmur to myself, inhaling the scent of leather and aged whiskey that permeates my office. Charlie's words still resonates within me, but there's a part of me that refuses to let go of the hope for something more, something beyond this life of crime.

"Isabella," I breathe her name like a prayer, as if invoking her presence could somehow soothe the tempest inside me. I allow my mind to wander through the tantalizing possibilities of a life with her, exploring every one of our darkest desires together, unraveling the mysteries of each other's bodies and souls. The mere thought sends a shiver down my spine, arousal coursing through my veins.

"Damn," I mutter under my breath, running a hand

through my hair in frustration. It's clear that these feelings for Isabella run deeper than I ever imagined, a wellspring of emotion I've never experienced before with any other woman. But how can I dare to dream of a future when its very existence remains uncertain?

"Focus, Primo," I chastise myself, forcing my thoughts away from the intoxicating allure of what might be and back to the reality at hand. There's work to be done, responsibilities to fulfill, and a life to salvage—if only I can find the strength to make the hard choices that lie ahead.

"Isabella's brilliant, but she's not infallible," I reason, acknowledging the forces conspiring against us, the enemies who would prefer to see me locked away for good. "I can't rely on her alone to save me. I need to take control of my own destiny."

With renewed determination, I dive back into the sea of paperwork and phone calls that consume my days, immersing myself in the relentless demands of my world.

## Chapter Twenty-Seven

*Isabella*

The sun dips low in the sky, casting a warm orange glow through my window. Papers are strewn across my desk, evidence of hours spent poring over trial preparations. My phone beeps, slicing through the silence of my apartment like a knife. I glance down at the screen, eyes widening as I read the text message.

> Throw the trial and your father's debts will be forgiven.

It's from an anonymous number, but the words are unmistakable. I know exactly who sent this message. My fingers tremble as they grip the phone, the cold metal pressing into my skin. The deal with Primo was always clear: win his trial, and he would take care of my father's debts. But winning the trial is far from certain, a stormy sea threatening to capsize us both.

Throwing the trial, though? That would be easy - almost too easy. I could do it in a heartbeat. A single slip-up, one misplaced word or document, and everything would come crashing down. I'd be free of the loan sharks for good. No more looking over my shoulder. No more living in fear. The temptation coils inside me, a serpent whispering foul promises.

"Stop it," I hiss under my breath, smacking my cheeks as if to physically chase away the treacherous thoughts. "What am I even thinking?"

Why would I allow myself to even consider this? I could never betray Primo like that, not when I'm starting to... I sigh, admitting the truth to myself. Fall for him. The thought sends warmth blooming through my chest, an unexpected burst of color against the stark black-and-white world I've been navigating since diving into his case.

"Absolutely not," I murmur, shaking my head. "I won't play a dirty game like this."

To throw the trial would make me no better than my father – perhaps even worse. The thought leaves a bitter taste in my mouth, and I force myself to set the phone aside, refusing to give the text message any more of my attention.

Instead, I turn back to the papers scattered across my desk, determination surging through me like a current. I will win Primo's trial on its merits, and I know – deep in my bones, with a certainty that burns like fire – that he will keep his word.

The phone rings, jolting me from my reverie. I pick up with cautious curiosity when I see the caller.

"Isabella," Primo's voice is like velvet on the other end, "how are you doing? How are the trial preparations coming?"

"Primo," I breathe, instantly feeling a pang of longing for him. It's been days since I've set foot in the mansion, immersed in the case and determined to remain undistracted. My mind constantly wanders back to him, yearning for him, but I know that if I go back there, I'll be pulled into another one of our darkly enticing scenes, unable to focus on what truly matters. "I'm good. Preparations are going well."

"Isabella," he says, his tone more serious, "I've thought about it, and I'm willing to take the route where we implicate Constantino to clear my name."

My heart leaps at his words, knowing this decision could cost him dearly in his tumultuous relationship with his brother. "Primo, I know how hard of a decision this must be for you. But, I do think you're making the right one."

"Thank you," he whispers, the vulnerability in his voice tugging at my heartstrings. "I'd like to see you again," he tells me. "Would tomorrow night work for you?" His voice trembles with anticipation. "If you have everything in order, we could spend the last night together before the trial."

"Tomorrow night," I agree, my pulse quickening at the thought. "I'll come to the mansion. Primo," I hesitate, "would you like to do another scene?"

A shiver runs down my spine as I remember our last rendezvous, but I wonder whether now is really the time for such distractions.

"Isabella, I would prefer to just spend time with you tomorrow night, if that's okay with you."

"Of course!" I reply.

"Good," he murmurs, relief evident in his tone. "We'll celebrate our special way after the trial is over and all of this is behind us."

"Until tomorrow night then," I say softly, hanging up the phone.

The moment I end the call, a wave of relief washes over me. Primo's decision to expose Constantino's treachery will undoubtedly help our case, but it's also a step toward finding justice for both him and his family. Determined to put those thoughts aside for now, I turn my attention to the final preparations for tomorrow.

In the dim light of my office, I jot down notes in my leather-bound notebook, reorganizing my thoughts and constructing a solid defense strategy. My fingertips dance across the pages, leaving behind a trail of ink as they weave together a story of truth and deceit. Finally satisfied with my work, I close the book with a soft sigh and gather my materials, filing them away for safekeeping.

Exhaustion settles upon my shoulders as I make my way to my bedroom. As I slip beneath the cool sheets, my mind begins to wander, imagining a life with Primo after the trial is over. Images of us together, exploring hidden passions and building a future free from the shadows of his past, flicker through my thoughts like scenes from an old film reel.

"Would that even be possible?" I murmur into the darkness, uncertain of what lies ahead for us.

My hand drifts to the rose gold necklace resting against my collarbone, its delicate chain warm against my skin. The symbol for St. Ives, which hangs at the center of the pendant, catches the moonlight streaming through the window, casting a soft glow on my chest. Though I may not be a practicing Catholic, the knowledge that Primo gifted me this token of protection, inspired by the patron saint of lawyers, brings me a sense of comfort.

"Watch over us, St. Ives," I whisper into the night, feeling the weight of the upcoming trial pressing down on me. "Guide my words so that the truth may be revealed. Only two more days," I think as I succumb to the darkness, my hand still clasping the necklace that binds us together. "Two more days, and we'll have our chance to change everything."

Sleep claims me quickly, and I drift through the abyss of dreams until the ghostly sound of footsteps down the hallway shatters my slumber. Blinking against the remnants of sleep, I try to focus on the unfamiliar noises, but dismiss them as the quirks of an apartment that has become almost foreign to me. Turning over, I allow my eyes to close once more.

Sudden, sharp pain sears through my arm as I'm wrenched out of bed, and a rough bag is shoved over my head. Panic blossoms inside me, tendrils of fear reaching into every corner of my mind. My heart beats a frenzied tempo against my ribs.

"Wh-what's happening?" The words leave my lips, muffled beneath the suffocating fabric.

"Shut up," a voice hisses. The cold steel of a knife presses against my throat, making me swallow any further protests.

As the world goes dark around me, I struggle to breathe, each inhale filled with the stale scent of the bag's confines. Time becomes an elusive concept, seconds stretching into eternity as I'm dragged somewhere unknown.

## Chapter Twenty-Eight

*Primo*

The dim light of the moon filters through the filmy curtains as I stand at the edge of my luxurious bed, the silky sheets inviting me to surrender to a night of rest. My fingers graze the cool fabric when an unfamiliar notification sound pierces the silence, startling me from my reverie. Heart pounding, I snatch up my phone, squinting at the screen as it reveals the unthinkable.

"Isabella," I whisper, my voice quivering with fear and disbelief. The blue dot on my phone indicates her rapid movements through the city, far from the safety of her apartment where she should be preparing for our trial or nestling into her own bed. Panic floods through me, adrenaline spurring me into action as I hastily dress, my thoughts racing alongside my pulse.

"Damn this place!" I hiss, cursing my secluded mansion

as I stride into the garage, losing cell signal in its depths. The low growl of my car's engine reverberates around me as I peel out, leaving black tire marks as a testament to my desperation.

The signal returns, my eyes locked on the pulsating blue dot guiding me towards Isabella. Driving recklessly, I attempt to dial her number, but there's no answer. Guilt gnaws at me; I knew she should've stayed here with me. But I also couldn't bear to deny her request, to suppress her fierce independence that had drawn me to her in the first place.

After an agonizing ten minutes, the blue dot stops moving. Dread churns in my stomach, a stark contrast to the distant hope that maybe, just maybe, she's simply taken a midnight stroll.

But deep down, I know that isn't true. Too much time has passed, too many things could've happened to her by now. And if they have, I'll never forgive myself.

The abandoned warehouse looms before me like a relic of a bygone era, its corroded walls and shattered windows testament to the ravages of time. As I pull my car up as close as I dare without being detected, the headlights briefly illuminate a rundown van parked nearby before I dim them. It's the kind of vehicle that screams nothing but trouble.

Stepping out of my car, I take extra care to muffle the sound of the door closing, aware that every second counts in this precarious situation. My hands are steady as I grip the gun in one hand, the silencer already screwed in place.

A fire burns within me, fueled by the thought of anyone daring to lay a finger on my Isabella. They won't survive the night.

I make my way around the van, peering inside only to find it empty. Voices echo from within the warehouse; it seems they're too preoccupied to notice my approach.

"Look, I don't know about this," one of them grumbles, his tone impatient.

"Shut up, no one asked you," another sneers.

I inch closer to the building, my anger mounting with each step. Their ineptitude is almost laughable – no outside scout, all of them bickering inside like children. At least their incompetence reassures me that Isabella is still alive.

"Whatever we end up doing with her," a third voice says, "we should at least have some fun with her first. Been a while since I had a good fuck, and she looks like just the type to satisfy."

That comment is enough to snap the last thread of my patience. My blood boils, fury coursing through my veins like molten lava. Whoever dared to abduct Isabella will pay dearly for their actions. The loan sharks had been dealt with, but maybe they didn't get the message clearly enough. Or perhaps this is motivated by the trial, a last-ditch effort to silence her and, consequently, me.

I grit my teeth at the realization that it's likely my connection with her that has placed her in such danger. The thought of losing her because of my own actions is unbearable. I can't – won't – let that happen.

"Alright, enough talk," one of them announces, his voice dripping with malice. "Let's have some fun."

"Over my dead body," I mutter under my breath.

As I breach the doors of the warehouse, gun raised and heart pounding, I know one thing for certain: tonight will end with either their deaths or mine. But no matter the outcome, I'll make sure that Isabella is safe.

## Chapter Twenty-Nine

*Isabella*

As I strain to make sense of the muffled voices around me, I realize that I'm tied to a rickety wooden chair, hands and feet bound with rough rope that digs into my skin. A gag presses against my lips, while a coarse bag obscures my vision. Through the fabric, I can just make out dim lights flickering, casting eerie shadows on the walls.

"Look, I don't know about this," a nervous voice breaks through the tense atmosphere. "Primo's lawyer goes missing, and you think he's just gonna sit back and do nothing? He'll retaliate, hard."

"Shut up," another voice snaps. "No one asked for your opinion."

From their fumbling conversation and haphazard plan, I can tell they're desperate, acting without proper forethought. This realization ignites a spark of hope within me, fueling my determination to escape.

"Whatever we end up doing with her," a third voice says, his words dripping with sinister intent, "we should at least have some fun with her first. Been a while since I had a good fuck, and she looks like just the type to satisfy."

As panic claws its way up my throat, my heart pounding wildly in my chest, I force myself to focus on wriggling my wrists against the ropes. Their careless binding works in my favor as I manage to free one hand. Just as I'm about to cautiously loosen the knots around my feet, the voices abruptly cease.

With bated breath, I wait, listening intently to the sudden silence.

Frozen in place, my heart hammers against my ribcage as I fear they've sensed my escape attempt. Instead, one of them mutters about an unexpected visitor at the door.

"Who the hell is that?" the nervous voice hisses.

"Nobody should be here," another growls.

And then, like the sweetest music to my ears, I hear Primo's smooth, commanding voice. Relief courses through me, threatening to bring tears to my eyes.

"Who do you work for?" he asks calmly, his tone laced with danger.

"Go to hell!" one of the captors snarls.

"Wrong answer."

The sound of a gunshot slices through the room, followed by a thud as a body hits the floor. I flinch, unease and hope warring within me.

"Next," Primo says coolly. "Who sent you?"

"I-I don't know!" stammers the second voice.

"Wrong again."

Another gunshot rings out, and I shudder as another lifeless form collapses onto the cold concrete. The third man, the one who threatened to violate me, begins to ramble desperately.

"Look, I don't know who gave the order, but I can find out! Just--"

"Actually," Primo interrupts icily, "I never intended on getting information from you. Not after what you said you'd do to my sweet Isabella."

The man's guttural screams pierce the air, but I can't see what's happening. My heart aches for Primo, torn between gratitude and horror. I sense him close by, and I choke back sobs.

A final gunshot silences the screams, leaving only Primo and me in the room. He comes to me swiftly, still keeping the hood in place for reasons unknown. Perhaps it's to save me from the sight of what he's done to my captors. His strong arms lift me up, carrying me up a flight of stairs. I can feel the chill of the morning air and sense the faint sunlight filtering through the fabric.

It's not until we're inside a car that he finally removes the hood. Overwhelmed, I collapse into his embrace, my body shaking with emotion. He holds me tight, murmuring apologies and reassurances as if to soothe away my pain.

Grabbing his phone, Primo calls Teddy, relaying the address before hanging up.

"Isabella," he whispers, his voice thick with emotion, "I'm so sorry I let this happen to you. You're safe now, and I swear I'll never let anyone hurt you again."

## Chapter Thirty

*Primo*

As I pull the car into the mansion's garage, my heart races in anticipation. I swiftly dial a doctor as I gaze at the imposing facade, the dark stone contrasting sharply against the velvet night sky. Isabella, still shaken from her ordeal, tries to protest, but I silence her with a firm yet gentle command.

"Isabella, don't argue. We cannot be sure that you weren't harmed," I say, my voice laced with concern. "I'm just lucky I got to you in time."

I scoop her up effortlessly, cradling her delicate form as I carry her into the mansion. As we pass through the extravagant foyer, Isabella looks into my eyes, her voice a mix of gratitude and curiosity. "How did you know I was kidnapped? And how did you know where to find me?"

I hesitate for a moment, the shadows dancing across

my face as I finally confess. "The necklace I gave you... it was more than just a token of my affection. It was a protective charm."

"Protective charm?" Isabella asks, her brow furrowing in confusion.

I sigh deeply. "The pendant has a tracking chip in it."

Suddenly, Isabella stiffens, pushing herself out of my embrace with fiery anger that catches me off guard. "How dare you put a GPS device on me like I'm a dog!" she exclaims, her eyes blazing with betrayal. "You should have told me! You lied to me about something this important. I thought we were supposed to have a deep connection built on trust. This doesn't make me want to trust you, Primo."

As she stands before me, her chest heaving with indignation, I feel a pang of guilt mixed with frustration. In my world, trust and safety were often at odds, but I hadn't expected Isabella to react so strongly to this. I struggle to find the right words to explain my actions while still respecting her feelings.

"Isabella, I don't understand why you're so upset," I say, my voice laced with confusion. "I monitor the movements of all my men. They're involved in dangerous business, and this is my standard of care. You mean more to me than anyone else working for me."

"Is that it then?" she asks bitterly, her anger simmering beneath the surface. "Am I just someone who works for you?"

The hurt in her eyes stings me, but I can't look away. I stumble over my words, trying to find a way to convey what she means to me without admitting the depths of my feelings. "No, that's not it at all," I say, frustration mounting as I struggle to express myself. "I can't explain what you mean to me, Isabella. But please, don't think that I don't care for you."

Her face falls, and I realize too late that she's misinterpreted my words as a rejection. The pain in her eyes is more than I can bear, but I know that I need to make things right between us.

"Isabella," I begin, my voice cracking with my emotions. But before I can continue, she tries to interject.

"No, Primo!"

A wave of anger surges through me, and I find myself yelling for silence. The sound echoes through the mansion, reverberating off the walls. She looks at me, stunned.

"Listen to me," I say, my voice now calm but firm. "I am *not* sorry for giving you a GPS device; I did it to protect you. I'm glad I did so because it may have very well saved your life. But I do apologize for not telling you about it." My heart aches as I add, "I care for you more than I care for my men, Isabella, and I don't want you to twist my words."

Just as I gather the courage to finally reveal the depth of my feelings for her, the doctor appears, his presence an unwelcome interruption. With a heavy heart, I reluctantly shift my focus from Isabella to the physician, knowing that the conversation we were having is far from over.

I lead the doctor and Isabella into the guest room where she'll be examined. The air in the room is thick with tension, a palpable reminder of the unresolved issues between us.

"Please, take care of her," I say softly to the doctor, my voice betraying both my concern and the vulnerability I've been trying so hard to hide. He nods solemnly and closes the door, leaving me alone in the hallway with my thoughts.

I pace back and forth, feeling like a caged animal. My mind races with worry for Isabella and anger at myself for allowing her to get caught up in my dangerous world. Minutes stretch into an eternity until finally, the door opens again and the doctor emerges.

"Mr. Maldonado, Isabella is okay," he says, his words a balm to my frayed nerves. "There's evidence she was chloroformed, but I see no signs she was violated in any way."

"Thank you, Doctor," I reply, relief washing over me like a tidal wave. "What does she need now?"

"Rest and reassurance," he answers, his gaze steady. "She's been through a lot, and her emotional state will need time to recover as well."

"Understood. Thank you, Doctor," I say, watching him leave before turning my attention back to the guest room. Taking a deep breath, I open the door and step inside.

Isabella lies in bed, her eyes closed, her chest rising and falling with each steady breath. The sight of her, fragile yet defiant, stirs something powerful within me. I can't help but be drawn to her.

"Hey," I whisper as I slip into the bed beside her, wrapping my arms around her trembling form. "I'm sorry for putting you in this position."

Her voice is barely audible as she replies, "Don't apologize, Primo. I knew who you were when I agreed to take your case."

"Then why?" I ask, my voice laced with confusion. "Why take on my case when you're trying to distance yourself from your father's legacy?"

She sighs, and I can feel the weight of her words before they even leave her lips. "At first, it was about the money, if I'm being honest. I needed the work to try and get out from the loan sharks. But as I got to know you and hear your side of the story, I couldn't ignore the injustice that had been done to you. Yes, you've done evil things, but you deserve a fair trial. You shouldn't be held accountable for things you didn't do."

Our intertwined bodies seem to breathe as one, our hearts beating in sync, as we lie together in the dimly lit room. The flickering candlelight casts a warm glow over Isabella's face, her vulnerability laid bare for me to see, and I realize just how much I need her by my side.

"Thank you, Isabella," I say, my voice soft and sincere. "You're one of the few people I can actually trust these days."

She looks up at me, her eyes searching mine, as if trying to see past the darkness that has consumed my life for so long. "I want to trust you too, Primo," she says hesitantly. "But that GPS collar... it's upsetting."

"I understand." My fingers brush against her cheek,

wiping away a stray tear. "But I need to know you're safe. I can't afford to lose you."

Her brow furrows, and she asks, "What do you mean by that?"

My heart races, my breath catches in my throat, and for a moment, I think I might finally reveal the truth of my feelings for her. But then, I stop myself. It would be cruel to burden her with this knowledge, especially when my future hangs in the balance.

"Let's talk about it after the trial," I tell her, tucking a lock of hair behind her ear. "For now, let's just rest."

We drift off into an easy sleep together, my arms wrapped protectively around her, my body shielding hers from the demons that haunt us both.

## Chapter Thirty-One

*Primo*

The first light of dawn seeps through the curtains, and I find myself awake before her. Isabella lies next to me, her breathing slow and steady in the depths of sleep. She is vulnerable, soft, a far cry from the fierce woman who fights for me in the courtroom. My heart aches with guilt, knowing it's my actions that have put her in danger.

Her red hair spills across the pillow, each strand a reminder of how connected our lives have become. As I watch her chest rise and fall, the decision crystallizes in my mind. When she wakes, I will tell her that I'm finding another lawyer. It's absurd, with the trial only a day away, but I can't risk her safety any longer.

"Primo?" Her voice is still thick with slumber as she turns her head to look at me, those bright green eyes searching mine. "What's wrong?"

"Isabella," I begin, trying to keep my voice steady. "How are you feeling?"

"Fine," she answers, rubbing her eyes. "Just nervous about what's ahead."

"About that..." I hesitate for a moment, gathering my courage. "I've been thinking...After everything that's happened, I can't allow you to be my lawyer anymore."

Her eyes widen, shock flitting across her face before being replaced with indignation. "What did you just say?"

"I can't continue to risk your safety for my sake," I repeat, steeling myself against the storm I know is coming. "I'll be hiring another lawyer to represent me in the trial."

In an instant, she's out of bed, her naked body flushed with anger. Her beauty is almost otherworldly, even when she's furious. I'd never admit it, but I secretly love it when she argues with me – she's the only one who's ever dared to go toe-to-toe with me.

"Primo Maldonado," she seethes, fists clenched at her sides as she stands before me. "You don't get to make that decision for me."

"Isabella, please understand, I'm doing this for your safety." My chest feels tight, our shared fears pressing down on me.

"Your safety is my concern too!" she snaps, pacing the room like a caged lioness. "We're in this together, whether you like it or not."

I admire her tenacity, even as it threatens to tear us apart. "I just want to protect you," I whisper, praying she'll understand.

"Then let me protect you too," she pleads, her eyes shining with unshed tears. "Let's face this together, as equals."

"This is not up for debate," I say, my voice firm but gentle.

"Like hell it's not!" she retorts, her eyes blazing with defiance. "You're really going to stand there and tell me you're doing this for my safety? I don't buy it. Is it that you don't trust me to handle the trial?"

"Of course I trust you," I insist, feeling my chest tighten with frustration. "But your safety comes first."

She continues to pace the room, her naked form a mesmerizing dance of shadows and light as she moves. "This is ridiculous! The judge won't even likely grant a motion this close to the trial!"

"Then I'll have to get the case moved to a judge who will take a bribe and grant such a motion," I reply, my words tasting bitter in my mouth.

Her anger boils over at that. "You're going back on everything we agreed upon! We were going to do this the right way – no bribes, no dirty tricks!"

"I have no other options," I plead, my heart aching at the thought of losing her. "I cannot risk your safety."

"That is my risk to take!" she all but screams, tears pooling in her eyes. "I made the decision to defend you knowingly. You can't rob me of that choice.

"If you do this to me, it will destroy my career. Everyone will think I'm being released because I'm incompetent, is that it?" Her voice trembles with a mix of rage and pain.

"If it does ruin your career, I will take care of you," I say, but that doesn't improve her rage.

"Well, I've got news for you: I don't need to work for you. I don't need to be a mobster's live-in fuck toy!"

"Isabella–" I try to interrupt, but she continues.

"I thought you knew me better than that. I want a better life, not just for myself, but for you, too. I thought that once this trial was over, maybe – just maybe – you might consider having a different sort of life. One that we could share together."

Her words pierce through my defenses, leaving me vulnerable and exposed. I can't help but imagine a future with her, one where the shadows of our pasts no longer haunt us. But is it possible? Can I atone for the sins of my family, the darkness that has consumed me for so long?

"Isabella," I breathe, reaching out to touch her arm, but she pulls away, the hurt in her eyes a reflection of my own. "I don't want to hurt you. I only want to protect you."

"Then trust me," she whispers, her voice barely audible above the pounding of my heart. "Let's face this together, as equals."

I'm quiet as I think about her words, feeling her gaze on me. She's waiting for a response, but my thoughts are tangled with images of the life we could've had if not for the choices I made. A life with my son, watching him grow up, and now, perhaps, a life with Isabella – full of love, laughter, and warmth. The thought warms my heart.

But when I don't give her the answer she seeks, her anger breaks down into tears. She sits on the floor, burying her face in her hands, her body shaking with sobs. I feel terrible for what I'm doing to her; I'm only trying to protect her.

I get up from the bed and go to her, my bare feet sinking into the plush carpet beneath us. Her tears sting my soul, and I yearn to wrap her in my arms and shield her from the world. Yet when I reach for her, she pushes me away, rejecting my comfort. We end up struggling against one another, a dance of desperation and pain.

"Stop," she says through gritted teeth, her fists clenched at her sides. "Just stop."

"Isabella, I–" But before I can finish, she tells me no and ends up punching me in the jaw.

The impact reverberates through my skull, and I stumble back a step. For a moment, we both just stare at each other, frozen in time. Then the silence is broken by her apology.

"I'm sorry," she whispers, her eyes wide with shock. "I don't know what came over me."

I laugh despite the lingering sting of her blow, rubbing my jaw tenderly. "You've got a pretty good right hook. If you ever tire of being a lawyer, you should consider cage fighting."

Her lips curve into a small, reluctant smile. "The professions are basically the same thing, aren't they?"

We share a laugh. But as the laughter fades, the silence returns, heavy and oppressive.

"Isabella," I say, my voice soft and full of regret. "I didn't mean to upset you or disrespect you. The events of last night were so troubling for me...finding you with that hood over your head, fearing those disgusting men may have touched you at all...it was too much for me to bear."

She looks at me, her eyes glistening with unshed tears, and nods. "I understand. That's how I feel about you in your line of work."

Her words hang in the air between us. The silence stretches between us, taut and fragile. Isabella's tear-filled eyes search my face, aching with vulnerability.

"Primo," she says softly, "you don't have to live this life."

I take a shaky breath, feeling my family's expectations bearing down on me. "As the firstborn son, there are certain expectations I must fulfill. I never really had a choice."

"Everyone has choices," she insists, her voice steady and determined. "They may be hard to make, but that doesn't mean they aren't options."

I swallow hard, unable to meet her gaze. "Can I hold you?" I ask hesitantly, needing the comfort of her touch.

She nods, relenting, and I gather her into my arms, cherishing the warmth of her body against mine. Her heartbeat is a soothing rhythm against my chest, a melody I could lose myself in.

Her words stick in my mind, even as I try to push them

away. I promise myself that I'll give them legitimate thought after the trial – if I end up going to prison, there won't be any more choices for me anyway.

"Isabella," I say, my voice thick with emotion, "I'm sorry."

"Are you serious about switching lawyers?" she asks.

"I just want to protect you," I reply, my heart aching at the thought of losing her.

She sighs, understanding but resolute. "That's not the way, Primo."

"Okay," I concede, knowing that I can't deny her the agency to make her own choices. "We'll keep things as they are."

"Maybe we should get a bit more sleep," I suggest, tenderly wiping the last of her tears from her cheeks. She agrees, and I lift her into my arms, carrying her back to our bed.

As I lay her down and pull the covers over us, I hold her close, feeling the steady rise and fall of her chest as she drifts back into sleep. The room is filled with the scent of her perfume, a delicate reminder of her presence.

My thoughts continue to race, consumed by her words and the possibility of a different life – one that I can scarcely imagine, yet yearn for with every fiber of my being. There's both a promise and a plea inside of me – a hope that, against all odds, we may find a way to bridge the distance between us and forge a future together.

But for now, I savor the sweetness of her embrace, allowing it to anchor me in the present moment, as I surrender to the darkness that beckons me from the edge of consciousness.

The afternoon sun filters through the curtains, casting dappled patterns on the wall as I watch Isabella sleep.

"Primo?" Her voice is groggy, but still music to my ears. She blinks up at me, her eyes slowly focusing on my face. "What time is it?" she asks, clearly sensing that we overslept.

"Nearly noon," I say, brushing a strand of hair from her forehead. "I had someone pick up everything you need for the trial from your apartment."

"Really?" She looks surprised, but there's a hint of gratitude in her eyes.

"I won't let you out of my sight for the next 24 hours," I tell her firmly. "Unless there's something left for you to prepare, how about we spend a relaxed day together?"

"Okay," she agrees, the corners of her mouth lifting into a small smile.

As we move through the day, I show her the hidden beauty of my home, the small sanctuaries that have offered solace in darker times. We talk, we laugh, and for a moment, it feels as if the shadows have retreated, leaving only light and warmth behind.

I lead Isabella through the grand archway that opens

onto the sprawling estate, her hand in mine. The sun bathes the gardens in a golden glow, casting intricate shadows where roses intertwine with ivy and birds sing their sweet melodies from the branches above.

"Wow," she breathes, entranced by the lush landscape before her. "I guess I never really appreciated how beautiful this place could be."

I guide her down the winding stone path and into a greenhouse, past vegetable boxes overflowing with ripe produce and vibrant flower beds that perfume the air. She stops to examine a cluster of delicate orchids, her fingers tracing their petals as if she's absorbing their essence. "This place seems very large for just one person."

"Ah, well, it used to be the family home and center of all our business," I explain, my gaze drifting over the familiar grounds. "But times change, and people want to move out and do their own thing."

"Your brothers?" she inquires, curiosity sparking in her eyes.

"Teddy comes and goes as he pleases; he's here most often," I say, picturing my youngest brother's bright smile. "Giovanni moved out as soon as he could. Constantino... he's mostly a mystery these days. I've only seen him at the mansion twice in recent months."

"Even your father left?"

I nod, recalling how my father moved out and purchased a home outside of Cambridge before his arrest. "Sometimes I wonder if I'm the only one still fighting for what this family once was," I admit, my voice tinged with melancholy. "Maybe I should let it go."

"No," she insists, gripping my hand more tightly. "Despite my frustrations with you in the beginning and even recently, I'm proud of the way you've handled this time. It cannot be easy to lead anyone from your situation. You've shown true strength in the face of difficult circumstances."

Her words wrap around me, offering solace I didn't realize I needed. "You're giving me too much credit," I murmur, my chest tightening.

"Your strength has helped give me my own," she continues, her gaze locked with mine. Her unspoken confession hangs heavy between us, and I can feel the thundering beat of my heart as she opens her mouth to speak again.

"Isabella," I interrupt before she can utter another word. I don't want any confessions now, not when the trial looms over us and uncertainty clouds our future. Instead, I silence her with a deep and passionate kiss, my lips meeting hers like the crashing of waves in a stormy sea.

As we pull apart, breathless and flushed, I know there's still so much left unsaid. But for now, we'll let the gardens hold our secrets, biding our time until the moment we can finally lay them bare.

We retire to the grand living room, the air infused with the tantalizing aroma of the takeout containers scattered across the coffee table. As I sink into the plush couch, Isabella flips through the collection of old movies, her eyes sparkling with delight at each title she recognizes. The sound of her laughter is like a symphony to my ears, filling me with an intoxicating blend of joy and longing.

"Let's watch this one!" she exclaims, holding up a worn DVD case. I nod, unable to resist the excitement in her voice or the way her cheeks flush when she smiles.

The movie begins, casting flickering shadows on the walls as its scenes unfold. I find myself more captivated by the woman beside me than the story on the screen. Her eyes are wide with wonder, her lips parting in soft gasps at the twists and turns of the plot. She laughs at the witty banter between the characters, her silver-toned giggles making my body respond.

"Isn't this scene just beautiful?" she murmurs, gesturing at the screen where two lovers embrace beneath a canopy of stars.

"Isabella," I reply softly, my gaze never leaving her face, "you outshine them all."

Her cheeks flush a deeper shade of pink, and she playfully swats my arm. "You're just saying that."

"Believe me, bella, I've never been more serious in my life."

For a fleeting moment, I allow my mind to wander, envisioning a life with her – free from the violence and danger that has defined my existence for so long. A life where we could grow old together, our love blossoming like the flowers in the garden, untainted by the shadows of my past. A life where my son could be a part of our world, without fear or hesitation.

But reality creeps back in, its cold tendrils wrapping around my heart. The trial looms before us, a storm on the horizon that threatens to tear us apart. I force myself to focus on the present, on the woman beside me who has brought light into my darkness.

"Isabella," I say as the movie ends and the room is bathed in soft, dim light, "come to bed with me."

"Are you sure?" She hesitates, her eyes searching mine for any hint of doubt.

"More than anything," I assure her, my hand reaching out to intertwine with hers.

We rise from the couch, our fingers locked together as we make our way to the bedroom. The crisp sheets welcome us, enveloping our bodies in their cool embrace. As I pull her closer, her warmth seeping into my very soul, I feel a sense of peace I haven't known in years.

"Thank you," I whisper into the night, my voice barely audible above the soft sound of our breathing.

"For what?" she murmurs, her head resting against my chest.

"For everything."

## Chapter Thirty-Two

*Isabella*

The scent of Primo's cologne lingers in the air. His strong arms wrap around my waist, securing me to his side as we lay tangled in the sheets of his bed. The events of the last 24 hours replay in my mind like a movie reel, each scene intensifying the connection between us.

"Isabella," he whispers into my ear, and I can sense a shift in him. It's as if the weight of the world has been temporarily lifted from his shoulders. Primo seems calmer now, steadier, even with the trial looming ahead. His newfound serenity gives me strength and confidence, and I find myself wanting more.

"Primo," I murmur, turning to face him. Our eyes meet for a brief moment before I lean in and press my lips against his, tentatively at first, then with growing urgency.

I know this could be our last night together, and I want to savor every second of it.

His response is immediate, his mouth molding against mine with a hunger that matches my own. We are locked in an electrifying dance, our tongues exploring and teasing, our breaths mingling as we grow more desperate for each other.

"Isabella," he gasps against my lips, his voice thick with desire. "I need you."

"Show me," I whisper back, my heart pounding wildly in my chest.

Primo wastes no time, his hands gliding over my body, feeling me beneath the thin fabric of the sheet. His touch ignites a fire within me, heat pooling between my thighs. As his fingers deftly unbutton my shirt, I wonder if I'll be able to experience all of him tonight.

"God, Isabella," he murmurs, his warm breath fanning over my exposed collarbone as he slides my blouse off my shoulders. "You have no idea how much I want you."

"Show me," I repeat, my voice barely audible.

His attentions are different now, tender and sensual, a stark contrast to the dominating force he can be during our passionate scenes. It's as if he's revealing another side of himself, a hidden vulnerability that draws me in even further.

"Primo," I sigh, my body arching into his touch as he gently cups my breast through the lace of my bra. "Please."

"Anything for you, bella," he promises, his words both a declaration and a plea. And as he slowly undresses me, piece by piece, I can't help but think that tonight, we might just find everything we've been searching for in each other's arms.

My body trembles under his gaze, every fiber of my being craving his touch. This time, Primo doesn't make me wait. His fingers, strong and skilled, tease my nipples. A gasp escapes my lips as the sensations ripple through me, a desperate need for more building within.

"Primo," I whimper, my voice thick with desire.

"Shh, bella," he murmurs against my ear, his warm breath sending shivers down my spine. He lowers his head to take one nipple into his mouth, and the world narrows to the sensation of his tongue flicking over the sensitive peak. As our eyes lock, I see the passion burning within him, but also a tenderness that steals my breath away.

"Open your mouth, Isabella," he commands, his voice a sultry whisper that sends a shiver down my spine. I comply without hesitation, and he slips two fingers inside, the taste of him filling my senses. "Get them nice and wet, just like that."

I suck on his fingers eagerly, wanting to please him in every way possible. He gives me a wicked smile before withdrawing his fingers from my mouth, trailing them down my throat, between my breasts, and further down until they reach their destination. The sensation of his slick fingers slipping inside me makes my back arch, and I bite my lip to stifle a moan.

"God, you're beautiful like this," he tells me, his voice filled with raw emotion. "Your breasts bouncing with my movements, your wet heat wrapped around my fingers... It's intoxicating."

"Primo, I want more," I confess, the words slipping out before I can stop them. "Please, give me everything."

"Anything you want, Isabella, will always be yours," he promises, his eyes dark with desire.

My heart swells with a longing I can't quite put into words. It's not just his body I want, but the man behind the mask – the heart he hides so well. But for now, I'll take what he gives me and cherish every moment.

As he works my body toward completion, he doesn't deny me the pleasure I crave. Instead, he lets my arousal build naturally, his fingers exploring every intimate curve and hollow until I'm teetering on the edge of ecstasy.

"Primo," I whisper, the feeling of everything we've shared tonight heavy in my voice.

"Let go, bella," he urges, his eyes locked onto mine, daring me to surrender to the passion that consumes us both.

And with those words, the dam breaks, and I soar, lost in the dizzying heights of the pleasure he's given me.

"Primo," I cry out, my voice breaking as the pleasure reaches its crescendo. His name lingers in my ears like a melody, and I can feel him drinking in my screams, savoring the connection that binds us together in this moment.

"Isabella," he murmurs, his lips leaving a trail of fire as they pull away from my trembling form. "You come so beautifully, and you're never more breathtaking than when you're screaming my name."

His words stoke the embers of my lust, transforming them into an inferno that threatens to consume me whole. With a newfound hunger, I slide down his body, my fingers deftly unfastening his silk sleep pants and revealing the hard arousal that matches my own.

"Let me taste you," I breathe, giving voice to the desire that courses through me. Taking him into my mouth, I delight in the weight of him, the way he moans my name, and the sensation of his fingers threading through my hair, guiding me.

"Isabella... you're incredible," he praises, the vulnerability in his voice only serving to heighten my need for him.

But before I can take him any further, he gently tugs at my hair, pulling me off his cock and back up to meet his gaze. There's a tenderness in his eyes that makes my chest ache, a longing that mirrors my own. He cradles me in his strong arms and positions me beneath him once more, our bodies fitting together like pieces of a puzzle.

"Look at me, bella," he whispers, and I find myself lost in the depths of his eyes, captivated by the emotions that dance within them.

Slowly, ever so slowly, he begins to enter me, inch by glorious inch. The stretch is exquisite, and I can't help but gasp as I feel my walls ripple around him, my body welcoming him home. When he finally starts to move, I find myself drowning in the rhythm and scent of him, my world reduced to this moment, this connection that binds us together.

"Primo," I whimper, as he continues to fuck me with a deliberate slowness that borders on torture. But just when I think I can't take it anymore, when I'm on the verge of begging for more, he increases his pace, driving into me with a force that leaves me breathless.

"Isabella," - *thrust* - "you," - *thrust* - "belong" - *thrust* - "to," - *thrust*, "me," he growls, his eyes never leaving mine.

His words act as a catalyst, shattering my control and sending me spiraling over the edge once more. As I come undone beneath him, he follows suit, our bodies trembling in unison as we ride out the waves together.

In the aftermath, I find solace in the tender way he brushes the hair from my face, the warmth of his gaze as he studies me, and the knowledge that, despite everything, we've found something precious within one another.

Our bodies, still entwined, begin to float back down from the heights of passion. Primo's breath, warm and steady, tickles my ear as his chest rises and falls against my back. I can feel his heart pounding in time with mine, a shared rhythm that seems to sing through the room.

"Isabella..." he murmurs, his voice barely audible above the sound of our breathing. I strain to make out his words but they're lost to the shadows – a secret whispered into the darkness.

I close my eyes, letting the memory of his declaration wash over me. The words he spoke while thrusting deep inside me ring through my mind, filling me with a sense of belonging that I've never known before. With each heartbeat, my desire to be his grows stronger.

"Please," I whisper into the night, my lips pressed against the sheets as I send a silent prayer out to whatever deity might be listening. "Let me win this trial for him, so we can have a chance together."

As slumber beckons, I find myself tracing the intricate outlines of Primo's tattoos with my fingertips – a tactile symphony of ink and skin that tells the story of a life lived on the edge. Each curve, each line, is a testament to the man he is; complex, ambitious, and unapologetically primal.

"Isabella?" His voice, soft and laced with curiosity, pulls me from my reverie.

"Sorry, I didn't mean to wake you," I say, my fingers stalling in their exploration.

"Your touch... it's soothing," he admits, his eyes heavy with sleep yet still filled with warmth. "I don't mind."

"Good," I smile, resuming my tracing as his eyelids flutter closed once more. "Because I don't want to stop."

Our whispered conversation drifts into the night, weaving in and out of our shared dreams like a thread of silver spun from moonlight.

I awaken, my throat parched as if I've been wandering through a desert. Primo's rhythmic breathing fills the darkness of the room, and I'm careful not to disturb him as I slip out of bed. The silk sheets whisper against my skin, their cool touch reminding me of his presence.

Padding softly across the plush carpet, I slip into Primo's discarded shirt and make my way to the kitchen. As I round the corner, my eyes widen in surprise: Charlie is there, his back turned to me as he stirs something on the stove. The dim light casts shadows along the contours of his face, adding years to the lines etched there.

"Charlie!" I exclaim, despite myself. At the sound of my voice, he turns, his crinkled eyes smiling warmly.

"Ah, Isabella," he says, holding his wooden spoon aloft like a conductor's baton. "You're up late."

"Couldn't sleep," I reply, running my fingers through my tousled hair. "My throat feels like it's been sandpapered. What are you doing up?"

"Old people never sleep," he chuckles, stirring his concoction once more. The scent of something savory wafts through the air, making my stomach rumble in anticipation.

"More like old people need their midnight snacks," I tease, grabbing a glass from the cabinet above. I fill it with water from the tap, the liquid glistening.

"Guilty as charged," Charlie admits with another laugh. He places a lid on his pot and turns to face me, leaning against the counter. His gaze grows serious. "How are you feeling about the trial?"

"Hopeful...and terrified," I confess, taking a sip of my water. It's cold and soothing, quenching the fire in my throat. "It's hard not to doubt myself."

"Understandable," Charlie nods, his eyes never leaving mine. "But don't be too hard on yourself. Primo's put you through the wringer, and you've come out stronger for it. Lesser people wouldn't have made it this far."

"Is that so?" I ask, feeling a little bolder. "And what was he like as a child? Just as enigmatic and demanding?"

"Ha!" Charlie laughs, the sound resonating in the otherwise quiet kitchen. "Primo was born with a fierceness most men only dream of possessing. He's always been loyal, determined to get what he wants...and protect those he loves."

I can't help but smile at the thought of a young Primo, already brimming with ambition and intensity. Perhaps it's that spark, hidden beneath layers of darkness, that makes him so captivating.

"Thank you, Charlie," I say, my voice soft and sincere. "For everything."

Charlie studies me for a moment, his warm gaze softening even further. "I've seen the way he looks at you when he thinks no one's watching, Isabella. He won't admit it, but he cares deeply for you too."

A smile tugs at my lips, an unexpected warmth blossoming in my chest. "That's a lovely thought, but we come from two different worlds. How could we ever make this work?"

"Worlds often collide, my dear." His smile is enigmatic,

his eyes twinkling like stars in the night sky. "What matters is how we navigate the chaos that follows."

His words weave themselves into the tapestry of my soul, filling me with a strange sense of hope and wonder. "Thank you, Charlie," I murmur, feeling his wisdom settle around my shoulders like a protective cloak.

"Goodnight, Isabella," he says softly, his voice fading as I turn away, cradling my water glass in my hands.

The hushed sounds of the house envelop me as I pad silently down the hallway, the floorboards cool beneath my bare feet. The flickering shadows cast by the moonlight dance across the walls, painting ethereal patterns that merge and separate, a visual symphony that mirrors the swirling emotions within my heart.

As I slip back into the bedroom, the sight of Primo sleeping peacefully takes my breath away. The sharp angles of his face are softened by slumber, and for once, the darkness that usually clings to him seems to have receded, replaced by an almost vulnerable tranquility.

I ease myself back into bed, taking care not to disturb him as I nestle against the sheets. As I lay there, my thoughts drift to Charlie's words and the secret truth I've only just begun to acknowledge.

## Chapter Thirty-Three

*Isabella*

The morning sun casts golden hues over the courthouse steps, its grand structure looming before me. I feel a frisson of nerves as Primo and I push through the clamoring crowd of reporters, their voices merging into an indecipherable cacophony. My heart thuds against my chest, expectation heavy on my shoulders.

"Mr. Maldonado, do you have anything to say before your trial begins?" one reporter manages to shout above the rest.

I step forward, my voice steady despite the trembling in my hands. "We are confident in our case and have no further comments at this time."

Primo maintains a completely cool outward appearance, but we manage to lock eyes and I can see the warmth and appreciation for me in their depths.

As we ascend the courthouse steps, I find myself scrutinizing the building with a newfound reverence. The familiar stone edifice feels different now; it's no longer just a workplace, but a battleground where my wits and dedication will be tested. I know I've spent countless hours preparing for this moment, but self-doubt still lingers inside me, a serpent whispering that perhaps I'm not ready.

Primo seems to sense my unease, and his hand finds my shoulder, its warmth seeping through the fabric of my blouse. His touch anchors me, reminding me that I am not alone in this fight. We share a look of mutual determination, and with renewed confidence, I square my shoulders and stride into the fray.

The courtroom doors swing open, revealing the hushed anticipation within. My eyes scan the gallery and briefly lock onto Greg's piercing gaze. His eyes widen in surprise as he takes in my presence, and I wonder why he's so taken aback. It's only natural for me to be here on the first day of the trial – unless he had a hand in orchestrating my recent kidnapping attempt.

"Isabella," he says, a forced smile tugging at his lips, "I didn't expect to see you here."

"Really? It's the first day of trial," I retort, curiosity and suspicion mingling in my chest. "Why wouldn't I be here?"

Before Greg can respond, Primo steps between us, his face a stony mask of barely contained fury. He leans in close, his voice low and dangerous. "If you ever try to harm her again, I'll happily plead guilty to crimes against humanity after what I'd do to you." The menace in his words sends a shiver down my spine, but there's also an odd sense of comfort in knowing how fiercely he would protect me.

Greg pales visibly, his anger simmering just beneath the surface. It's clear that Primo has struck a nerve, only further cementing my suspicions about his involvement in the kidnapping plot. As we take our seats at the defense table, I feel that we're not only facing the prosecution, but also fighting an unseen war against those who would seek to undermine us from within.

"Primo, you shouldn't have done that," I whisper urgently as he settles back into his seat beside me. "I don't want you implicated for those three men."

He meets my gaze with a steady one of his own, the fierceness in his eyes softening just a fraction. "Isabella, I'm not worried about that. If they come after me, it implicates Greg for kidnapping, too. This is the game of criminal activity – mutually assured destruction." He offers a brief, humorless smile before turning his attention to the front of the courtroom.

My heart still races from our encounter with Greg, but Primo's words offer some solace. I take a deep breath, laying out all my materials as the chatter around us dies down and the room falls silent.

"Order in the court!" the bailiff calls out, and everyone rises as Judge Dolan takes his place behind the bench. As we sit back down, the jury instructions are given, and the air in the courtroom grows tense.

The prosecution stands, taking center stage. My grip tightens around the edges of my notes, but I force myself to listen to their opening arguments. They paint a picture of Primo as a man with murderous intent, someone cruel and ruthless who wouldn't hesitate to kill his own business partner. It's a twisted caricature of the man I've come to know, but I can see the doubt creeping into the jurors' eyes.

As the prosecution concludes, I rise, leaving my carefully crafted speech on the table. Instead, I look each juror in the eye, speaking from the depths of my heart. "Ladies and gentlemen of the jury, over the course of preparing for this trial, I've had the privilege of getting to know the man that is Primo Maldonado. He is fiercely loyal and protective, a far cry from the monster the prosecution would have you believe."

I pause, letting my words sink in before continuing. "The person who kills someone close to them is not the same person who risks everything to protect those he cares about. The evidence will show that Primo was set up by someone lacking his moral compass, someone desperate to see him fall. Someone who had personal motive to get him out of the way, no matter the cost. I ask that you look past the show the prosecution is trying to put on, and truly examine the man beneath the suit."

As I take my seat once more, I can feel the energy shift in the courtroom. My words have struck a chord with the jury, and I can only hope it's enough to turn the tide in our favor. The battle has just begun, but with each passing moment, I am more determined than ever to see justice prevail.

The gavel strikes and the first day of trial concludes. The courtroom empties, leaving only its cold, sterile atmosphere behind. Primo is escorted away, his eyes lingering on me for a moment before he disappears from sight.

I make my way to my my hotel room, one right next to the courthouse since my apartment is too far of a drive. My body is heavy with exhaustion. My hand trembles as I unlock the door, and the moment it swings open, I'm greeted by an unexpected sight. Teddy Maldonado sits in the dimly lit room, his lean form sprawled across a plush armchair.

"Teddy? What are you doing here?" I ask, my voice barely above a whisper.

"Really, Isabella? By now I thought you'd have learned that Primo doesn't just let bad things happen to the people he loves," he replies with a smirk.

"Love?" I stammer, taken aback by his choice of words. "No one said anything about love."

He shrugs and leans back in the chair, his light eyes twinkling with amusement. "Call it what you want. But don't think Primo would leave you unprotected."

"Are you staying here tonight?" I glance around the room, wondering where Teddy plans to sleep.

"Right by the door," he answers, sensing my unspoken question. "To make sure no more pesky kidnappers come after you."

A mixture of gratitude and relief settle deep into my bones. Primo's forethought and Teddy's presence provide a sense of security I didn't realize I needed. The day finally catches up to me, and I sink into the soft mattress, allowing the darkness to claim me.

Over the next week, the trial drags on, each day bringing fresh challenges and revelations. Witness after witness is called to the stand, their testimonies scrutinized and dissected. Constantino watches from the stands his predatory gaze on my back unnerving, but I feel confident in our case. We're saving the final blow for last – exposing him and his treacherous schemes.

As the sun sets each evening, I return to the hotel room, my body and mind aching from the day's battle. Teddy is always there, a silent sentinel guarding my door. Our conversations are sparse, but there's comfort in the familiarity of his presence. With every passing day, I grow more determined to bring the truth to light, fueled by the support of those who believe in me.

The final day of witness testimony dawns, and I can feel the electric anticipation crackling in the air as I step into the courtroom. My heart races with a mixture of excitement and dread, knowing that today will be the culmination of all my efforts. The room seems bathed in an eerie, golden light, casting a surreal glow over the proceedings.

"Constantino Maldonado," I call out, my voice steady and resolute despite the pounding in my chest. There is a collective hush among the audience as he rises from his seat, his eyes locked onto mine. As he makes his way to the witness box, I notice the wolfish glint in those icy orbs – a stark reminder that I'm dealing with a dangerous man.

He places his hand on the Bible, and I observe how his movements are cold, deliberate, and calculating, even for such a simple act. I take a deep breath, drawing in the scent of old wood and musty leather that fills the courtroom, and steady myself for the battle ahead.

"Mr. Maldonado," I begin, meeting his gaze with unwavering determination. "Can you tell us where you were on the night in question?"

"Of course," he replies, his voice smooth and practiced. He rattles off a series of quick, simple answers, clearly prepared for every query I might throw his way. But I am not deterred – I know that beneath that polished veneer lies a web of deception, and I'm determined to untangle it.

As I guide him through the events of that fateful night, he follows along easily enough, providing each expected answer with effortless charm. But then, I see it – the chink in his armor that I've been searching for. Unable to resist the opportunity, I turn the tables on him, catching him in an inconsistency that leaves him faltering.

"Mr. Maldonado, you claim that you were visiting your Father on the night of the murder. Isn't that correct?"

"Yes," he replies coolly.

"Permission to approach the witness," I ask the judge.

"Granted," Judge Dolan replies.

I make my way over to Constantino and hand him a ledger.

"Can you inform the Court what this is, Mr. Maldonado?" I ask.

He looks at it briefly and then tries to hand it back to me.

"It appears to be a log of visitors," he says.

"Hold onto that just a little bit longer," I say to him. "And if you could direct your attention to your entry on the night in question."

He scans the page and I continue.

"How long does it say you were visiting with your father on the night in question, Mr. Maldonado?"

He considers the page. "Approximately four hours."

"Wow! Four hours," I exclaim, turning to look at the jury briefly. I turn back to Constantino. "That's a pretty long visit, and quite late at night, don't you think?"

He shrugs, never one to lose his composure. "We had a lot to talk about, I guess."

"No doubt," I reply. "Could you inform the jury how long your visit was the week prior."

He looks at the document, his brows furrowing as he starts to catch on with where this is going. "Seventeen minutes," he responds curtly.

"And the week before that?"

"Twenty-three minutes," he says.

"Other than the night in question, has there ever been an entry for longer than one hour, Mr. Maldonado?" I ask, turning again to the jury.

"No," he replies.

"Is the prison in the practice of allowing visitors to stay for four hours?" I ask incredulously.

"I couldn't say," he replies, irritation coating his voice. "I'm not in charge at the prison."

"No, I suppose not," I reply.

"Can you tell the jury why, on the night of the murder, your visit was so much longer with your father?"

"As I said," he replies, staring me down, "I guess we had a lot to talk about that night."

"Is it possible, Mr. Maldonado," I ask, my voice dripping with implication, "that you cannot account for this inconsistency because you – conspiring with your father, no less – orchestrated this entire setup for your brother?"

He opens his mouth to respond, but I press on relentlessly, a tidal wave of questions crashing down upon him. "And is it not true that Primo did not kill Beau Bennett, but in fact, it was you who pulled the trigger?"

Constantino's face pales as he stumbles over his words, the mask of composure slipping away before our very eyes. Silence stretches taut between us, and I know I have him.

"Please listen carefully, Mr. Maldonado, and tell me if the events as I outline them are consistent with your recollection. Following your father's guilty verdict, control over the family business fell to Primo, his first born son. But, that didn't sit well with you. And, neither did it sit well with your father, with whom you've always had a closer relationship than Primo. So, you both needed a way to get Primo out of the way so that you could take over.

"Axe Michelson created a perfect opportunity for your father to lay a trap. He asked Axe to lure Primo to Miami to handle a business meeting. Primo, suspecting that this agent had double crossed him, was prepared. Someone tipped the police off to the meeting and the police showed up and everyone scatters.

"Primo escaped your trap, so you need to lay another. The feds showing up in Miami gave you the perfect excuse. You started to conspire with Beau Bennett and word is passed to Primo that Axe has gone rogue and is working with the feds. A meeting at a safehouse is set up to take out Axe. You, quite conveniently, are in a four hour meeting at the prison, so you could not possibly be at the safehouse, where you expect Axe to be killed.

"But, Axe isn't killed. He escapes, and this time he really does go to the feds. Angry over the second failure, you decide that you need a body that you can pin on Primo. Beau Bennett was *your* victim, wasn't he Mr. Maldonado? He trusted you, so you were able to pull the trigger at close range, because he never suspected it would come from you.

"An anonymous tip was given to the police, Primo's DNA, which you have easy access to given that you live in the same residence, was found at the crime scene, and away he goes, in the back of the squad car. Did I get it right, Mr. Maldonado?"

"I invoke the protections of the Fifth Amendment, and decline to answer your question, Ms. Moretti," Constantino says with ice in his eyes.

Turning to the judge, I announce, "No further questions."

I return to my seat next to Primo, feeling like I've just stepped off a roller coaster. His hand finds mine under the table, squeezing gently in reassurance. It's been ages since we've had any meaningful interaction, but this small gesture fills me with renewed hope and strength.

As closing arguments begin, the prosecution once again paints a picture of a cruel and heartless man, attempting one last time to sway the jury against Primo. When they finish, I rise once more, ready to speak from my heart.

"Members of the jury," I address them earnestly, "the prosecution is trying to put Primo Maldonado on trial for who he is, rather than what he's done. But we are here today because he stands accused of killing Beau Bennett – a crime for which the evidence clearly shows he has been wrongly framed by his own family." My voice swells with passion as I implore them to see past the smoke and mirrors, to find the truth buried beneath the lies.

I look at each juror in turn, my gaze steady, as I make my final plea. "I implore you to see through the smokescreen the federal agents have cast over this case, obscuring crucial facts from your view. Consider how they have manipulated the truth to serve their agenda, ignoring the inconsistencies and glaring omissions in their presentation.

"Ask yourselves," I continue passionately, "if there remains even a shred of doubt in your minds that Primo was not the one to pull the trigger, can you honestly sentence him to a life behind bars for a crime he did not commit?"

The room is heavy with anticipation, an electric charge buzzing in the air as I finish speaking. It feels as though the eyes of every person present are boring into me, but my focus remains solely on the jury, hoping beyond hope that my words have struck a chord.

I make my final plea and return to my seat, my pulse in overdrive.

"Very well, Counselors," Judge Dolan replies, giving a firm nod. "Court is adjourned for the day. The jury will begin deliberations tomorrow morning. Everyone is dismissed."

As I gather my papers and close my briefcase, my heart races in my chest, a wild symphony of hope and fear. Primo places a hand on my shoulder, his touch warm and reassuring despite the world bearing down on him. I can see it in his eyes, that flicker of gratitude and admiration.

"Thank you, Isabella," he murmurs softly before leaving the courtroom under heavy guard.

As the oak doors close behind him, the room empties out, leaving me alone with my thoughts and the whispers that cling to the air like ghosts. The fate of the man I've come to know so intimately now rests in the hands of twelve strangers.

# Chapter Thirty-Four

## *Isabella*

The sterile scent of the windowless conference room hangs heavy in the air as Primo and I wait, a quiet tension settling over us like an invisible shroud. It's been several hours since the jury began its deliberation, and I feel a glimmer of hope. They say that when the jury takes time to decide, it's a good sign for the defense. But still, I keep my hopes in check, trying not to let them run wild.

Lunch has come and gone, the forgotten remnants of our meal discarded into the trash bin in the corner. We've spent these long hours sitting in silence, each lost in our own thoughts. The incessant ticking of the wall clock is the only sound that accompanies our vigil.

Primo suddenly rises from his chair, his tall frame casting a shadow over the polished surface of the conference table. He begins to pace the room, his dark eyes reflecting the anxiety clawing at him from within. I reach out to him, wanting to ease his worry somehow. "I understand your anxiousness, Primo," I say softly, watching as he stops mid-stride.

He turns to me, concern etched into the lines of his face. With a boldness that surprises me, he crosses the room and kneels before me, his strong hands gripping my knees. "Isabella," he murmurs, sincerity lacing his voice, "I am incredibly grateful for everything you've done for me. No matter the outcome, you are a fantastic lawyer, and I'm lucky to have had you by my side throughout this case. I knew you wouldn't take the bait," he murmurs softly, his voice like velvet against my skin. His dark eyes seem to pierce through mine, their depths holding secrets I'm not sure I want to uncover.

I give him a confused look, my brow furrowing in uncertainty. "The bait? What bait are you talking about?"

"The loan sharks," he reveals with a casual shrug, as if it were a mere inconvenience. "I know they offered to absolve you of all your debts if you threw my case."

I stare at him incredulously, my heart thundering in my chest. "You knew? How did you know?"

"I have eyes and ears in a lot of places, my dear Isabella," he replies with a sly grin. "The moment they laid a hand on you, they were under constant surveillance until this trial was over, and I could deal with them without raising suspicion."

Confusion overwhelms me, and I shake my head, my fingers absentmindedly playing with the edge of my blouse. "But, if you knew, why didn't you say anything to me? Ask me ahead of time what I was going to do?"

"Did I need to ask you?" he counters, the corners of his mouth lifting in a knowing smile. "No," he answers for himself, "because I had no doubt in my mind that you would never throw my case."

My breath catches in my throat as his words sink in. "You trusted me that much?" I manage to whisper, my eyes searching his for any hint of deceit.

"Of course," he sighs, his gaze never leaving mine. "I trust you with my life." A pause, and then he adds, almost as an afterthought, "And my heart."

The weight of his confession hangs heavy in the air, mingling with the scent of his cologne that now feels intoxicating. My pulse races, a wild symphony playing beneath my skin, as I consider the implications of his trust and what it means for us. My heart swells with emotion, and I lean forward, wrapping my arms around him. Our lips meet in a tender kiss that quickly deepens, our tongues dancing together in a passionate exchange.

The tension in the room is palpable, and as Primo's hands roam my body, I shiver with anticipation. "Maybe we shouldn't be doing this here," I whisper, glancing around the empty conference room, my heart pounding in my chest. "We could be caught."

"Ah, Isabella," he breathes against my ear, his lips sending a shudder down my spine. "That's what makes it so exciting, don't you think? Besides," he says, his fingers tracing the curve of my hip, causing me to feel a surge of desire for him, "what more can they really do to punish me at this point? Can I continue?" he asks, his voice low and filled with promise.

My hesitation dissolves, and I nod, eager to submit to him once more. I want him to give me everything he has, even if it may be the last time.

"Alright," he says, his eyes darkening with determination. "I'll do what I can within reason, given our setting. But don't worry, there will be plenty of time for us to explore further in the future." The hope that ignites in my chest at his words is unexpected and powerful.

"Show me what you have in mind," I challenge him, feeling bolder now. He smirks and pulls back, looking me up and down as if appraising a prized possession.

"Today, I want to do things to you instead of giving commands," he tells me, his eyes flicking over my face, searching for any signs of discomfort. "If you want to be my good girl, you should be my little fuck pet—happy and waiting for anything I decide to give you." He reminds me of the stoplight system, and I nod in understanding, grateful for the safety measures he's put in place.

Primo doesn't remove my clothing, but rather opens my blouse and hikes up my skirt, pulling my bra down to expose my breasts and pulling my panties aside to reveal my pussy. I'm still fully clothed, but this somehow feels even more intense, as if he's stripping away not just the fabric, but the layers of pretense that separate us.

"Beautiful," he murmurs, his gaze traveling over my

exposed skin. The vulnerability I feel is exhilarating, and I can hardly contain my desire for him.

"Please, Primo," I beg, my voice barely audible. "I need you."

"Patience, my love," he whispers, his fingers brushing against my collarbone, making me shiver with anticipation. "We have all the time in the world."

Primo sits me up on the table, my legs dangling over the edge, and gazes at me with a wicked smile. His fingers trace my skin, starting from my collarbone down to my chest, deliberately avoiding my nipples. The sensation sends shivers coursing through my body, making me squirm in anticipation.

"Tell me what you want," he teases, his voice low and sultry. "I want to hear you say it."

"Touch me, Primo," I plead, desperate for the feel of him on my skin. "Please, I need it."

He chuckles softly, enjoying my desperation. "I want to see just how hard I can make them before I finally get to torture them properly," he says, looking directly into my eyes as he speaks.

The way he says it makes my heart race, and I can feel the heat pooling between my legs. It's torturous waiting for him to give in, but the anticipation is intoxicating.

"Patience, Isabella," he taunts, and then, when I think I can't take it anymore, he finally palms my breast and tweaks my nipple, sending a jolt of pleasure through me. Before I wanted his touch so badly, now he won't stop touching me, and I worry that I might come just from this stimulation alone.

"Primo," I gasp, my breaths coming in short pants. He takes the opportunity to lean forward and capture one nipple in his mouth, biting gently enough to leave marks on my soft flesh.

"I love marking you," he murmurs against my skin. "I'd love to mark you permanently." My mind races, wondering what he means by that, but I don't have time to process because he's pushing me down onto the table. The cold surface against my back contrasts sharply with the heat of his body above me.

"Open your legs for me," he commands, and I obey, spreading my thighs wide and bending my knees to fully expose myself to him. Primo's eyes darken with lust as he admires the view.

"Your pussy is beautiful," he says softly, "but I know it tastes even better."

"Are you going to tease me forever?" I ask, unable to hide the desperation in my voice.

"Maybe," he replies with a smirk. But then his fingers finally graze my pussy, making me moan. "Work your nipples for me while I taste you," he instructs, and I comply, whispering, "Yes, Sir."

"Good girl," he praises me, and I preen at his approval. Then he kneels down, his breath hot on my sensitive folds before he begins to eat my pussy. As his tongue explores me, my thoughts dissolve into pure sensation, and I surrender to the passion building inside me, knowing that this moment is one I'll never forget.

I marvel at the way Primo eats me. His enthusiasm is unmatched, his desire to taste and savor every part of me intoxicating. He's unlike any other lover I've had—the few who have agreed to go down on me treat it as a chore, but not Primo.

"God, you're so good at this," I moan, unable to contain my appreciation.

"Only for you, Isabella," he murmurs against my slick heat, sending shivers up my spine. His tongue enters me with purpose, his fingers working my clit in tandem, leaving me gasping and begging for more.

"Please, let me come," I plead, desperate for release. But he shakes his head, his dark eyes locking onto mine.

"Patience, my beautiful girl." He drives me closer and closer to my edge, my body trembling and my breath coming out in short, ragged gasps. I know I'm not allowed to come yet, but God, it's so hard to hold back.

Suddenly, Primo stands, pulling me down from the table. His hands move roughly over my breasts, fingers digging into my sensitive flesh. He tilts my chin up, forcing me to meet his gaze. "Open," he commands with a wicked smile.

I obey, and he spits into my mouth. I drink it down without hesitation, surprising even myself with how much I love being his slut. Primo's grin widens as he sees my reaction. "You truly are a dream come true, Isabella."

"Thank you, Sir," I reply, my voice quivering with both

gratitude and arousal. He flips me around, urging me to bend over the conference table. The cool surface presses against my chest as I comply, feeling exposed and vulnerable under his commanding presence.

"Such a perfect view," Primo murmurs, his hand tracing the curve of my spine. I shiver at the contact, anticipation building inside me as I await his next move.

"Please, Sir," I beg once more, needing him to take control and push me over the edge. But even now, teetering on the brink, I know that I am his to command —and I couldn't be happier.

"Prepare yourself, Isabella," Primo whispers in my ear, his breath hot against my skin. "I'm going to fuck you hard against this conference table. Make sure you scream my name loud; I want everyone to know just what a little slut you are for me."

His words make me shiver, and I can feel the heat pooling between my legs. I nod silently, unable to speak as anticipation courses through me.

Taking a step back, Primo surveys me with an appreciative eye. "I love owning you," he confesses, voice low and commanding. "Using your body for my pleasure... The thought of your pussy has always made me hard."

"Please, Sir," I manage to choke out, my heart pounding in my chest. "I need you."

"Good girl," he replies with a smirk, positioning himself behind me. As he enters me, I scream his name, the sensation of him filling me completely overwhelming my senses. But I don't come, despite the desperation that threatens to consume me.

Primo's movements are not slow like last time; they're fast and insistent, each thrust driving me further into the edge of ecstasy. My breasts bounce with the force of his actions, and he slaps and squeezes my ass as leverage for each powerful thrust.

"Your ass feels so good in my hands, Isabella," he growls, his voice laced with lust. "I love the way it looks marked with my prints."

As he spanks me again, I whimper, the pain only heightening my arousal. Primo praises me, his voice a mix of tenderness and authority. "You're a joy to own, Isabella. My perfect little slut."

"Thank you, Sir," I gasp out, my mind reeling from the pleasure coursing through my body. I can't help but marvel at the intensity of this moment, the raw connection between us as he takes control and dominates me. And in the midst of it all, I know that I'm exactly where I want to be—completely under Primo's spell, embracing every part of the darkness we share.

"Are you going to come for me, Isabella?" Primo asks, his voice a low growl.

"Only with your permission, Sir," I reply breathlessly. The tension between us is palpable as he continues to thrust into me relentlessly, my body aching for the sweet release of orgasm.

"Such a good girl," he praises me, his fingers finding my nipples and tweaking them, making me gasp in pleasure.

"You deserve to come for me. Let yourself go and speak freely; tell me every filthy thought on your mind."

I let loose, words spilling from my lips like a broken dam. "I love being your pet, Primo. I crave it when you fuck and degrade me. Being your needy slut is all I want, and the feeling of your cock inside me... God, it's amazing." As I scream his name, my orgasm crashes over me, waves of pleasure coursing through every nerve in my body.

He turns me around so that he can see my face as he enters me once more, my slick opening welcoming him eagerly. Glancing down, I notice the mess my arousal has made on the table. Primo follows my gaze and smirks.

"I can't wait to watch you clean that up," he says, a wicked gleam in his eyes. He turns me around again and pushes my face into the mess on the table. "In fact, clean it up while I continue to fuck you."

My tongue laps at the wetness on the table as he thrusts into me, his grip on my hips firm and unyielding. Soon enough, he spins me around again, capturing my breasts in his hands and teasing my nipples to the point of near pain.

"God, you're incredible," he groans, his thrusts becoming even more powerful than before. I'm left breathless, my body quivering with the intensity of it all. I feel another orgasm building within me, every nerve ending alight with anticipation.

"Come for me, Isabella," he commands. "I love how much you come for me. Do it once more, and then I'm going to fill your needy pussy with my seed. Your panties should always be soaked with my cum."

As I reach my peak once again, crying out his name among a litany of filthy words and desires, I feel Primo's cock pulse inside me. He presses deep, spilling his release into me, an intimate mark of ownership that leaves me feeling both sated and hungry for more of him.

Just as our breaths begin to steady, and the remnants of our orgasms still linger on my skin, a knock on the door shatters the moment. Panic floods my veins, a stark contrast to the lustful heat that had consumed me only moments ago.

"Shit," Primo hisses, hastily fumbling with his clothing as we scramble to put ourselves back together. My hands tremble as I button my blouse, trying to conceal the evidence of our reckless tryst.

"Give me a second," I call out, my voice wavering slightly. I pray that it doesn't betray the frantic pounding of my heart.

I glance at Primo, who shoots me a reassuring smile, though I can see the apprehension in his eyes. We share a brief, silent exchange, our faces flushed with a mix of desire and anxiety.

"Ready?" he asks, his voice low, his hand resting on my shoulder to steady me.

"Ready," I nod, inhaling deeply before turning the handle and opening the door.

The bailiff stands there, his stoic expression unchanged, as if he's unaware of the scandalous scene that had unfolded just beyond his reach. "The jury has reached a verdict," he announces, his words slicing through the tension like a knife.

"Thank you," I reply, trying to sound composed despite the whirlwind of emotions swirling within me. My mind races, shifting from the passionate encounter with Primo to the potential consequences of the trial. What if they find him guilty? Will this be the last time I can feel his touch, taste his lips?

"Isabella," Primo whispers, his fingertips grazing my arm. "You did everything you could. No matter what happens, remember that."

His words ground me, anchoring me to the present. I force a small smile, even as fear twists in my stomach like a viper. We step out of the conference room, side by side, preparing to face the verdict that will change both our lives forever.

"Ready?" he asks once more, his warm gaze meeting mine.

"Ready," I repeat, taking a deep breath. Together, we walk into the courtroom, hand in hand, ready for whatever fate has in store for us.

## Chapter Thirty-Five

### Primo

As Isabella and I return to the courtroom, escorted by the stern-faced bailiff, the comforting cocoon of our recent rendezvous has been torn away. My heart races beneath my carefully composed facade. Our family's power has waned, and I know that if I'm truly convicted, it's very likely I'll be killed before I ever see the inside of a prison cell.

As we step inside the courtroom, I watch the jurors file in, each one more ordinary than the next. Their faces betray nothing as they take their seats—twelve people who hold my fate in their hands. I take a deep breath, sending up a silent prayer for strength. No matter what happens, I'm grateful that Isabella is standing beside me for this.

"Order in the court," the bailiff calls out, and the room

falls silent. The tension is palpable, a heavy weight pressing down on every soul present.

The foreman of the jury rises, solemn and stoic, handing a folded paper to the bailiff. It's passed to Judge Dolan, whose leathery face remains impassive as he opens it with deliberate slowness. My heart hammers in my chest, completely at odds with the measured pace of the unfolding scene.

"In the matter of Commonwealth of Massachusetts v. Maldonado," Judge Dolan reads, his voice gravelly, "we the jury find the defendant not guilty of murder in the first degree."

I blink, unable to process the words. The courtroom erupts into a cacophony of noise, a tempest of emotion swirling around me as some scream in outrage while others celebrate. Isabella leaps into my arms, her beautiful body pressing against mine as she wraps her arms around me. I catch her, the disbelief still fogging my mind.

"We did it! We did it, Primo!" she cries, a cascade of joyous tears streaming down her face. Her eyes meet mine, filled with elation and relief.

My heart races as Isabella clings to me, her breath hot and sweet on my neck. I savor the warmth of her embrace, feeling her strong arms tighten around me. With a reluctant sigh, I turn to survey the room, our bodies still entwined.

Over the heads of the dispersing crowd, I spot Charlie standing near the back, his eyes glistening with what must be happiness. He raises a shaky hand in salute, and I return the gesture, filled with gratitude for his support. But the joy I feel shatters like fragile glass when my gaze falls upon Constantino.

My brother's eyes lock onto mine, dark and dangerous. I see him look between me and then at Charlie. Fury pulses from him like an electric current, causing goosebumps to rise on my skin. Without warning, he whirls around and storms out of the courtroom, each step heavy with menace. My blood runs cold; I know that we've driven him into a corner, and the consequences will be dire.

"Primo," Isabella whispers, drawing my attention back to her. Her voice is soft, but there's a determination in her eyes that speaks volumes. "We'll deal with your brother later. For now, let's just enjoy this victory."

As the courtroom empties, Charlie ambles over, his smile warm and inviting. "Congratulations, you two. Let's head back to the mansion and celebrate, huh? I'm too old for all this commotion."

"Sounds perfect," I reply, my voice steadying as the initial shock begins to wane. "We'll see you there soon."

"Looking forward to it," Charlie says with a nod before disappearing into the crowd.

As the last of the spectators filter out, Greg approaches us, his expression sheepish. I can tell he wants to say something, but I cut him off before he has the chance.

"Cut your losses and move on, Greg," I warn, my voice low and dangerous. "Otherwise, we'll create real problems for you, considering what you did to Isabella."

He looks uncomfortable, his eyes darting between us like a cornered animal. Wordlessly, he slinks away.

"Primo," Isabella murmurs, her fingers tracing patterns on my arm, "I know you want to make him pay, but please, be careful."

"Of course, Isabella," I promise, her concern settling in my chest. I may have won the battle today, but the war against my own family has only just begun.

Just as the last sound of footsteps fades away, leaving Isabella and me alone in the cavernous courtroom, an explosive sound shatters the silence. Gunshots. The air is suddenly thick with fear, screams tearing through the once-peaceful atmosphere.

"Primo!" Isabella gasps, her eyes wide and full of terror. We exchange a frantic glance before sprinting toward the exit, leaving our belongings behind.

As we burst through the heavy doors, the world outside is a chaotic blur of movement. My heart pounds violently in my chest, the adrenaline coursing through my veins like fire. And there, lying motionless on the pavement, is Charlie, a crimson stain spreading around him.

"Charlie!" I choke out, my voice barely a whisper. A storm of rage builds within me as I look up to see Constantino's car speeding off into the distance. The anger threatens to consume me whole, and I can scarcely think straight. "I'll meet you back at the mansion," I tell Isabella, my voice shaking with fury.

"Primo, stop!" she cries out, grabbing my arm. Her eyes brim with unshed tears, and my heart aches at the sight. "You can't just run off and implicate yourself in another murder. This is exactly what your brother wants."

"Isabella," I begin, but she cuts me off, her voice desperate and pleading.

"Listen to me," she insists. "He wants you to chase him, so he can lead you into more trouble. He won't make the same mistakes again, Primo. You need to think smarter than him." She swallows hard, her grip on my arm tightening. "Stay here with Charlie. Talk to the authorities. Give him the honors he deserves. We'll deal with your brother later."

Her words resonate deep within me, cutting through the red haze clouding my thoughts. I know she's right, but the urge to avenge Charlie is an almost unbearable weight on my shoulders. With a sigh, I reluctantly nod in agreement.

"Alright," I concede, my voice thick with emotion. "I'll stay."

The morning sun filters through the curtains, casting a muted glow across Isabella's apartment. The warmth is deceptive, a mere illusion that does little to alleviate the crushing guilt of Charlie's death bearing down on me. I find myself pacing the small space, my thoughts consumed by the uncertainty of what lies ahead.

"Primo," Isabella murmurs softly, her hand reaching out to touch my arm, halting my restless movements. "You can't keep torturing yourself like this. We need a plan."

I glance at her, eyes full of gratitude for her support. "I know. It's just...difficult," I confess, my voice faltering. "Charlie was like family. And I can't trust anyone right now."

"Except Teddy," she reminds me gently.

I nod, acknowledging the truth in her words. My phone buzzes with an incoming message, and as if summoned by our conversation, it's Teddy. He's managed to gather information on Constantino's whereabouts and intentions. Though I'm hesitant to act on anything just yet, the knowledge offers a semblance of control amidst the chaos.

"Talk to Teddy," Isabella urges. "Stay close to him. Together, we'll figure out a way to handle Constantino without causing more harm."

The day passes in a blur of anxious planning and hushed conversations, the tension between us slowly beginning to dissipate as we focus on the task at hand.

Two days later, the sky weeps as if mourning the loss alongside us. Raindrops patter against the windows, mirroring the heaviness in my heart as we prepare for Charlie's funeral. Isabella stands beside me, her expression a mix of concern and determination.

"Are you sure about going?" she asks, her fingers brushing against mine in a gesture of comfort. "It could be a trap."

"We may be a mafia family, but we have rules. One of which is respect for the dead. Constantino is a lot of things, but he wouldn't break the truce at a funeral," I reply, my voice laced with conviction. "Besides, I need to be there for Charlie."

"Then I'm going with you," she declares, her eyes resolute as they meet mine.

"Isabella, it's dangerous," I protest, but she cuts me off with a shake of her head.

"I know the risks, Primo," she says firmly. "But I won't let you face this alone. We're in this together, remember?"

My heart swells with gratitude and affection, even as guilt gnaws at the edges of my consciousness. She deserves so much more than the darkness that now taints our lives. I reach for her hand, entwining our fingers together, grounding myself in her touch.

"Thank you," I murmur, fighting the urge to pull her into my arms. "I don't know what I would do without you."

"Let's hope you never have to find out," she replies, her lips curving into a ghost of a smile.

As we step out into the rain, our clothes quickly dampened by the downpour, I silently vow to protect Isabella at all costs.

The rain pours down in a relentless cascade, matching the heaviness in my heart as we make our way to the graveside. Each step feels laden with memories of Charlie, the man who had stood by me through thick and thin. As I stand there, soaked to the bone, the somber weather is a reflection of the darkness that now engulfs my life.

Isabella's presence at my side offers a small sense of comfort, her hand gripping mine as if she too draws strength from the connection. The funeral service proceeds, each word etching itself into my memory as Constantino and I lock eyes, our gazes dueling amid the rain.

"Primo," Isabella murmurs as the service comes to an end, "be careful."

I nod and gently disengage our hands, unwilling to let her be pulled any deeper into this mire. "Wait for me beneath that oak tree," I tell her, pointing to its protective canopy. She hesitates for a moment before nodding and making her way there, leaving me to confront my brothers.

The four of us make our way together through the rain.

"Constantino," I begin, my voice barely audible over the sound of the rain, "Charlie's death is on your hands."

He smirks, the arrogance in his expression sending a chill down my spine. "I know. And it was no big loss."

The rage inside me threatens to boil over, but I force it back down; I will not dishonor Charlie's memory by starting a brawl here. Instead, I turn to Teddy, who stands silent, his usual humor absent from the situation. I know how much he cared for Charlie, the bond they shared stronger than blood.

"Teddy," I say, my voice softening, "I'm so sorry."

He just nods, sorrow evident in his eyes.

Unexpectedly, Giovanni chimes in. "Enough of this," he interrupts, his voice steady and commanding. "I have something to say." We all turn to look at him, the rain dripping from our brows, our clothes clinging to us like second skins.

"Go ahead," I prompt, still reeling from Constantino's callousness.

"I'm taking control of the family," he announces, his gaze dark.

Constantino scoffs, his disdain palpable. "You? You've got to be kidding."

But Giovanni is far from joking. He expertly lays out the details, how he has meticulously seized control of all the family's assets through legitimate means. My shock is mirrored in the faces of my brothers; we never expected Giovanni to make such a move.

"Impossible," I sputter, trying to argue with him. "You don't want this life."

"Primo, there's no argument to be had," he rebukes me. "I have control now, and I will lead the family as I see fit."

My mind races, trying to process the implications of what he's saying. If Giovanni is truly in control, then perhaps we can rebuild our faltering empire on a more solid foundation, free from the darkness that has tainted it for so long. But first, there's the matter of Constantino.

Giovanni turns to our treacherous brother, and his voice takes on a chilling edge. "Constantino, you have until the end of the day to flee. By killing Charlie, a made man, without permission, your life is forfeit, and I have no power to protect you."

"Run far, Constantino," I warn him through gritted teeth, my voice a whispered promise of retribution. "I will never stop hunting you for what you've done."

The four of us stand there in the rain, an uneasy truce hanging between us. I can feel our collective grief and betrayal pressing down on us, threatening to suffocate us beneath its crushing burden. With a final nod, we part ways, the rain washing away any lingering traces of camaraderie.

I return to Isabella, her figure a beacon of hope beneath the ancient oak. As I approach her, she senses the shift in me, the storm that still rages within my heart.

"Let's go," I say, guiding her back to the car, seeking solace in the privacy of its confines. The moment we're inside, the rain pounds against the windows, as if the heavens themselves weep for the fractured bonds of brotherhood left shattered in the wake of our meeting.

# Chapter Thirty-Six

*Primo*

Impatiently, I watch the sunset through my office window while waiting for news from Teddy. My heart pounds in my chest as Teddy finally calls, reporting the latest on Constantino. Isabella, a vision of strength and beauty, stands beside me, gripping my hand tightly.

"Constantino has fled the country," Teddy says, his voice tense. Relief washes over me, but it's quickly replaced by seething rage. My brother has once again escaped justice, leaving behind a trail of destruction and pain.

I thank Teddy and hang up the phone.

I glance at Isabella, and in her eyes, I see hope blossoming like a delicate flower. "Giovanni taking over could mean a fresh start for us," she says softly. "A life away from the criminal world. We could move forward together."

"Impossible," I reply, bitterness tainting my tone.

"Constantino must be brought to justice. I'm the first-born son; I cannot simply cede power to Giovanni without a fight." As the words leave my lips, I see anger flicker across her face, darkening her features.

"Is vengeance more important than happiness with me?" she demands, her voice sharp as a knife. "We've been given this chance, and you would throw it all away?"

"Isabella, we can still be happy together," I try to reason with her, but she shakes her head, her eyes filled with disappointment.

"No," she asserts firmly. "I won't be with someone who chooses to be consumed by a mafia civil war. I refuse to become like my father." The hurt is evidence in her eyes. "Is this the sort of life you want? Don't you want to be able to see your son? Have a relationship with him? One you both can be proud of?" The frustration in her voice stings, and I can feel my own anger beginning to boil beneath my skin.

"I should go," I say curtly, trying to suppress the hurt that threatens to overwhelm me.

As I walk away from her, our conversation hangs heavy in the air, leaving me with a deep sense of regret and longing. My heart aches with the knowledge that the path I've chosen may lead me away from the one person who has ever truly understood me.

The halls of the mansion feel empty as I return, the air heavy with the absence of Charlie's presence. The silence is deafening, and my heart aches with each step I take. I make my way back to my study, where bottles of aged scotch line the shelves, their amber liquid beckoning me.

"Fuck it," I mutter to myself, grabbing one of the bottles and pouring a generous amount into a glass. The alcohol burns my throat, but it doesn't matter – I need the numbness it brings. Glass after glass disappears down my throat, my thoughts spiraling around Charlie's death and Isabella's words.

"Primo, what the hell are you doing?" Teddy's voice cuts through the haze, and I look up to see him standing in the doorway, an amused grin on his face.

"Drinking," I slur, gesturing to the bottle in my hand. "Join me?"

Teddy chuckles and walks over, sitting down beside me on the floor before grabbing a bottle for himself. He takes a swig directly from the bottle, wincing at the burn. "So, what's your plan now, big brother?"

"I don't know," I confess, the words tasting like ash in my mouth. "Isabella wants me to just . . . walk away. But I can't. Not with Constantino still out there."

"Is that really what she wants?" Teddy probes, his eyes searching mine for the truth.

"More or less." I shrug, unable to elaborate further. "She made her choice."

"Did she? Or did you?" Teddy challenges, and I feel a

flash of anger, but it quickly dissipates under the alcohol. I avoid his gaze, unwilling to confront the question.

"Let's not talk about it," I mumble before downing another glass. The world begins to spin, and I let the darkness claim me.

I wake with a start, disoriented and stiff from sleeping on the floor. Teddy's hand is on my shoulder, shaking me awake. "Rise and shine, sunshine," he says, his voice oddly chipper for the early hour. "I've got a clean-up job, and you're coming with me."

"Wha— Why?" I groan, rubbing my aching head.

"Because Carmine's grieving Charlie, and I'm not gonna ask him to help me with this one." Teddy's eyes are somber as he speaks of Charlie's son and his normal partner on jobs, and I know I can't argue.

"Fine," I mumble, dragging myself to my feet and following Teddy out to his van. It's a carpet cleaning van, complete with a cheesy slogan painted on the side. I smile, thinking about how Teddy chose this life all those years ago, much to our father's chagrin.

"Whatcha thinkin' about?" Teddy asks as he starts the van and begins to drive.

"About how you got into cleaning," I reply, still

marveling at the decision that set him on such a different path from mine.

Teddy laughs, a genuine, warm sound that cuts through the lingering haze in my mind. "Yeah, that sure was an interesting time, huh?"

The van comes to a stop outside an old, abandoned warehouse on the outskirts of town. The sun is just beginning to cast its first rays of light, painting the sky in a mix of orange and pink. My heart sinks as we step out of the van and I see the warehouse door slightly ajar; this was a place where death seemed to linger, like a specter waiting for another soul to claim.

"Stay sharp," Teddy warns me as we make our way inside. The warehouse is dim, the morning light barely creeping through the cracks in the walls, casting long shadows across the large space. My eyes adjust quickly, and I'm immediately confronted with the sight of three gunned-down bodies lying next to a pile of ammunition. Their lifeless eyes stare into the void, faces frozen in expressions of shock and horror.

I swallow hard, suddenly understanding the gravity of Teddy's job. It's not easy dealing with so much death, yet he manages to maintain his upbeat attitude – something I find more impressive now than ever.

"Keep watch by the entrance," Teddy instructs as he pulls out a pair of headphones. "And don't let anyone in."

"Those don't go in your ears?" I ask, trying to distract myself from the grisly scene before me.

"Ah, these are the new bone-conducting headphones,"

he explains, beaming with excitement. "They let me listen to my tunes without blocking out any important sounds. Pretty neat, huh?"

"Definitely. So, what song do you start with for a cleanup job like this?" I inquire, curious about how he copes with such grim circumstances.

"Steal My Sunshine, always," he replies, grinning. "Gotta keep that '90s pop vibe alive, right?"

I chuckle, remembering how much Teddy loved that kind of music growing up. As he gets to work, meticulously rolling the bodies in plastic with practiced precision, I find myself deep in thought. My loyalty to the family and my desire for a life with Isabella are at odds, and I find myself opening up to Teddy about it.

"Teddy, I feel torn between the family and wanting a life with Isabella," I confess, my voice barely above a whisper. "It feels impossible to have both."

"But maybe it's not," Teddy replies, pausing for a moment as he considers his words. "Giovanni taking over might actually give you the chance to have both worlds. If you support him, you can still be a part of the family business without losing everything you've built with Isabella."

I watch Teddy work, contemplating his words. It's true that Giovanni wants to steer the family away from things like this – the violence and death that taints our legacy. As I look at Teddy, I realize how wise he truly is, despite his laid-back demeanor.

"Stop being a simp for me," he teases, catching my gaze. We share a laugh, the sound ringing through the warehouse and temporarily relieving the tension that hangs heavily in the air.

"Alright, alright," I chuckle, shaking my head as we finish loading the bodies into the van and make our way to the funeral home we own to cremate them.

As the last body is consumed by the fire, I find myself entranced by the dancing flames. The heat prickles my skin, and for a moment, it feels as if all my sins are being burned away with them. A bitter taste fills my mouth as I realize that I don't want this life of crime anymore. The anger toward Constantino still rages within me, but deep down, I know that Charlie would be more disappointed if I threw away the freedom I had just reclaimed, all for vengeance.

"Teddy," I say, swallowing down the lump in my throat, "I've made up my mind."

His eyes widen a fraction before he asks, "What's that?"

"I'm going to take your advice," I continue, my voice steady despite the storm of emotions brewing inside me. "I'll support Giovanni in his bid to turn our family business legitimate."

Teddy studies me for a moment, then nods slowly. "It won't be easy, you know."

"I know," I concede. "But Giovanni hasn't been

involved in the criminal side of things, and he'll need someone who knows that world to watch his back."

"Hey," Teddy says softly, placing a hand on my shoulder. "I'm proud of you."

"Thanks," I murmur, clapping him on the back before turning away from the fire. We leave the funeral home behind us, each step feeling lighter than the last.

***

The weekend sun casts a golden glow over the city as I drive toward the office building where Teddy said I'd find Giovanni. Towering glass windows reflect the sunlight, bathing the sleek, modern structure in a warm radiance. I marvel at the clean lines and minimalist design as I make my way through the expensive building. It's like stepping into another world – one defined by power and wealth rather than blood and violence.

As I ride up to the top floor, I realize how little I know about Giovanni's business. When the elevator doors slide open to reveal an entire floor owned by him, I'm taken aback. A sense of pride swells within me as I step into his lavish office, finding my brother standing by the floor-to-ceiling windows, staring out at the sprawling city below.

I knock on the door, my knuckles rapping against the glass. Giovanni whirls around, his hand instinctively reaching for the gun at his belt. I'm surprised to see him armed; it's a testament to the seriousness of his decision to take over our family's empire.

"Whoa, easy there," I say, raising my hands in surrender. "I come in peace."

Giovanni relaxes slightly, eyeing me with a mix of suspicion and curiosity. I step into his luxurious office, taking a seat across from him. The scent of expensive leather fills my nostrils as I sink into the plush chair.

"Listen, Giovanni," I begin, my voice firm yet gentle. "I want you to know that I support you taking over the family. I really do."

He raises an eyebrow, skepticism etched across his face. "Why? What's changed?"

"Isabella has," I admit, a soft sigh escaping my lips. "I want a life with her, and I believe this is the only way I can have it. We've already agreed that we should take the family toward more legitimate practices, and I want to help you make that happen."

Giovanni leans back in his chair, his gaze never leaving mine. "You think I can't handle it on my own?"

"Of course not," I reply quickly. "You've built an entire empire by yourself, and I'm damn impressed. But the criminal world is different, and I have connections that could be valuable to you. I've been leading our family's operations for years, after all."

He nods slowly, conceding the point. "I won't lie, I'm out of my element when it comes to some of our... darker dealings. And turning the family legit won't happen overnight."

"Exactly," I agree. "If you cut ties with other families too abruptly – the Irish, the Russians, the Chinese – we could end up with a mob war on our hands. We need to do this the right way so there's not more blood spilled."

Giovanni studies me for a moment, as if weighing my words and intentions. "Are you serious about helping me?"

"Absolutely," I assure him, my voice steady and sincere.

He extends his hand, and I grasp it firmly. The deal is sealed, a new chapter in our family's history beginning. "Come back to my office Monday morning," he says, a hint of determination creeping into his voice. "We'll get started then."

"Deal," I reply, feeling a newfound sense of purpose welling up inside me. As I leave Giovanni's office, I feel a sense of hope that, together, we might just be able to forge a brighter future for our family – one that doesn't involve bloodshed and darkness, one where Isabella and I can have a future together.

## Chapter Thirty-Seven

### Isabella

It's been a week since I last heard from Primo, and I can't contain my anger any longer. I need to talk to someone about it.

"Can you believe it?" My voice cracks into the phone as I pour out my heart. "After everything, after all the work I did, he chooses his life of crime over me." Hot tears cascade down my cheeks, the sting of betrayal leaving its mark. I really thought he wanted more – with me, for himself.

"Isabella," Eve says gently, her voice soothing to my aching heart, "we should meet and talk about it over breakfast. You need fresh air."

I wipe my tears with the back of my hand. "I don't know if I can eat right now," I confess.

"Then it's definitely a sign you're really upset. Come

on, let's meet at our usual spot. You'll feel better once we talk."

"Fine," I relent, "but I'm going to look like a mess."

"Who cares? We're sisters. Just come," she insists.

As I drive to meet Eve, I consider the fancy car Primo gave me – a symbol of the ritzy world he inhabited. Anger, sadness, frustration – every emotion churns within me, swirling together in an overwhelming storm. Part of me feels guilt for even driving it.

I park the car and head to the café, where my sister is already waiting. Her warm smile and open arms welcome me, enveloping me in a big hug. "It's going to be okay, Bella," she whispers into my ear. "We don't need men because there is bread."

Her attempt at humor brings a small, grateful smile to my lips. The knot in my chest loosens ever so slightly as we sit down in the farthest booth in the back of the café. Surrounded by the aroma of freshly brewed coffee and the soft background hum of conversation, Eve orders for us.

"Listen," she says, leaning in, her eyes filled with concern, "you need to talk about what's happened - everything you're feeling. Let it out."

I look down at my hands, my emotions heavy on my shoulders. "I just... I really believed he wanted more, y'know? And now it's like all of that was just a lie."

I take a deep breath as I gaze at the steaming mug of coffee in front of me, its warmth seeping into my hands, grounding me. "Primo and I... we had so much left to explore together. There were things we wanted to do –"

my voice falters, "– I wanted a life with him. To travel, to explore. I wanted him to meet you. He's got a son, did I tell you that? I thought he'd finally be able to reconnect with him. With his brother taking over the mob, we finally had a chance at all that. But instead of choosing me, he decides to start what will surely turn into a civil war within the mob. It's dangerous, not just for him, but for everyone in the city. Why wasn't a life with me enough? Why does he feel like he still needs to be a mob boss?"

Eve listens intently, her fingers wrapped around her own cup as she leans in closer. "Do you love him, Bella?"

Her question shocks me, and I find myself at a loss for words. Do I love him? My heart races as I try to make sense of my feelings. Eve watches my struggle and clarifies, "Actually, I didn't mean that as a question. I know you love him."

"How can you tell?" I ask, feeling exposed and vulnerable.

"It's obvious. That's why this hurts so much. He's completely broken your heart." She pauses, then asks tentatively, "Do you think he feels the same way about you?"

"I thought he did," I admit, fighting back tears. "But how could he, if he could just walk away from everything we had together?" I recount the morning before the trial when Primo suggested he get another lawyer because of my kidnapping.

"Wait, what?" Eve exclaims, shocked. "You were kidnapped? Was it the loan sharks? Why didn't you tell me?"

"I'm sorry," I apologize, feeling guilty. "It was just a blur with the trial. No, it wasn't the loan shark people. Actually, I haven't heard from them since the last incident and I have a feeling they've been handled. I can't prove it, but I'm pretty sure it was the prosecution behind the kidnapping. Primo wanted to switch lawyers because of it. I told him it would ruin my career, and he said I didn't need one because I could just live with him."

As I speak, I can feel my words hanging in the air between us. The café's cozy ambiance seems to fade away, leaving me feeling exposed and raw. In this moment, I realize just how deeply interwoven Primo has become in my life – and just how difficult it will be to untangle myself from his world.

"Bella, you're not just a live-in house call," Eve insists, her eyes fierce with conviction. "You know that, and Primo knows that too."

"Maybe he does, but–" I throw up my hands in exasperation. "I can't figure this guy out. Maybe it's better if I just move on and stop trying." I sigh, feeling my words sink in. "I don't want a life filled with risks, where I constantly worry about my safety and any children we might have. That's not what I want."

Just as the words escape my lips, a voice – one I haven't heard in a week – echoes over me. "Is that how you truly feel?"

I look up, locking eyes with Primo. He's standing there, looking polished and impossibly handsome as always. My heart rate spikes just from seeing him.

"Are you going to introduce me to your sister?" he asks, his voice low and smooth.

"Absolutely not," I retort, my heart pounding in my chest. "I don't even want to talk to you right now."

Primo raises an eyebrow, unfazed by my anger. "I understand, but I would like to have a private conversation with you."

"Too bad." I cross my arms, defiant. "I'm having breakfast with my sister, and things shouldn't always be on your terms."

He nods, acknowledging my point. With a deep breath, he introduces himself to Eve, who seems instantly captivated by his charm. "May I join you?"

"Of course!" she exclaims, much to my annoyance. I shoot her a dirty look, which she dismisses with a sheepish shrug.

As Primo slides into the booth beside Eve, their conversation begins to flow effortlessly. He asks about her work, learning that she is indeed a doctor. "Ah, quite the smart pair of sisters," he comments, a hint of admiration in his eyes.

Eve beams, her cheeks flushed with excitement. She shoots me discreet glances, mouthing the words "he's so handsome" as if I could somehow forget the magnetic pull of Primo's presence.

As they continue to chat, I find myself caught in a whirlwind of emotions – anger, sadness, and an undeniable longing for the man sitting across from me. The café's warm atmosphere seems to grow heavier, the air thick with unspoken words and desires that threaten to swallow me whole.

I shake my head, trying to clear my thoughts. How can one man have such a powerful hold over me? And more importantly, will I ever be able to break free?

As we finish our food, Primo smoothly insists on paying the bill, making it impossible for me to argue. As the three of us step outside into the crisp morning air,

I watch Eve and Primo exchange pleasantries with an unsettling ease.

"Eve, it's been a pleasure meeting you," he says, his eyes warm and sincere. "I apologize for interrupting your breakfast."

"Please, don't worry about it," she replies with a smile, her earlier awe replaced by genuine fondness.

She pulls me into a tender hug, her breath tickling my ear as she whispers, "Give him a chance – at least hear him out." I grumble indistinctly, reluctant to admit that there might be merit in her words. We exchange goodbyes, and I promise to keep her updated.

"May I walk with you?" Primo asks, his voice tentative but hopeful.

"Fine," I snap. "I'm walking. I can't control what you do."

As we stroll side by side toward my car, the silence between us is heavy, pregnant with unspoken emotions. Unable to bear it any longer, I stop and confront him. "How did you know where I was?"

His smile is bittersweet as he glances down at my chest. "You're still wearing my necklace," he reminds me gently.

My fingers trace the delicate chain, and I realize with a jolt that I never took it off, despite knowing it had a GPS chip hidden within. Why? What hold does this man have over me?

We continue walking, the distance between us both physical and emotional. As we approach my car, Primo speaks up. "I've decided to return to the family business—"

"Is that why you came here?" I cut him off, anger flaring inside me. "To tell me you're choosing crime over me? You could've saved us both the trouble and just stayed away!"

"Wait, I didn't—" he starts, but I don't let him finish.

"Save it," I snap, yanking open the car door. "There's nothing you can say that will make this right." With those words, I slam the door shut and drive off, leaving him standing in the parking lot, a forlorn figure against the backdrop of the city.

As I make my way back to my apartment, a small part of me feels guilty for treating him so harshly. But then I remind myself – he's the one who broke my heart, and I won't let him get away with that.

## Chapter Thirty-Eight

*Primo*

The sky above is a melancholy gray as I make my way down the narrow cobblestone street in a quiet section of Boston. My footsteps click against the brick walls of the surrounding buildings, converging at the entrance to the little shop. It's tucked away discreetly, like a secret waiting to be unraveled. A weathered wooden sign hangs above the door, announcing its purpose with an intricate design of inked roses and skulls: The Iron Quill Tattoo Parlor.

As I push open the door, the familiar scent of antiseptic and ink envelops me, welcoming me back to a place that had become something of a sanctuary over the years. The owner, a man with a permanent half-smile creasing his face and a beard peppered with silver, looks up from behind the counter. His dark eyes glint with recognition, and warmth fills his voice as he greets me.

"Primo! It's been too long. What brings you here today?"

His arms, covered in a tapestry of vibrant tattoos, bear testament to his life's work. There's a sense of quiet strength in his gaze, the sort of wisdom one acquires after decades of listening to stories etched into skin.

"Hey, Joe," I say softly, feeling an unexpected tightness in my chest. "I lost someone very special to me recently. Charlie. I'd like to honor him properly."

Joe's smile falters for a moment, and he nods solemnly. He gestures to the worn leather chair in the center of the room, inviting me to sit. "Tell me about Charlie," he says, his voice gentle and understanding. "What did he mean to you?"

"Charlie...he was more of a father to me than my actual father," I begin, my voice shaking slightly. "He taught me many things, always watched out for me. We were navigating through a dangerous world, and he was my compass."

As the words spill out of me, a heavy weight settles in my heart. "He died, Joe," I choke out. "And it was my fault."

Joe listens intently, his eyes never leaving mine as I speak. He picks up a pencil and begins to sketch something on a piece of paper. It's a fluid motion, his hand guided by years of experience and an innate understanding of the human soul.

"Your grief is clear, Primo," he says quietly, presenting

the design he has created. "Let this be a testament to him and to your bond."

My breath catches as I take in the intricate artwork: a black rose intertwined with a golden compass, its needle pointing north. The petals of the rose are tinged with crimson, representing both love and loss. At the center, in delicate script, is a single word: 'Charlie.'

I nod at him, giving him the approval he needs to get started. A lump forms in my throat as I marvel at the beauty of the design. Somehow, he has captured the essence of Charlie and our relationship in a way that transcends mere ink and skin.

"Let's get started then," Joe murmurs, preparing his tools with practiced ease. As the tattoo gun comes to life, buzzing like a swarm of bees, I brace myself for the familiar sting – a small price to pay for the permanent tribute that will soon adorn my body.

The hum of the tattoo gun ceases, and I feel the cool touch of Joe's gloved hand as he gently wipes away any excess ink from my skin. The pain has dulled down to a faint ache, a reminder of the story now etched into my flesh.

"Done," Joe announces, stepping back to admire his work. The black rose and golden compass gleam under the soft lights of the shop, seeming to come alive with every beat of my heart. Charlie would have been proud of this tribute, a symbol of our unbreakable bond that remains even after death.

"Thank you, Joe," I say, my voice thick with gratitude.

He nods solemnly, understanding the gravity of what he's just given me.

"Is there anything else I can do for you, Primo?" Joe asks, already starting to clean up his workspace.

A flash of determination sparks within me, fueled by the memory of Charlie and the need to honor him in every way possible. "Actually, yes," I reply, meeting Joe's gaze unwaveringly. "I'd like one more tattoo."

He raises an eyebrow, curiosity flickering in his eyes. "What do you have in mind?"

I hesitate for a moment, the image of the second tattoo clear in my mind but the words difficult to find. It isn't just about honoring Charlie; it's about embracing the part of myself I've kept hidden for too long. With Isabella's acceptance of my secret desire, I feel a newfound courage rising within me.

"Something...personal," I finally say, a hint of vulnerability seeping through my usual stoicism. "A symbol of who I am and what I want."

Joe nods slowly, understanding dawning on his face. "Alright, Primo. I trust you'll know it when you see it."

"Thank you, Joe," I breathe, preparing myself for what comes next. It's a step into the unknown, the uncharted territory of my heart.

As Joe begins to gather his tools once more, I find myself lost in thought, considering all the ways this small act will change me - and the world around me. My life is a web of decisions, a tapestry woven from strands of love, loyalty, and sacrifice. This new tattoo will be another thread, tying me to the person I am becoming.

"Ready when you are," Joe says softly, his eyes filled with the wisdom of a thousand stories inked into skin.

I nod, and we begin again.

---

A week has gone by, and the silence between Isabella and me stretches like a weighty chasm. Stubborn as ever, she refuses to answer my texts and calls, her voice a fading melody in the cavernous halls of my mind. Even when I gather the courage to approach her in person, she stands like stone, beautiful but immovable. The flower deliveries I've sent pile up outside her apartment door, creating a vibrant barricade that still fails to reach her heart.

I find myself sitting in Giovanni's office, my focus slipping away like sand through my fingers. We work side by side, our desks facing each other, and he catches my distracted gaze more than once. Today, his eyes hold a glimmer of concern as they meet mine.

"Alright, what's going on?" he asks, leaning back in his chair.

"Nothing," I lie, but Giovanni isn't buying it.

"We've got a pretty substantial mental health program here at the company," he says. "You can refuse to tell me, but before the end of the day, you'll be telling somebody, because frankly, all your moping around is a huge bummer."

I give him a look. "You sound like Teddy."

He shrugs. "We could both use a bit more of his perspective in our lives."

I sigh heavily, my worry pushing the air from my lungs. "I fear that I have lost Isabella completely."

Giovanni shakes his head, offering a reassuring smile. "That's not the case, I'm sure. Perhaps she just needs time to come around."

The frustration builds inside me, a storm waiting to break. I run my fingers through my hair, gripping the strands tightly. "I don't want to wait any longer for her. I want her now."

He laughs, his voice light and teasing. "You need to learn patience. You're used to being the head of the mafia, with all its perks, but now in the real world, you'll have to be patient and kind to get what you want."

My lips twist into a wry grin. "I've made a terrible mistake, haven't I?"

"Too late to go back now," Giovanni chuckles. His gaze softens, and he leans forward, elbows resting on his desk. "Look, I'm not the person to ask about women."

"Yet I've seen you with a woman I don't recognize," I counter, raising an eyebrow.

He waves a dismissive hand. "Yes, but let's not change the subject. If you really want guidance in this situation, of the four of us, Teddy has always had a way with women."

"Excellent idea," I say, standing up from my chair.

"Make sure you fit it in your lunch break," he calls after me, a teasing note in his voice.

I glance back at him, incredulous. He laughs, waving me off. "I'm joking! Go on, sort this out. You're a pile of shit with this still on your mind."

With that encouragement, I leave Giovanni's office, determined to find Teddy and seek his advice.

I make my way to the mansion, uncertainty heavy on my chest. The gym is a familiar sight, full of worn equipment and memories of sweat-drenched afternoons. Teddy is there, as I expected, his fists pounding a punching bag with a rhythmic intensity that speaks of deep focus.

"Teddy," I call out, but he doesn't seem to hear me over the sound of his strikes. It's only when he glances up and sees me waiting by the door that he stops, his expression shifting from concentration to concern.

"What's the matter?" he asks, wiping the sweat from his brow as he approaches. "You look even sadder than usual."

"Isabella," I admit, my voice barely more than a whisper. "I need your advice."

"Come on then," he says, motioning for me to follow him. "This won't be a short conversation. Let's take it up to the kitchen."

We climb the stairs, the silence between us punctuated only by the distant sounds of our footsteps. The kitchen is bright and airy, sunlight streaming through the windows and casting warm shadows across the gleaming countertops. Teddy starts making himself a protein shake, the blender roaring to life with a deafening whir.

"Can you hear me?" I shout over the noise, but Teddy just shakes his head and gestures for me to wait.

When the machine finally falls silent, he grins and leans against the counter, his biceps flexing beneath his t-shirt. "So what's going on?"

"Isabella refuses to talk to me," I say, frustration seeping into my voice.

"Smartest of us all, then," Teddy quips, and I glare at him.

"Can we be serious? Please."

"Alright, alright, relax," he says, raising his hands in surrender. "What have you done so far to try and get her to talk to you?"

"Visited her, sent gifts and flowers," I list off.

"Doing it all wrong," he says, shaking his head. "Are these just generic gifts?"

"Y-yes," I stammer, taken aback by his bluntness.

"Showing up unannounced to force her to talk to you?" Teddy raises an eyebrow, and I nod, feeling my cheeks burn with shame. "See, women don't want generic gifts when their men screw up. They want something special that shows you're really sorry. Anyone can buy her flowers. Every woman wants a guy who makes her feel special."

I frown, pondering his words. "Why do flowers seem so popular then?"

"Because there's a fool born every minute," Teddy shrugs, a wry smile playing on his lips.

"Teddy, I'm not sure what I can do for her based on this advice."

"Put actual thought into it. Women like being thought about and all that," he says as he takes a sip of his protein shake. "Personalize your approach."

"Speaking of women," I say, smirking at him, "why don't you have a girlfriend? You seem to know it all."

He grins. "I have many."

"Of course," I retort, rolling my eyes. "Thanks for the insight, Teddy." With that, I head back upstairs to my office.

As I sit down at my desk, I try to focus on work, sifting through my emails. It feels surreal to have a legitimate work email address now. My fingers hover over the keyboard as I scroll through, pausing when I see an email from Giovanni. He wants to discuss the upcoming charity fundraiser.

Every year, our family throws a lavish charity event. In the past, it was merely an excuse for mafia families to mingle socially, with the funds never actually reaching those in need. This year, however, Giovanni intends to change that. A spark ignites within me as I realize this might be the perfect opportunity to show Isabella that I truly care and want to set things right.

The next morning, I find Giovanni in his office, looking over paperwork. "Did you sort out your issue with Isabella?" he asks without looking up.

"Sort of," I say. "About the charity fundraiser, we need to pick a cause, right?"

"Yes," he replies, setting down his pen. "Have something in mind?"

"Actually, I do." I take a deep breath. "I'd like to raise money for the Innocence Project."

Giovanni raises an eyebrow. "Why that of all causes?"

"Isabella works on it pro bono," I explain. "I want to support her and her initiatives. Show her how much she means to me."

He studies me for a moment, then nods. "Alright. I hope this works for you."

"Me too, Giovanni. Me too."

# Chapter Thirty-Nine

## *Isabella*

The invitation arrives like a dark specter on my doorstep, heavy and embossed with silver filigree. The Maldonado family crest, a proud lion with a crown, graces the front of the black cardstock. I trace its edges, feeling the expectation within its glossy surface.

"Please join us for an elegant evening," I read aloud, my voice quivering. I turn the card over in my hand, and there, dancing across the back in little silver script, is a handwritten note from Primo.

*I hope you can attend.*

The audacity of it all leaves me breathless. Irritation courses through me as I realize that he still isn't getting the message. His attempts to woo me back only make it harder to get over him, but who am I kidding? I'm not getting over him at all.

I collapse into the armchair of my small apartment, the walls seeming to close in around me. A sad laugh escapes my lips. It's been quite the opposite of moving on, really. No matter what I do, I can't seem to stop thinking about him. My work suffers; cases pile up, untouched, while I obsessively check news sites reporting on him and his brother making great business strides. I'm confused by his choice to work with Giovanni, but Primo made it clear he was returning to crime. And I cannot support that life.

My heart aches for him, and every inch of my body craves his touch. When I close my eyes at night, I can't help but explore myself, reliving the way he dominated me. I want more of that with him, to delve deeper into our desires together. But I know this will never be, not while I refuse to live a life of crime.

"Damn you, Primo," I whisper into the quiet of my apartment, feeling the tears well up in my eyes. I wipe them away, trying to regain some semblance of control over my emotions.

"Get a grip, Isabella," I chide myself. "You are stronger than this."

And yet, as I sit there holding the invitation, I wonder if attending the fundraiser might be the final push I need to move on from Primo Maldonado once and for all.

I study the invitation more closely, noticing it includes a plus one. A wicked grin tugs at my lips as a devious thought crosses my mind.

"Two can play this game," I murmur under my breath.

I quickly text my sister, asking if she knows any doctors who wouldn't mind attending a fundraiser with me as a date. She replies almost immediately, assuring me she can find someone suitable. I send her a picture of the invitation and she responds with a note of caution:

> I hope you know what you're doing.

My fingers fly across the screen, typing out a message that I'm pretty sure I do.

The night of the fundraiser arrives, and a nice but painfully boring doctor named Isaac stands at my doorstep. He's tall and skinny, glasses perched on the bridge of his nose. We exchange pleasantries, and he escorts me to his car.

As we drive toward Primo's mansion, I attempt conversation. But Isaac barely responds to my questions, making me yearn for Primo's passion and imposing character. "This is for the best," I remind myself. "Primo needs to see me with another man. Only then can we both move on."

We pull up to the valet, stepping out of the car and walking arm in arm toward the entrance. It feels strange entering Primo's mansion with another man, but I'm determined to see this through. I'm wearing an exquisite gown—a daring, blood-red number that hugs my curves and leaves little to the imagination. The fabric clings uncomfortably, but I know it will make me irresistible tonight. Despite everything, I still wear the pendant Primo gave me, unable to part with the memory it holds.

"Isabella, you look stunning," Isaac says, breaking our prolonged silence.

"Thank you," I reply, forcing a smile. "You clean up nicely yourself."

We continue to exchange small talk, but my thoughts are elsewhere. I wonder what Primo's reaction will be when he sees me with Isaac. Will it finally drive him away or push him further into the darkness? And can I truly let him go?

"Is everything okay?" Isaac asks, drawing me back to the present.

"Of course," I lie through a tight smile. "Just trying to mentally prepare myself for the evening."

As we step into Primo's mansion, I take a deep breath and square my shoulders, ready to face the man whose presence continues to haunt me.

I'm struck by how different the mansion feels from my previous visits. The cold, austere atmosphere has been replaced by a warm and inviting ambiance. Soft, golden light spills from elegant chandeliers, casting a romantic glow on the room. The walls are adorned with tasteful artwork, and the air hums with the lively chatter of well-dressed guests.

"Isabella, look at this place," Isaac says, his voice barely audible over the din. "It's like stepping into another world."

I nod in agreement, but my thoughts are elsewhere.

My eyes scan the room, taking in the silent auction set up along one wall, where people are bidding on various items ranging from fine wines to exotic vacations. I know there will be a live auction later in the evening, and I can already sense the anticipation building among the attendees.

Waiters weave through the crowd, offering delicate hors d'oeuvres on silver platters. The scent of gourmet cuisine mingles with the expensive perfumes and colognes of the guests. Surprisingly, I don't see any familiar faces from the mob families – an unexpected relief considering the Maldonado name.

"Who's that?" Isaac asks, pointing toward the door.

I glance over and see Primo's younger brother approaching us. He looks sharp in his tailored suit, yet a hint of anxiety lingers in his eyes. As he reaches us, I greet him with apprehension, unsure of how he'll react to Isaac. "An acquaintance," I respond quickly to Isaac.

"Welcome, Isabella," Giovanni smiles warmly, though the tension between us is palpable. "And who is your handsome companion for the evening?"

"Isaac," I introduce, trying to keep my voice steady. "He's a doctor."

"Ah, a doctor," Giovanni nods, sizing Isaac up with a curious gaze. "Well, it's good to see you, Isabella. I hope you enjoy the evening."

"Thank you," I reply, exchanging a courteous smile before we move further into the room.

Despite the captivating surroundings, I can't help but search for Primo. My heart skips a beat when I finally spot him, standing by the bar. He's the picture of a perfect man – tall, dark, and devastatingly handsome. His high-end tuxedo fits him like a glove, accentuating his broad shoulders and narrow waist. His hair is slicked back, giving him an air of sophistication that makes my breath catch in my throat.

Our eyes meet across the room, and I feel a jolt of electricity run through me. His gaze is intense. But then he notices Isaac at my side, and his expression darkens with anger. I realize, in that moment, that maybe I've made a big mistake.

"Isabella, would you like a drink?" Isaac asks, oblivious to the storm brewing between Primo and me.

"Sure," I mumble, hoping against hope that Primo won't cause a scene. But as he strides toward us, his jaw set and his eyes burning with fury, I know that tonight is about to take a turn I hadn't anticipated.

Primo approaches us, his anger tightly controlled just beneath a veneer of civility. "Isabella," he murmurs, leaning in to press a gentle kiss to my cheek. The heat of his touch sends arousal coursing through me like wildfire.

"Primo," I manage to say, my voice betraying none of the turmoil roiling within me. "This is Isaac, my date for the evening."

"Isaac," Primo replies, shaking his hand with an iron grip that belies his polite tone. "What do you do for a living?"

"I'm a doctor," Isaac answers.

"Ah," Primo says, feigning interest. "And how long have you known Isabella?"

"Only a short while," Isaac admits.

"Interesting. What are your intentions toward her?" Primo's eyes bore into Isaac now, and I can see my date starting to squirm under the pressure.

"Primo, that's enough," I interject, unable to take the interrogation any longer. "I need to use the restroom. Excuse me."

As I slip away from the two men, I make my way toward the restrooms but quickly find myself veering off course. The familiarity of the mansion tugs at my heartstrings, and I find myself wandering through the halls I once complained about.

I end up outside Primo's office, the door slightly ajar. The same dark wood furniture dominates the room, and his meticulously organized desk remains untouched. It feels odd to be standing here alone, without him by my side.

Continuing my solitary journey, I reach the room where I used to sleep. My breath catches in my throat as I take in the sight before me – everything is still in perfect order, as if I had never left. The soft sheets on the bed are folded neatly, and even my favorite book lies on the nightstand, a bittersweet reminder of the nights I spent here.

Unable to resist the pull any longer, I find myself outside Primo's master bedroom. As I push open the door, his scent overwhelms me – that intoxicating mix of cologne and masculinity that used to drive me wild.

Memories of our passionate encounters flood my mind, the darkness we explored together both thrilling and terrifying in equal measure.

Tears prick at the corners of my eyes as the weight of everything I've lost comes crashing down upon me. I really do miss him. But I know I can't go back to the life we once shared – not when he's chosen crime over the possibility of a future with me.

I wipe away my tears, steeling myself to return to the party below. As I turn to leave, there he stands – Primo, in all his dark, irresistible glory, blocking the doorway.

"Isabella," he says softly, his voice tinged with pain and longing. "Why did you come tonight?"

"Primo," I whisper, my heart aching with the love I still feel for him. "I don't know."

## Chapter Forty

*Primo*

The hours of the evening stretch on, like tendrils of darkness creeping through my very soul. I stand by the grand fireplace, trying not to let my gaze linger too long on the door, as if Isabella might walk in at any moment. My heart is a hummingbird trapped within a cage of anticipation.

"Relax," Giovanni murmurs, his voice low and calming. "You're making yourself sick with all this waiting."

"I know," I whisper, but even my own voice sounds foreign to me. "But I can't help it."

"Take a breather," he suggests, his eyes flicking to the bar across the room. "Grab a drink, try to ignore the clock ticking away in your head."

I nod, finding solace in his wisdom, and make my way over to the bar. The amber liquid swirls in the glass as I sip my whiskey, forcing myself to look forward and away from the guests. Time becomes an elusive concept, slipping through my fingers like sand.

And then, I hear her voice.

It feels like a siren's call, drawing me out of the tempest of my thoughts. I turn to look at her. She is a marvel in a blood-red silk dress that hugs her curves. The gown falls off one shoulder, baring her smooth skin to my hungry eyes. It cinches at her waist before flowing down to the floor in a river of crimson, leaving a trail of desire in its wake. Seeing her in it makes my body ache with arousal.

My breath catches in my throat, but then my arousal is quickly filled by anger as I see that she has come with a date. There's no holding myself back. I stride over to them, each step fueled by the fire of jealousy and possessiveness.

"Isabella," I greet, my voice barely restrained as I press a kiss to her cheek. Her soft skin against my lips pulls me into fantasies that are far too dark and delicious to indulge in around people. To my surprise, I notice that she still wears the pendant I gave her—a symbol of our shared secret.

"Primo," she replies, her eyes guarded but unable to hide the flicker of something deeper. She introduces her date, a doctor, who seems to shrink under my intense gaze.

"Interesting. What are your intentions toward her?" I ask him, unable to keep the venom from my words.

"Primo, that's enough," Isabella cuts in, clearly irritated by my line of questioning. I can tell that this man is squirming under my gaze, intimidated by the unspoken challenge I'm issuing. He's not fit for my Isabella.

"I need to use the restroom. Excuse me," she says, this time aimed at me before storming off.

Her date's relief is palpable as he walks off to the bar rather than accompany her to ensure her safety. My heart races, torn between the anger at her presence with another man and the desperate desire to have her close once more.

I follow Isabella into the mansion, my heart pounding as I watch her every move. She walks past the bathroom and starts to meander through the halls we once walked together, lost in a world of memories. I keep a careful distance, not wanting to be seen, but unable to tear myself away from her alluring presence.

She goes first into my office, her delicate fingers wrapping around the door frame as she peers inside, as if searching for traces of the man I once was. My chest tightens at the sight of her exploring this space that has been empty without her. Then, she makes her way to her old room, pausing at the threshold before continuing on.

In a surprising move, she enters my master bedroom, her slender figure disappearing behind the heavy wooden door. She remains inside for what feels like an eternity, and curiosity gets the better of me. I walk into the room to see her on the verge of tears, her emerald eyes shimmering with unshed emotion. It breaks my heart to see her this way. Maybe she hasn't moved on as much as she would like to appear.

"Isabella," I say softly, and she startles slightly, wiping the water from her face with the back of her hand. "Why did you come tonight?"

"I... I don't know," she admits, her voice barely above a whisper.

She tries to slide past me, but I can't let her go so easily. I reach out, daring to touch her soft skin exposed by the plunging neckline of her dress. The sensation sends a shiver down my spine, fueling my desire. Our gazes meet and, for a moment, time seems to stand still.

I want to hold her, to kiss her, to rip this dress off and fuck her senseless until she's screaming my name and promising never to even think about leaving my side again.

"Primo," she murmurs, "you should be getting back. Your guests will wonder where you are."

"Fuck the guests," I growl, my need for her consuming me. "I care about you and us."

"Us?" She scoffs, her eyes flashing with anger. "There is no 'us,' and that was your choice."

She's right. I fucked up, consumed by grief and hatred, but I've changed. I try to convey this through my gaze, through the desperation in my voice. "Isabella, I've changed."

"Changed?" She scoffs again, disbelief etched on her beautiful face. "This entire ordeal has proven to me that you're incapable of change."

"Please, Isabella," I plead, my heart breaking at her words, "give me a chance to show you that I *am* capable—for you."

Isabella moves to leave, but I can't bear the thought of losing her again. I drop to one knee, tears streaming down my face as I beg her to listen to me. My words come out in a torrent of desperation.

"Isabella, I've agreed to support Giovanni as the head of the family. I've given up my position and we're moving the family away from crime and into legitimate business. I'm helping him transition safely so there won't be civil war or violence in the streets. I messed up when I chose vengeance over a life with you, and I don't deserve another chance with you, but please... just give me one more chance to show you that I want this with you."

I take a deep breath, steadying myself before continuing. "I organized tonight's fundraiser in your honor, and all the proceeds raised are going to be donated to the Innocence Project because I remember how much you supported that cause through your pro bono work. I know it doesn't even begin to make up for what I put you through, but I love you, Isabella, and I can't live another day without you."

She pauses, her eyes searching mine. "Repeat what you just said," she demands.

I start from the beginning, telling her about giving up crime, but she cuts me off. "No, the last thing."

"I love you," I confess, my heart pounding in my chest. "I can't live another day without you. I don't want to go on living if it means I have to see you with another man."

"Y-you love me?" She stammers, her voice barely a whisper.

"Yes," I reply, my voice thick with emotion. "The word doesn't even begin to describe how I feel about you."

"Since when?" she asks, her eyes still locked with mine.

"Probably from the first time you picked a fight with me," I admit, a small smile tugging at my lips.

"Why didn't you tell me before?" Her voice trembles, tears brimming in her eyes.

"Because I wasn't sure if I was going to die in prison," I confess. "How could I admit something like that to you before I was taken from you? I thought it would be better for you to live your life, fall in love, and have a family without thinking about what could have been with me."

As my words settles between us, we're left to confront the possibility of a future together--one that only seemed like a fantasy before.

"Life with you," she whispers, her eyes searching mine for any hint of insincerity. "I can't stop thinking about what it could be like."

Her words send shockwaves through my veins, making my heart flutter and hope bloom in the darkest corners of my soul. I swallow hard, trying to find my voice. "Do you really want a life with me?"

She nods, biting her lip as she studies my face. "I do. But I won't be some mobster's wife. That's not the life I want."

"I don't want that for you, either," I assure her, my heart pounding with my admission. "I want a life with you. I want to see my son without fearing that I'm corrupting him. I want us to grow old together without worrying about being gunned down on the street like Charlie was."

The mention of his name sends a pang of guilt through

me, but I push forward. "I want to honor what he gave up because of me, and I want to do it with you."

"Are you saying...?" she trails off, her voice laced with disbelief.

"Yes," I say, my resolve strengthening with each word. "I want you to be my wife. I want you to belong to me and no one else. I don't want to see another man touch you ever again. I want to see you pregnant, swollen with my child, and I want to fuck you until we're so old we can't fuck anymore—but then still even try."

Tears fill her eyes as she crumbles before me, falling to the floor in a heap of raw emotion. Risking everything, I pull her into my arms and she lets me. As we cling to each other, our tears fall together, releasing the pent-up emotions we were never able to share after the acquittal—and Charlie's death.

"You don't need to answer me now," I tell her, my voice hoarse with emotion. "In fact, you shouldn't—I don't even have a ring to give you."

She shakes her head, tears streaming down her cheeks. "I don't need a ring. Your words and your promises are all I've ever wanted. I don't care about the money, the cars, or the fancy house. I only ever wanted you."

Her confession wraps around my heart like a lifeline. "I couldn't stop thinking about you, no matter how much I tried to get over you," she admits. "Isaac is just one of the doctors who works with my sister. I thought by showing up here with another guy, it might help both of us move on...but I can't." Her voice breaks, and she looks up at me, her eyes filled with a desperate longing. "I just can't."

"Is that so?" I ask gently, hardly daring to breathe as I wait for her answer.

"Yes," she whispers, her breath warm against my neck. "It means...it means I love you too."

# Chapter Forty-One

## *Isabella*

Primo's confession hits me like a stormy tide, as though I've been submerged in an ocean of emotions and finally emerge gasping for air. My heart swells with a happiness I haven't felt in what feels like an eternity. He pulls me into him, our bodies melding together like two pieces of a puzzle long separated. His lips find mine, a gentle kiss that mingles with the salty wetness of our tears. But soon, the kiss deepens, becoming more insistent, hungry even. We both have been starved of each other's touch for far too long, and now that we are reunited, denying this moment would be impossible.

The sounds of partygoers laughing and chatting filter through from downstairs. The thought of us making love upstairs while everyone else remains oblivious sends a shiver down my spine, igniting a fire within me. Primo's fingers deftly work at the fabric of my dress, peeling it away from my body while he whispers to me how gorgeous I look. But his voice takes on a dark edge. "Although," he says, his fingers grazing down my shoulders, "this dress is far too revealing. You should only expose yourself in such a way for me." The way he speaks to me, both degrading and adoring, stirs something primal in me. I've missed the way his words can make me feel both dirty and cherished all at once.

"Primo," I moan softly, "I've missed being your dirty little pet."

He growls in response, the sound vibrating against my ear. With one swift motion, he lifts the dress up and over my head, leaving me bare before him.

His eyes widen as he realizes I am not wearing any undergarments, completely exposed to him. He traces his fingers along my curves. "I look forward to exploring every one of our fantasies together in the years to come, mia cara. I promise to collar you and then you will officially be my little fuck pet. You will be mine forever, in both body and soul."

"Primo," I breathe, my voice trembling with desire, "that's all I want – to serve you and let you use my body."

Our gazes lock, and I see a storm of passion brewing within his dark eyes. This moment feels like the beginning of a journey we're about to embark on together, a journey filled with love, lust, and the promise of a life intertwined.

My heart races as I look at him, his dark eyes full of desire. He pulls me to him, guiding my thighs down so that I'm hovering above his face. "Sit on my face, bella," he commands, his voice rough and gravelly, "I need to taste you – it's been too long."

Bashfulness floods through me, but his strong fingers grip my thighs tightly, pulling me down onto him. As soon as his tongue makes contact with my sensitive flesh, I gasp, my hands instinctively moving to tease my nipples. I've fantasized about this moment for weeks, but nothing could have prepared me for the way Primo makes me feel.

"Ride my tongue, baby," he urges, smacking my ass gently. I rock my hips against him, my body growing closer and closer to release. His talented tongue, combined with two of his fingers expertly working my g-spot, pushes me to the edge. It doesn't take long before I'm coming undone, my climax washing over me in waves. His growls of approval vibrate against my skin as he laps up every bit of me, leaving no trace of my pleasure behind.

When Primo flips me over, his eyes are alight with a ravenous hunger. I know that we're far from finished, and the anticipation of what's to come makes me ache for more.

"Primo," I whisper breathlessly, "I want to taste you."

He shakes his head, gripping my chin firmly. "No, I need to fuck you now. It's been too long since I've been inside your sweet pussy."

"Please," I beg, my eyes pleading with his, "I miss the taste of you."

"Look at yourself," he degrades me, his words dripping with lust, "You're such a pitiful little sub that you can't even go a few weeks without the taste of my cock in your mouth. I love how horny and needy you are for me."

I open my mouth wide, showing him exactly what I crave. A dark chuckle escapes his lips as he decides to give me just that. He lifts me up, and I squirm in his strong arms, but a hard smack on my ass reminds me to be a good girl. He tosses me onto the bed and unzips his pants, pulling me until my head is hanging off the edge.

"Get ready, pet," he warns, before pushing himself into my eager mouth. The angle makes it difficult for me to take him completely, but his praise and degradation spur me on. As he fucks my face at a punishing pace, his fingers find their way between my thighs, reigniting my arousal. Another orgasm builds within me, and I know I won't be able to hold back for long.

"Such a good girl," Primo murmurs, his voice laced with satisfaction, "taking me so well." He continues this way as I choke on his cock.

"Enough," he breathes, withdrawing from my mouth with a wet pop. He flips me over onto my stomach, my body tingling with anticipation. I watch as he sheds his clothing, his muscles gleaming in the low light, all those delicious tattoos glinting like forbidden treasures. The sight of him sends a shiver down my spine, my arousal flaring anew.

He climbs on top of me, entering me from behind with one slow, deliberate thrust. Our bodies meld together, his strong arms wrapping around me as he caresses my skin, nipping at my neck. He starts out slow, but soon his pace increases, our bodies colliding with each frantic thrust. My moans fill the room, and I start to worry that those downstairs might hear us.

"Say my name, mia cara," he growls into my ear, his voice commanding and irresistible. "I want to hear you scream it when you come for me again."

The heat rises within me, his relentless rhythm pushing me closer and closer to the edge. As he twists my nipples and plunges into me again and again, I finally let go, crying out his name as my orgasm moves through me. The pulsing of my walls sends him over the edge too, and he releases himself deep inside me with a guttural groan.

We collapse onto the bed, our bodies slick with sweat and desire. I'm all smiles as he turns me over, cradling me in his arms. The intimacy of the moment has me tracing the edges of his tattoos, curiosity piqued by their intricate designs.

"Will you tell me now what each one means?" I whisper, my fingers dancing across his inked skin.

"Of course," he replies softly. He begins to explain each one, his voice low and soothing. "This one is my family crest. This one—the wolf—I got from a monk while traveling. It represents loyalty and protection of my pack."

"Your pack?" I tease, grinning up at him.

"Si, my family, my friends—like Charlie, who I got this tattoo for recently." He points out each one as he speaks, his fingers brushing the inked tributes to those he loves. "And this one is for my mother, still in Italy, and my son."

My gaze lingers on a fresh tattoo, curiosity piqued. "Who is that one for?"

A slow smile spreads across his face. "That one is for you, bella. Lady Justice, holding a single scale with my heart inside it."

Tears well up in my eyes as I ask him when he got it. He tells me it was a few weeks ago.

"But," I say looking at him in confusion, "we didn't know that we would end up together then."

"Bella," he murmurs, his eyes locked onto mine, "that doesn't mean I stopped loving you, or ever would."

As our breathing slows and our hearts find their rhythm once more, I realize just how deeply Primo has woven himself into the fabric of my life. And I wouldn't have it any other way.

As we come back to our senses, I feel the need to ask him about something he mentioned earlier. "Primo, what did you mean by collaring me?" I inquire, my voice soft and curious.

"Ah," he murmurs, his eyes darkening with excitement. "Collaring is a BDSM tradition, symbolizing a deep commitment between a Dominant and their submissive. It's like a wedding ring, but for our kind of relationship."

He pauses, gauging my reaction. "I would love to do that with you, if you'd be willing to."

"Wait," I say, furrowing my brow in thought. "If I'm willing to marry you, doesn't that mean I'd be willing to let you collar me?"

He shakes his head, giving me a tender smile. "Not necessarily. Marriage is a public commitment, while collaring is an intensely personal one. It doesn't have to be for everyone, but it can be a powerful expression of our bond."

The idea intrigues me, awakening something within me that hungers for more. "I'm very interested, Primo. I can't wait to learn more about it with you."

"Me too," he says, his eyes alight with anticipation. "We'll explore all our fantasies together and work slowly toward that step in our dynamic, at our own pace."

Feeling refreshed and reconnected, we clean up and put our clothes back on. As we make our way downstairs, hand in hand, the live auction has already begun. The room buzzes with excitement as people place their bids, the atmosphere electric.

"Isaac," I call out to my date as I approach him. "Sorry I was gone so long."

He waves off my apology with a smile. "No worries, I hardly noticed."

"Thank you for being such a great date tonight, but I won't be needing a ride home," I tell him, hoping he understands.

Isaac glances between Primo and me, a knowing grin

spreading across his face. "I see. Well, I really do wish you both the best." He leaves us with a nod, and Primo's attention returns to me.

We walk the halls of the mansion, our fingers intertwined, when we run into Teddy looking sheepish. Primo tries to express his gratitude for the advice Teddy had given him, but Teddy attempts to brush it off.

"Really, it was nothing," he mumbles, shifting uncomfortably.

That's when I notice what Teddy is trying to hide: a girl tucked behind one of the statues. Primo seems slightly irritated by the situation, but I just laugh. With a lighthearted tug on Primo's hand, I lead him into the gardens.

The gardens come alive at night, the moon casting a silvery glow on the impeccably groomed hedges and blossoming sprintime flowers. The scent of roses mixed with the crisp night air creates an intoxicating aroma.

"Here," Primo murmurs, bending down to pluck a delicate bloom from its stem. He places the flower gently in my hair, his fingers lingering for a moment as he adjusts its position. His eyes meet mine, filled with warmth and adoration, and I feel my heart swell in response.

"Thank you," I whisper, just before his lips find mine in a tender kiss beneath the moonlight. The world around us fades away, leaving only the sensation of his mouth against mine, gentle yet full of unspoken promise.

As he pulls back, I take a deep breath and share what's been on my mind. "I'm not giving up my law career, Primo."

He smiles softly, understanding in his eyes. "I would never ask you to."

"Instead of private practice, I've decided to work for the public defender's office." My voice is firm, resolute. "I know people are being taken advantage of by prosecutors like Greg, and I can't just stand by and watch that happen to them."

"Isabella," Primo says, his voice filled with admiration, "I'm so proud of you. You're an incredibly smart attorney, and they'll be lucky to have you. And I am so lucky to have you."

His words send a shiver down my spine, a mix of anticipation and exhilaration coursing through me. As we continue our stroll through the garden, hand in hand, I imagine the life we're going to build together – one where we support each other, challenge each other, and grow together.

"Primo," I say, my voice barely more than a whisper, "I can't wait to spend the rest of my life with you."

"Neither can I, bella," he replies, his grip on my hand tightening ever so slightly. "And I will spend every day proving just how much you mean to me."

The End.

# Epilogue

## *Isabella*

It's Primo and my wedding day, and I can barely contain my excitement. We talked about having just a small ceremony of family and friends, but he really wouldn't hear of it. He told me that he wanted as big of a ceremony as possible because he wanted the entire world to know that I now officially belong to him. I couldn't say no to him; I never really can.

I didn't have to do any planning for it. Primo did everything from start to finish, leaving me only in charge of picking out my dress and making sure he didn't get to see it before the wedding day. Primo, being Italian, was very much into traditions and extremely superstitious. He gave me an unlimited budget to pick out my dress, and even though I wanted to be careful with his money (especially because we've really had to earn our own these days), I ended up getting something definitely on the pricier side.

As I stand in front of the mirror, taking in the sight of myself in the most exquisite wedding gown I've ever laid eyes on, I feel like a queen. The gown is a vision of delicate lace and silk, hugging my curves just right, with a subtly seductive plunging neckline. The long sleeves are adorned with intricate embroidery, trailing down to the tips of my fingers. The train cascades behind me, a waterfall of fabric shimmering with every movement.

My hair is styled into an elegant chignon, adorned with tiny pearls that catch the light beautifully. My makeup is flawless: subtle smoky eyes, rosy cheeks, and soft pink lips. I feel both powerful and incredibly vulnerable at the same time.

"Damn, sis," Eve, also my maid of honor, says as she beams with pride. "You look amazing! Who knew you'd clean up so well? I'm sad I didn't find my own hot mobster before the family went legit – I'm tired of working."

I roll my eyes playfully. "Hey, you never know. You might still find the right criminal to turn you into a trophy wife."

"One can dream!" Eve exclaims with a laugh, and we share a knowing smile.

We join Tammy, my other bridesmaid, in the foyer as we wait for the music to start playing. The anticipation is almost overwhelming, but I'm so ready to begin this new chapter of my life with Primo.

The music swells as I stand at the entrance to the grand

church, my heart pounding in my chest. Eve gives my veil one more graceful flourish before winking at me and stepping down the aisle ahead of me. The warmth of her love and support fills me up.

Taking a deep breath, I begin my slow walk down the aisle, each step measured and deliberate. I've seen so many brides cry on their wedding day, but not a single tear escapes me today – only pure happiness radiates from within. My gaze sweeps over the crowd, finding the happy, familiar faces of our loved ones. I spot Lucas, Primo's son, smiling proudly among them. I was so proud of him, but he worked up the courage to call his son and they've been reconnecting ever since.

It's been three months since Primo started working with Giovanni, and everything feels safer, more secure – the family is finally moving in the right direction.

As I reach the altar, my heart leaps into my throat at the sight of Primo. He stands tall and regal, his jaw set and eyes fierce with determination. His dark hair is neatly styled, and the sharp lines of his tailored suit accentuate his strong physique. His gaze locks onto mine, and in that moment, I feel an all-consuming love that sets my soul alight.

"Welcome, family and friends," the officiant begins, his voice resonant and warm. "Today, we gather to celebrate the union of Isabella and Primo."

The service is a blur as I keep my eyes locked onto his. Finally, it's time for us to exchange vows.

"Primo," I start, my voice trembling with excitement as

I launch into my vows. The words tumble from my lips in a torrent, my heart racing so fast that I can barely remember what I've said. But it doesn't matter – the raw emotion speaks louder than any well-crafted phrase could.

"Isabella," Primo replies, his voice steady and controlled, just like the man himself. "You have made me a better man. You have saved me from the darkness that once consumed me. I vow to spend my entire life trying to live up to you and everything you've done for me."

The sincerity in his words is palpable, the depth of his emotion resonating through every syllable.

Before I know it, Primo's strong arms encircle my waist, pulling me into him as his lips crash against mine. The passion ignites within us, an insatiable fire that consumes us both. He dips me back, deepening the kiss further, our love on full display for everyone to witness.

"By the power vested in me," the officiant declares, "I now pronounce you husband and wife."

As we break apart, our breaths mingling in the air between us, I know without a doubt that this is the beginning of a beautiful, passionate life together – filled with love, devotion, and a connection that transcends time itself.

"Congratulations!" Our friends and family cheer as we make our way to the limo, their faces alight with joy. The reality of being Primo's wife fills me with a warmth I've never experienced before.

Once inside the limo, Primo's arms wrap around me, pulling me into a heated kiss that leaves me breathless. His voice is low and sultry, tinged with the darkness I've grown to crave. "I can't wait to rip this dress off you and fuck you until you're begging for mercy."

My core clenches at his words, the filthiness contrasting with the purity of my wedding gown. He pushes me down onto the backseat, lifting my skirt and burying his face between my legs. My hands grip the soft leather as his tongue delves into me, sending shivers up my spine.

"Primo," I moan. His fingers slide into me, curving to hit that perfect spot. "I want to scream your name every time I come."

He pulls away, his eyes dark with lust. "I'll make sure of it, my needy little wife. Your body belongs to me now, and I'll use it every single day."

Without another word, he unzips his pants and takes out his cock, fully erect and glistening with precum. I move toward him, my mouth watering at the sight. As I take him in, the taste of him overwhelms me, and I suck him with abandon.

"Such a good girl," he groans above me, his hands gripping my hair. The dirtiness of the act only fuels my desire.

I feel like a goddess, powerful and sensual, even as I submit to him.

Just as he's about to cum, he pulls me off, his breathing ragged. "Climb on, Isabella," he orders, his voice husky. "I want my cum dripping down you for the entire reception."

I climb onto his lap, straddling him as the limo glides through the city streets. His hands grip my hips, guiding me as I bounce on his cock. He pulls my wedding dress down, exposing my breasts to the dim light of the limo. His mouth latches onto my soft flesh, biting and marking me as he groans in pleasure.

"God, Isabella, you belong to me now. And I'm so fucking thankful for it," he murmurs between bites.

My body trembles with each thrust, feeling the orgasm building within me like a tidal wave. "Primo, I... I'm trying to hold on," I gasp, clutching at his broad shoulders.

"Wait for me," he commands, his voice strained. His fingers pinch my nipples hard, sending jolts of pleasure through me. "Now, come for me."

We come together, our cries mingling in the air as we lose ourselves in the intensity of the moment. As though on cue, the limo stops in front of the reception hall. I right myself, but I can feel his cum dripping down my thighs.

"I love the idea of my cum dirtying up your wedding dress," Primo whispers, his eyes dark with desire. "You're mine now, Isabella."

As we enter the reception, Primo is immediately pulled aside by Giovanni. I watch them talk business, their expressions serious. Teddy approaches me, a mischievous grin on his face.

"Hey, they're talking business. We gotta break it up, but first... shots!" He laughs, and I join him. Together, we down our glasses before moving toward the two brothers. I place a hand on Primo's arm, urging him to relax and enjoy the celebration.

"Come on, boys, drink up and have some fun," I tell them playfully. We cut the cake, and Primo feeds me a bite with a gentle touch. He gives me a warning look as I grin, daring him to think I'd smash it in his face. Instead, I dab icing on his nose, and he smiles, though a promise of punishment lingers in his eyes.

"Can't wait," I murmur, the anticipation thrilling me.

We dance, our bodies moving in sync to the rhythm of the music, but soon enough, Primo's lust is too strong to contain. He pulls me close, whispering in my ear, "I need you again, Isabella."

He announces to the gathered guests that he appreciates their presence but must take his bride away.

Upon entering the hotel room, my senses are flooded with the rich scent of roses and the flickering glow of candles. Primo pulls me close, his eyes reflecting a love that both warms and consumes me.

"Isabella," he whispers, "I love you more than anything. I'm so incredibly lucky to have you as my wife."

He presses his lips to mine, a gentle kiss that speaks volumes. As we break apart, Primo gazes into my eyes, making me feel like the most precious treasure in the world.

"Before we do anything else tonight, I want to give you all the attention you deserve," he tells me. "You've made me the happiest man alive, and now it's my turn to make you happy."

With that, he guides me to the sumptuous bathroom, where a steaming Jacuzzi. The water is infused with fragrant oils, and petals float delicately on the surface. Primo helps me out of my wedding dress and eases me into the bath, the warmth enveloping me.

"Relax, my beautiful bride," he murmurs, massaging my shoulders before reaching for a bottle of scented oil. He pours it into his hands, warming it before applying it to my skin. His strong fingers work their magic, kneading away any tension and leaving me pliant and sated under his touch.

As my eyes flutter closed, I can't help but apologize. "I'm sorry, Primo, I'm just so tired..."

"Shh, bella," he soothes, cradling me in his arms. "There's no need to apologize. We have a lifetime ahead of us to explore each other, to learn and grow together. Tomorrow, we leave for our honeymoon, and we'll start our new life as husband and wife."

His words are soothing to my weary soul, and I allow myself to drift into the realm of dreams, knowing that when I wake, Primo will be by my side, ready to face whatever challenges life may throw our way.

Want more of Isabella and Primo?
I wrote an exclusive extended epilogue about their honeymoon!

Click here to read it!

or

Scan the code below!

# Acknowledgments

*To Lacey:* Thank you for always believing in me and my books and being there to help me when I was feeling really alone! I am so lucky to have you on this journey!

*To my alpha and beta readers:* Yelena, Tal, Jamie, Kels, Kandace and Maria, thank you all for taking the time to read and provide me feedback! This book would be so much worse without your amazing help and input!

*To Valentine PR:* Thank you for all the amazing marketing help in getting this book and series up off the ground!

*To Dante Black:* Thank you for giving me permission to riff off your car audio and create one of my favorite scenes I've written thus far! I still can't remember if you said you would do voice work for this or not, though...

*To YOU, the reader:* Thank you for taking a chance on Primo and Isabella. I wouldn't be here if it weren't for you!

# Also by Ivy Wild

### Kings of Capital:

**The Estate**

A billionaire romance

**Infamous**

A second chance romance

**Brightly Burning Bridges**

A bully romance

**Beautiful Surrender**

A BDSM romance

**My Fiancé's Bodyguard**

A forbidden, mafia romance

**Total Obsession**

A dark, stalker romance

# A Vicious Rumor

A high school academy romance

# About the Author

USA Today and a Top 15 Amazon bestselling author, Ivy Wild writes angsty, sometimes dark, contemporary romance with guaranteed happily-ever-afters. As a practicing corporate attorney for a global law firm, Ivy loves combining her real world experiences with her fictional worlds.

When she's not working—who are we kidding?—she's never not working. She currently lives just outside of Washington, D.C. with her husband, her German Shepherd, and a sassy rescue cat named Cobalt.

Ivy loves connecting with her readers and is as active as possible on the following platforms:

- amazon.com/author/ivywild
- tiktok.com/@ivywildauthor
- instagram.com/ivywildauthor
- facebook.com/ivywildromance
- bookbub.com/profile/ivy-wild
- twitter.com/ivywildauthor
- youtube.com/ivywildauthor

## You are beautiful

Printed in Great Britain
by Amazon